TAMING HER IRISH WARRIOR

MICHELLE WILLINGHAM

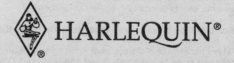

HARLEQUIN®

TORONTO • NEW YORK • LONDON
AMSTERDAM • PARIS • SYDNEY • HAMBURG
STOCKHOLM • ATHENS • TOKYO • MILAN • MADRID
PRAGUE • WARSAW • BUDAPEST • AUCKLAND

To all the readers who asked me for Ewan's story.
Thank you so much for all of your
support and encouragement.

Recycling programs
for this product may
not exist in your area.

ISBN-13: 978-0-373-29566-1

TAMING HER IRISH WARRIOR

Someone grabbed her. His hand clamped over her mouth, the other arm gripping her waist as he spun her around. A blade of moonlight slipped from behind the clouds, casting a beam upon his face.

She froze at the sight of Ewan MacEgan. By the Rood, she'd never thought to see him again. What was he doing here?

His sculpted bare chest gleamed silver, his pectoral muscles rising and falling as he breathed.

"Looking for something?" he accused.

The last time she'd seen Ewan, he'd been a gangly boy of sixteen. The boy had become a man. A handsome one at that. His dark blond hair was cut short, emphasizing a lean face and a strong jawline. Broad shoulders revealed a tight strength she hadn't remembered. Ridged muscles lined his abdomen, down to...

Oh, dear God above. He was naked.

With that, every coherent thought left her. He looked like a savage Celt. Ewan had a wildness about him that made her uneasy.

He released one wrist and ripped her hood free.

"You're a woman."

She couldn't gather up her thoughts to answer and before she knew it, his mouth came down upon hers.

* * *

Taming Her Irish Warrior
Harlequin® Historical #966—October 2009

Author Note

When I first began writing the Irish medieval stories of The MacEgan Brothers, the youngest brother, Ewan MacEgan, always held a special place in my heart. I've been eagerly awaiting the day when I could give this awkward, boyish and fiercely loyal hero the heroine of his dreams. Now that the adolescent boy has grown into a strong, passionate man, Ewan is about to meet his match in Honora St. Leger.

As a girl, Honora dreamed of wielding a sword and fighting alongside her father's men. As a widow, she wages her own battle against losing her heart to Ewan, the man she loved many years ago. She can only be with Ewan if he sacrifices everything, and she refuses to let him surrender his future.

I hope you enjoy Ewan MacEgan's tale, and I also invite you to download the love story of Honora's sister Katherine and her handsome knight Sir Ademar, *The Warrior's Forbidden Virgin,* available now in eBook form from Harlequin Historical Undone! You can also find behind-the-scenes information about my books and the other four MacEgan brothers on my Web site: www.michellewillingham.com. Trahern MacEgan will be next, and I look forward to writing his book.

I love to hear from readers, and you may e-mail me at michelle@michellewillingham.com or write to me at P.O. Box 2242, Poquoson, VA 23662.

Praise for Michelle Willingham

HER WARRIOR SLAVE

"Michelle Willingham writes characters that feel all too real to me. The tortured soul that is Kieran really pulled at my heartstrings. And Iseult's unfailing search for her lost child made this book a truly emotional read."
—*Publishers Weekly*

"Willingham skillfully combines a cast of wonderfully original characters with a refreshingly different, meticulously detailed setting to create a vivid tale of love and danger in medieval Ireland."
—*Chicago Tribune*

HER WARRIOR KING

"The MacEgan tales just keep getting better. With *Her Warrior King,* Michelle Willingham has set a new standard of excellence. We will all be impatiently awaiting the next novel."
—*CataRomance,* 4.5 stars

THE WARRIOR'S TOUCH

"[A] thought-provoking tale of love in the second installment of The MacEgan Brothers."
—*Romantic Times BOOKreviews,* 4 stars

"I know we all wish we could have a MacEgan for our very own but since we cannot, be sure and pick up this not-to-be-missed tale of The MacEgan Brothers, *The Warrior's Touch.*"
—*CataRomance,* 4.5 stars

HER IRISH WARRIOR

"Willingham not only delves into medieval culture, she also tells the dark side of being a woman in that era… The bright side is that in romantic fiction, a happy ending is expected, and it's delivered in this excellent, plot-driven, page-turner of a book."
—*Romantic Times BOOKreviews,* 4 stars

**DON'T MISS THESE OTHER
NOVELS AVAILABLE NOW:**

Chapter One

The wood creaked, a faint noise that hardly anyone would notice. But Honora St Leger had trained herself to perceive details such as this, the underlying hints of a man's presence.

He was here. The thief she'd been waiting to capture.

Her knees ached against the cold stone floor of the chapel, and though she pretended to pray, she inched her way closer to the altar and the sword she'd hidden beneath it.

A sennight ago, the thief had stolen a wooden cross from the chapel. And last night, a chalice had gone missing. Her father's men had found nothing, not a trace of the thief.

The hairs stood up on the back of her neck, her instincts roaring. Closer now. Her breathing grew steadier as she mentally steeled herself for battle.

She reached beneath the altar cover, finding the cool metal hilt of the sword. The candles extinguished from a sudden gust of air.

Honora leapt to her feet, poised to strike. The soft sound of footsteps betrayed the man's presence. Darkness shielded both of them, and she used her other senses to her advantage. Although she could not see her opponent, neither could he see her.

The rhythm of footsteps shifted, and fear suddenly arced through her. Oh, Jesu. There were two of them.

The air within the chapel shifted without warning, and instinct made her swing the sword behind her. Her blade struck steel, and the thief parried, the blow numbing her arm.

Where had the cur gotten a sword? A sword meant he was no ordinary thief—he was a trained fighter. Her pulse quickened, her fear rising. Though she had full confidence in her skills, fighting blind made it more challenging.

And there was still someone else in the chapel, someone she couldn't see. The footsteps quickened, though she could not tell if they were running towards her or running away.

She swung the blade and was rewarded with a hiss of pain. 'Who are you?' she demanded. 'What do you want?'

Silence.

When she sliced the sword again, it missed. She halted the blade, listening. Nothing remained but the coolness of air coming from the open door. Not a footstep, not a foreign breath marred the stillness. Both men had vanished.

Why?

Unless one of the men had driven the other off. Like an unseen protector.

She frowned, dropping to her knees again. The sword hilt warmed beneath her palm while her heart pulsed with energy. It had been half a year since she'd fled her husband's home, Ceredys, and returned to her father's *donjon*. She'd thought she was safe here at Ardennes. Now, she wasn't so certain.

It unnerved her that this thief kept returning, as though he were searching for something. But what?

Honora contemplated returning to her chamber, but her sister Katherine was still abed. She couldn't endanger her by leading the attackers there.

Instead, she lit the candles once more, trying to calm

herself while the familiar scent of beeswax and old incense filled the space.

With her sword in hand, she sat against the stone wall. Though it was freezing and uncomfortable, she tucked her feet beneath her skirts.

It was then that she noticed the missing chest. She had brought it back from Ceredys, a gift given by her mother-in-law, Marie St Leger.

Now stolen.

Furious, she eyed the empty space where it had rested only moments ago. As she murmured a silent prayer for Marie's soul, she vowed she would bring the thief to justice.

'She won't wed you.'

Ewan MacEgan shielded his eyes against the glare of the sun beginning to sink below the horizon. His brother's prediction came as no surprise to him. He was the youngest son, with not much more than a tiny plot of land. What right did he have, thinking he could win the hand of an heiress? None at all.

But this was Lady Katherine of Ardennes, the woman he'd idolised since he was a lad of sixteen. While others had mocked his clumsiness, she had smiled at him, reassuring, 'You'll beat all of them one day.'

Though she was only a girl of fourteen years, Lady Katherine's quiet faith had sustained him. Now that she had grown up to be a lady worthy of a thousand suitors, he intended to wed her.

'I've known her since we were children,' Ewan told his brother.

Bevan drew his horse to a stop by the river and let the animal drink. 'That was five years ago. Her father will want her to wed a wealthy nobleman, not a penniless Irishman.'

'I'll gain my own wealth,' Ewan answered. 'Enough to build whatever kingdom she desires.' Though he spoke with confidence, like Bevan, he had his doubts that Lord Ardennes would even consider him as a suitor for Katherine. The only thing in his favour was his royal bloodline, for his eldest brother, Patrick, was king of their province in Éireann.

Bevan rested his arm upon the horse and regarded him. 'Let us help you. Take the land Patrick offered.'

'I won't take what I haven't earned. I'll get the land myself, or not at all.' He would not be a leech, feeding off the family's wealth.

'Too proud, are you?' The scar upon Bevan's cheek tightened. 'It won't do you any good here. The girl's family possesses wealth beyond your imaginings. She'll marry a nobleman of the highest rank. You haven't a chance.'

Ewan refused to believe it. 'I have to try.' He stiffened, keeping his gaze fixed upon the horizon. Urging his mount forwards, he tried to behave as if he didn't see the pity on his brother's face.

'There are others who might be more suitable,' Bevan continued, softening his tone. 'Someone from Éireann. You don't need to live here, among enemies. Wed an Irish *cailín*.'

Give up this Herculean task, was what his brother meant. *Don't reach for what you cannot possibly achieve.*

It was what his brothers had counselled him, long ago when he'd expressed his desire to be a warrior. He had not possessed the natural talents of Patrick or Bevan. And though he'd poured himself into the training, his skills came from brute strength rather than finesse. Despite all the failures he'd suffered, he had overcome his weaknesses to become the man he was now.

Could he not do the same with winning a bride? Persistence counted for something, didn't it?

He turned to Bevan. 'She is the one I want.'

His brother expelled a sigh, drawing his horse to a stop. Although they were less than five miles from the *donjon*, Bevan turned his gaze westwards. 'Be sure of it, Ewan.'

They travelled alongside one another for the remainder of the journey, not speaking. The landscape was familiar to him, verdant fields that rolled into hills. In five years, none of it had changed.

It struck him suddenly that he'd been content here. Though most of his kinsmen viewed Normans as the enemy foreigners, Ewan had never seen them as such. He'd spent three years among them, after Bevan's wife, Genevieve, had arranged it. He'd finished his fostering with her father, Thomas de Renalt, the Earl of Longford. There, he had finally learned to fight.

A sense of unease passed over him, and he glanced at the scars upon his palms. Although the wounds had healed long ago, his hands were stiff. Grasping a sword took his full concentration, and he'd had to compensate for his awkwardness in other ways.

But he deserved the scars, for what he'd done to Bevan. He risked a glance at his older brother, wishing to God he hadn't betrayed him. And though Bevan had forgiven him, he felt unworthy of it.

Ahead, he spied the castle that belonged to the Baron of Ardennes. The fortification was a blend of stone and wood. The outer bailey wall stretched high, perhaps the height of two men. The inner *donjon* held stone battlements and wooden outbuildings. Though he had not dwelled within the fortress, he had visited a time or two, along with his foster-father.

He tensed as they drew close to the barbican gate, wondering if Katherine would remember him.

Or Honora.

His grip tightened on the reins. During his fostering, Honora had nearly killed him on three different occasions. Accidents, she'd claimed. Though it was forbidden for women to train, that did nothing to stop her. She'd wanted to learn swordplay, like him, and he'd reluctantly offered instruction.

She was married now, he'd heard. Perhaps to a husband who could tame her wildness. He'd never met a woman so eager to wield a blade. And though he'd tried to avoid her, Honora had followed him everywhere.

Would that her sister had worshipped him so.

Despite the number of men vying for her hand, he intended to win Katherine first—no matter what it entailed. Anticipation rose up inside him, for soon he would conquer her heart.

The thief was among the suitors who had come for her sister; Honora was certain of it. With so many strangers, it would be simple enough to avoid notice.

She'd waited many hours until darkness shrouded the castle once more. In the ebony cloak of night, she moved soundlessly. Past the guards, keeping to the shadows while they conversed and played games of dice.

Find the chest, find the thief. It was as simple as that. Already, she had searched the Hall, but there was no trace of it among the low-born knights and retainers. All that remained were the private chambers reserved for guests of noble birth.

Not a sound did she make when she entered the first chamber. After searching the men's belongings, she found nothing. She slid against the wall, moving towards the next chamber. Ahead, she spied the guard standing by the staircase.

Honora held her breath, praying he wouldn't see her. Her father would murder her if he knew what she was doing.

When she reached the next chamber, she opened the door. Inside, silence permeated the space. She moved closer to a pile of belongings, staring at the shadows for a glimpse of the chest.

Abruptly, someone grabbed her. His hand clamped over her mouth, the other arm gripping her waist as he spun her around. Honora fought, kicking at his legs, but he lifted her up, pressing her back against the wall. A blade of moonlight slipped from behind the clouds, casting a beam upon his face.

She froze at the sight of Ewan MacEgan. By the Rood, she'd never thought to see him again. What was he doing here?

His sculpted bare chest gleamed silver, his pectoral muscles rising and falling as he breathed. Her heartbeat pounded, her skin prickling with gooseflesh, despite the warm summer heat.

'Looking for something?' he accused. His muscles did not appear taxed in the least by her body weight.

The last time she'd seen Ewan, he'd been a gangly boy of sixteen. Tall and thin, she remembered him as an awkward fighter, driven to succeed. He'd trained night and day, struggling to gain expertise.

The boy had become a man. A handsome one at that. His dark blond hair was cut short, emphasising a lean face and a strong jaw line. Broad shoulders revealed a tight strength she hadn't remembered. Ridged muscles lined his abdomen, down to…

Oh, dear God above. He was naked.

With that, every coherent thought left her. She gaped at him, unable to stop herself from stealing a long look. Her husband had never looked like this. Like a savage Celt, Ewan had a wildness about him that made her uneasy.

He eased her down the wall, still holding her wrists trapped. She had stopped struggling, too disconcerted at being near him. He released one wrist and ripped her hood free.

'You're a woman.'

She couldn't gather up her thoughts to answer.

'Who are you?' he demanded.

Her tongue caught in her throat. Didn't he remember her? After all the years she'd humiliated herself, tagging along and trying to defeat him in swordplay? But then, the darkness hid her features from him. He couldn't see her clearly.

'Katherine?' he asked gently.

Anger surged through her. No, she wasn't her beautiful, saintly sister. He ought to have figured that out, from her unexpected entrance into his chamber. Her sister wouldn't dream of entering a man's bedchamber, much less hunt a thief.

Before she could deny it, his mouth came down upon hers. A shocking sensation rushed through her skin, as though every part of her had caught fire. She forgot what she was seeking, forgot what was happening. The world around her crumbled, with nothing else, save his kiss.

She didn't know how to respond, and her lips remained frozen. Gentle and coaxing, Ewan slid his hands through her hair. His powerful thighs pressed up to her body, the hot length of him suddenly reminding her why it was unwise to awaken a sleeping man.

His hands caressed the hollow of her back, slipping beneath the man's tunic she wore. A light shiver rose up on her skin while his hands roamed her body, caressing her as though she were made of silk. The touch of his rough palms aroused her, and an aching warmth bloomed between her thighs.

The unfamiliar sensation caught her without warning. His rough palms stroked her spine, and she longed for his hands to move upwards. To fill up with her breasts, easing the heaviness and the shocking need.

Never had a man touched her in this way. Especially not her husband.

The memory slashed through her, shattering the moment. She pushed him away, her lips swollen and her body restless. 'I'm not Katherine.'

'Honora.'

She nodded, not trusting her voice. She reached for her dagger, but discovered it wasn't there.

Ewan raised the blade, the steel reflecting in the moonlight. 'Looking for this?'

'I didn't come here to harm you.'

'No. Only to rob me.'

'I didn't even know you were here,' she protested. 'I came looking for—' She almost said *a thief*, but silenced herself. For all she knew, Ewan was the thief. Doubtful, but she could not rule it out.

'Looking for your husband?' he queried. Accusations filled up his voice, as though she were a little girl caught stealing sweets.

'My husband is dead.' She pulled his hand off her other wrist and held out her palm. 'Give me back my dagger.'

'No.' Ewan held it out of reach, and Honora lunged for it. With her full weight bearing down on him, she took him down. Before she could grab the blade from his grasp, he rolled over, his body crushing hers.

Trapped, she felt every line of his body. And the dangerous glint in his eye made her aware that she had made a very bad decision.

'I'm not the boy I was, Honora.' He kept her pinioned, and tossed the knife away. 'You won't defeat me in a fight. Not any more.'

Her face flushed. Apparently, he hadn't forgotten how she'd bested him. More than once she'd disarmed him, her fighting skills equal to his. But that was long ago.

'Let me get up.' She tried to sit, and Ewan rolled off her. He sat beside her on the floor, seemingly at ease.

She tried to straighten her clothing, regaining her composure. 'Why are you here?'

'I'm going to wed your sister.'

She bit back the argument that he was but one man among many. Her father hadn't settled the betrothal yet, nor would he, until he had taken each man's measure.

'I'm sorry I kissed you,' he said. 'I mistook you for Katherine.'

His apology only heated up her temper. Honora knew she wasn't as comely as her sister, but she didn't need to be reminded of it. 'Katherine would never enter a stranger's bedchambers.'

'Unlike you.' There was a hint of humour beneath his tone, but she didn't acknowledge the teasing. It made her feel insulted, and she regretted her impulsive behaviour.

The door opened, and Honora jerked to her feet. Oh, heaven. Another angry MacEgan brother was staring at her.

'Am I interrupting something?' He glanced at Ewan, who didn't seem at all embarrassed to be naked with a woman beside him.

'Honora was just leaving.' Ewan gestured towards the door, and she took the invitation gratefully. She didn't even bother about the dagger, so thankful was she to flee their presence.

Bevan closed the door behind Honora, setting a torch within an iron sconce. Ewan didn't miss the questioning look upon his brother's face. 'Wrong chamber,' was his only offer of explanation.

Bevan didn't believe a word of it, and waited for him to elaborate. Frankly, Ewan didn't feel like it. He'd been awakened by the sound of Honora's intrusion, and hadn't at all expected to find a woman in his chamber.

His uneasiness escalated, for he'd acted on impulse, kissing her. At first, he'd tricked himself into thinking Katherine had come to see him. Fool. Katherine was shy and demure, not nearly as brazen as her sister.

Honora. He rested his fingertips against his mouth, thinking of the kiss he'd stolen. The taste of her lingered, soft and sweet. Completely unlike the stubborn girl who had plagued him so many years ago.

'Her father won't be pleased,' Bevan said. 'I drank nearly half a barrel of ale with him this night, pleading your case.' He grimaced at the late hour, running a hand through his hair. 'You'd best ensure that he doesn't find out about this. I doubt if he'll let you wed his youngest daughter if you were dallying with her sister.'

'Honora intruded upon my sleep.' Ewan returned to his pallet, flipping the woollen coverlet over himself. 'It wasn't my fault.'

'What was she doing?'

'Looking for someone.' He shrugged, as though it were of no importance. Though now that he considered it, he wondered precisely whom she had sought. 'What else did her father say?'

'He will consider your suit. Thomas de Renalt also spoke with him and offered his approval of the match.'

Ewan's tension eased a bit at the mention of his foster-father. 'Good.'

Sinking back onto his pallet, he stared at the ceiling while Bevan retreated to his own sleeping place. The torch flickered shadows on to the walls, while all around, he heard the noise of other guests. In the distance, a dog barked, its cries mingling with the sounds of night.

Honora's hair had been short, barely touching her shoulders. Ragged and silky, he hadn't expected that. He was accustomed to seeing her with a veil. The intimacy of her bare head reminded him of how he'd kissed her, winding his fingers through the softness.

Her hair was the colour of a midnight sky, her skin milky pale. Large, full lips had kissed him back, and she'd tasted like apples, succulent with a hint of sweetness. Her arms were not the soft skin of most women, but they held a lean strength. So often she'd tried to best him when they were fostered together. She'd won, more times than he wanted to remember.

Not any more.

He shifted upon the bed coverings, trying to force his thoughts back to Katherine as he drifted off to sleep. Even so, he couldn't forget Honora's kiss.

Chapter Two

'**Y**ou were seen leaving the MacEgan bedchamber last night.' Nicholas de Montford, the Baron of Ardennes, set his goblet firmly upon the table in his private chamber. He folded his hands, the morning sunlight reflecting on his gold rings.

Honora's cheeks burned, and she fumbled for an excuse. 'It was a mistake. I was merely trying to find—'

'Your rooms are on the opposite side of the *donjon*. Don't offer lies.'

Caught. Her father was many things, but he was not a fool. His harsh expression regarded her as if weighing a decision. Honora folded her hands and waited for him to go on. When he didn't, her agitation heightened. Was he going to punish her? What did he want?

'Nothing happened,' she offered. 'I left immediately.'

'That does not matter. You are a widow and must comport yourself with virtue.'

He made it sound as though she'd invaded MacEgan's bedchamber with the intent of deflowering him. Her cheeks burned brighter at the memory of his strong, naked body. Ewan had never looked like that as an adolescent. But now… Her body tightened at the memory of his kiss. Her fingernails dug into her wrists as she fought to subdue the thought.

'Is it your intention to remarry?' her father was asking.

'No!' she blurted out. Hadn't she endured marriage once before? Her husband, Ranulf, hadn't lived for more than a year, praise be. And, God willing, she would never have another husband.

Her father steepled his hands. 'I thought Ranulf would be a good husband for you, that he would provide you with a comfortable home. None of us expected him to die so soon.'

Honora didn't admit she was glad Ranulf was dead. But why would Nicholas think she'd want another husband? There was no need.

She crossed herself, in a half-hearted gesture of forgiveness. 'I don't want to wed again.'

Nicholas regarded her with a serious expression. 'You cannot remain here forever, Honora. It's been half a year since you left Ceredys.'

And yet, it didn't seem long enough. Her shoulders lowered, the guilt bearing down on her.

'One third of Ranulf's estate belongs to you by law,' Nicholas continued, narrowing his gaze at her. 'A pity you didn't have any sons of your own. You'd have gotten more.'

And thank Heaven for that. She wanted no son of Ceredys blood, no permanent reminder of Ranulf St Leger. Her husband had left most of the land to his son John, who was born of a former marriage.

Like a serpent John was, sleek and deceptive. She shivered at the memory. He could have her third of the estate and her dowry land, if it meant getting rid of him.

She blamed herself for what had happened at Ceredys. Even with the influence of John's grandmother Marie St Leger, she'd been unable to stop him from stripping away every last penny of rents from the villagers.

What kind of a warrior could she call herself, if she let her people endure such a fate? Time had slipped away from her, and she still had not managed to conceive of a suitable plan.

'How much longer do you intend to hide behind my walls?' her father asked softly.

'I'm not hiding.'

He cast a look that said he didn't believe her.

'I will go back,' she said quietly. 'Soon enough.' If John were removed from power, she could try to repair the damage he'd done. But she couldn't overthrow him without help. 'I would ask you again, to lend me soldiers.'

'No. It isn't my place, nor yours, to meddle with John's... difficulties at Ceredys.'

'He's robbed them of their food,' she protested. 'You cannot stand by and do nothing. There are innocent folk suffering from what he's done.'

His expression hardened. 'Then perhaps you should marry a man with an army.'

Honora expelled a sigh of frustration, shaking her head. She would find a way to help them without relying upon another man.

Nicholas continued on, oblivious to her refusal. 'It would be the sensible thing to do. You're young enough to bear many sons.'

Honora reached to her side, but she'd forgotten her dagger wasn't there. Squeezing the grip usually brought her comfort, but she doubted if anything could calm the temper rising this time.

'Father, please.' She closed her eyes, wishing there was some way to make him understand. 'I need time.'

She would not marry again. Never could she forget the ten months of hell she'd suffered, nor the months afterwards of avoiding John.

'You're not getting any younger. And if you want any children at all, you've no choice.'

Honora swallowed, not facing her father. The idea of bearing a child terrified her. She hadn't made a good wife— why would she expect to be a good mother?

Her father didn't seem to notice her silence. 'No, I believe it is God's will, Honora. I chose poorly for your first husband. For the second, I'll allow you to choose. You may select first from among the suitors here.'

'But those men are here for Katherine!' she protested. Did he expect them to simply change their minds? It would never happen. She knew what she was. A woman who was far too impulsive, too impatient to be a wife. She didn't care about the household accounts or about mending clothing. Her interests lay in the castle defences and whether or not the men were well trained.

Her hands reached around her waist, as though holding back herself. Asking her to wed again meant facing that humiliation once more, of being an unworthy wife.

'I won't do it,' she said softly.

Nicholas sighed, refilling his tankard with ale. 'All you need is a real man in your bed and a babe swelling beneath your skirts. Then you'll be happy.'

A real man in her bed? She ground her teeth, longing to tell him just how she felt about that. What did her father know about choosing the right man for her?

Nothing at all. He'd married her off to the first man who'd asked. Her stomach soured at the memory of the disastrous marriage.

'You cannot force me to marry.'

'No, but I can force you to return to Ceredys.' Nicholas drained his cup, confident in his decision. 'You are of little use to me here. You've an estate of your own to manage.'

She didn't argue that she'd never been allowed to manage any part of Ceredys. She'd been more of a prisoner than a wife.

'But I am not without a heart, Honora,' her father went on. 'If you have your eye upon someone, I can arrange your marriage sooner than Katherine's. Ewan MacEgan, perhaps?' A smug look crossed Nicholas's face.

'Never.' The denial ripped from her mouth without a second's hesitation. Ewan was here for Katherine. He didn't even like her, not after all she'd done to him while they were fostered together. 'As I told you, I didn't mean to be in his room. It was an accident.'

'Hmm.' Her father did not appear convinced. 'Well, there are seven other men, all of them from noble families.'

He truly wasn't listening to her, was he? She tried another tack. 'Even if I did agree to remarry, my inheritance complicates matters. A new husband would have to dwell alongside John, else he'd have to surrender the land entirely.'

And she'd rather die than live with John St Leger again.

'True enough. But that's the way of marriage, isn't it? I married your mother for her estates here and in Normandy.'

'I married once for duty. I won't do it again.' Honora set her mouth in a firm line.

Her father's face darkened, and he puffed up with his own obstinacy. 'Aye, you will. For I'll not let Katherine wed until you do.'

Had he struck her in the throat, she could not have been more stunned. Why would he do this? What could he hope to gain from it?

'That isn't fair.' She spoke quietly, feigning the gentle quality he preferred. But inwardly, she was raging.

'I am hosting a feast on the morrow,' her father commented. 'I expect you to be there. There will be a tournament, and the suitors will compete for your entertainment.'

Oh, Jesu. Not that. She had no desire to look like a fool while the suitors fawned over her sister. Was she supposed to sit beside Katherine on a dais, hoping that a man would ask for her favour? Perhaps one man would show pity.

She had her pride. No, it mattered not what her father wanted. She'd not suffer through such a humiliation.

But Nicholas read her thoughts. 'If you do not come, I will have you dragged out of your chamber and brought forth.'

He meant it, too. She gripped her skirts, wanting to rend the fabric out of frustration. 'Yes, Father.'

She was about to leave, when he added one more warning. 'Behave yourself, Honora.'

She had no appetite for breaking her fast, no matter that the rest of the guests were partaking of the delicious array of foods. Honora strode through the Hall, trying to ignore the men enjoying their meal.

Her father's vow made it impossible not to notice them. Most were younger, and all wealthy.

Well, all, save one. Her gaze flickered upon Ewan MacEgan. His blond hair was slightly tousled, as though he'd raked his hand through it. From the way his sleeve tightened against his upper arm… Holy Virgin, there was no denying his strength.

Ewan reached for an apple, adding it to the food he'd already selected to break his fast. Honeyed cakes, bread, braised lamb and fresh salmon were piled high before him.

It was a wonder there was any food left, Honora thought to herself. Ewan had always been one to enjoy a meal, but from the look of him, there was not a trace of fat—only raw muscle.

'Did you find the man you were looking for?' he asked, when she was forced to walk past him.

Honora pretended as though he hadn't spoken. Blood rushed to her face at the memory of last night. It was easier to remember Ewan as the boy, not the man. When she walked past the trestle table, he reached out and caught her wrist.

'Let me pass.'

'Not yet. Where is your sister? I've not seen her this morn.'

Honora took his palm, trying to force her way out of his grasp. 'I imagine she is surrounded by her other suitors, listening to them describe the pearl of her skin or the silk of her hair. Now if you'll excuse me—'

Ewan stood, still holding her wrist. If she twisted away, the skin would bruise. But standing this close to him, she could smell the clean scent of him, like summer rain. He wore a forest-green tunic and brown trews, rather like a huntsman. His fair hair was cut short, resting against his neck. Vivid green eyes warmed as they looked upon her.

'Your father spoke of a tournament. To prove my strength and ability to protect his daughter, so he said.'

No, it was more like parading the men in front of them. Like animals for the choosing, Honora thought sourly.

'Let go of me, Ewan.'

He turned over her palm, studying the rough calluses from years of wielding a sword. 'Are you still as good as you used to be?' There was a hint of challenge beneath his words.

She knew what he meant. And though she had kept it hidden from her father, she trained among the men at least once every sennight. 'Better.'

'I am glad to hear it.' His shrewd expression revealed that he hadn't forgotten any of the sword matches they'd fought against one another. And though she had won often, Ewan had never once complained about being bested by a woman. Many a time he could have revealed her secret. Instead, he'd held his silence and trained even harder.

Now, she wasn't so certain she could win against him. His body was larger, his muscles firm. When he'd lifted her up, it was as if it took no effort at all.

As he bit into a piece of bread, she found herself watching the way his tunic clung to his body, tightening across his chest. She remembered Ewan's warm skin pressing close to hers, and his ardent kiss, the rush of sweet aching.

The direction of her thoughts was disconcerting, and Honora forced her mind back to the present. At Ewan's side, she spied a familiar weapon.

'I want my dagger back.'

He shrugged. 'And you'll have it. Once you've told me what I wish to know.'

'I already told you. I don't know where Katherine is.'

'That isn't the price of your dagger.'

'Then what is?'

'Tell me more about your sister. What does she covet? What gifts can I bring her that will give me an advantage over the others?'

Honora didn't answer at first. A sliver of anger balled up inside, wounding her pride. She didn't want to give him information about Katherine, didn't want to aid his courtship.

But it wasn't jealousy, she told herself. No, it was simply that Ewan wasn't the man for Katherine. He was far too aggressive, too bold for her sister's gentle ways.

'What about an animal?' he suggested. 'Perhaps a kitten. I haven't seen many cats around, and it might be useful to her.'

'A kitten,' she repeated, while mad thoughts of vengeance flowed through her mind. Her conscience prickled, but she stamped it down. It would serve him right for kissing her, stealing her dagger and demanding information about Katherine.

'No one has given her a kitten, thus far,' she admitted.

Jesu. Now she would have to go to confession. Thank goodness Father Louis was nearly deaf. She could confess to murder, and the priest would offer the same absolution as ever.

Ewan released her wrist. 'Was that so difficult?' He unsheathed the dagger and handed it to her, pommel first. 'And you should have the blacksmith adjust this weapon. The balance is off.'

'It was broken once.' Her husband, Ranulf, had destroyed the blade in a fit of temper, tossing it into the fire. Honora had never expected to see it again, but she'd found it among her belongings shortly after she'd left Ceredys. Marie St Leger must have ordered it repaired, though Honora didn't know why. Though she was grateful for the dagger's return, she disliked the large pommel the blacksmith had added, preferring a simpler design.

Honora rubbed her wrist and tucked the weapon into her

girdle without another word. She strode away, trying to push her way past the irrational anger. What was it about Ewan MacEgan that tangled up her sense of reason? As a child, she'd lost her head over him. As a woman, she found him entirely too confident.

Entirely too handsome and strong.

Oh, she needed to bash her head against the stone wall. Perhaps that would knock some sense into her. She didn't need a man like him, or any man. Despite her father's wishes, she would never marry again.

But if she didn't, Nicholas would force her to leave Ardennes and return to Ceredys. The very thought made her skin turn to ice. She wasn't ready yet. Nicholas wasn't about to lend her men against John, and she didn't have soldiers of her own.

She'd tried to hire mercenaries two moons ago, believing that they could remove John from power and allow her to return to Ceredys. But she'd learned the darker side of soldiers, for they'd stolen her money and done nothing in return. Her naïvety had cost her dearly.

No, she needed men of honour. And men of that nature required more coins than she had.

Her father's suggestion that she wed a man with an army wouldn't do, either. A new husband would have no interest in going to war against John of Ceredys.

There was no one to help.

A *frisson* of grief curled over her. Marie St Leger, John's grandmother, might have known what to do, had she lived. She had been one of the most intelligent ladies Honora had ever known. Strong-willed and furious with her own sons, Marie treated her like a daughter. And it was because of Marie that she'd managed to escape at all.

It broke her heart to think of the woman's death, only a single moon ago. She'd kept her vow to pray for Marie's soul each night.

Honora blinked back the wetness rising in her eyes. She

needed a moment to herself, a chance to think. Perhaps if she rode out from the castle, she'd find a solution for the people of Ceredys.

She walked to the stables and ordered a groom to prepare her palfrey. When the horse was ready, she urged the animal away from the castle grounds. Two guards joined her as escorts, but she ignored them, pretending for a moment that she was alone.

A light summer rain began to fall, misting her cheeks as she rode. The scent of horse and musty earth made her throat tighten. Why did this have to happen? Was God punishing her for her disobedience as a girl? She'd gone against the natural order of things, wanting to be more like a warrior than a woman.

And it was wrong, wasn't it? Why couldn't she content herself with womanly things? Why was there such a need inside, to be as strong as a man?

Unwanted tears mingled with the rain. All she'd ever wanted was to please her father. She had worn the silk bliauds and jewels, pretending to be feminine and everything he'd wanted in a daughter. But he'd hardly noticed her. Only when she argued with him did he pay her any heed.

Katherine had never lacked for attention. Their father had given her everything she'd ever desired, lavishing her with gifts and affection. And though Honora never admitted it, she envied her sister.

She slowed the horse, letting it stop by the river to drink. Her veil was damp from the rain, the water clinging to her skin.

It was her penance, she supposed. She'd come to accept that her father would never love her. Though he would never say it, she knew he blamed her for the death of her twin. The daughter had lived, while the coveted son had died.

In a way, it was why she wanted to fight so badly. She wanted to atone for her brother's death, to become the warrior he would have been. And perhaps then, her father would find something worthy inside her.

In secret, she'd learned to fight, with Ewan's help. Now, she watched the men train each day. She borrowed swords from the armoury, practising until her arms burned with exhaustion.

Never once had she shown Nicholas her skill. She was afraid of dishonouring her father, of embarrassing him in front of everyone. How could he ever be proud of a daughter who behaved like a man?

No. He'd hate her even more. And so she'd hidden it from him. For now, she could only use her fighting skills to protect the castle from petty thieves. That is, if she could catch the man.

As the rain intensified, Honora reluctantly turned her horse back to the castle. The ride had helped to clear her head, but now she had to decide what to do about her father's threat.

She could feign acceptance of her father's wishes, pretending to consider a suitor. Once Katherine was safely wed, she could try to escape the arrangement. The only problem was finding a man willing to go along with her ruse. Honora didn't like the thought of lying or causing anyone to feel humiliated.

She would have to find the right person. Honesty was best for such an arrangement.

Her hand closed upon the grip of her dagger. And in the meantime, she still had a thief to catch.

There were seven other suitors. Seven, for the love of *Críost*. Ewan stood watching the men, each bringing Katherine a gift. She'd already bestowed smiles upon those who had given her silks and ribbons.

Gerald Elshire, heir to the barony of Beaulais, had brought her an emerald. From the clouded surface of the gemstone, Ewan wondered if it was coloured glass.

Not that Ewan could afford gems or silks. Instead, he'd bribed one of the serfs to fetch him a kitten from the village. His brother's wife, Isabel, loved her cats, and no doubt

Katherine would feel the same. The mewing animal rested within a basket, lightly covered with a cloth.

Katherine sat within the solar, her white veil hiding the length of sable hair. Pearls adorned her sapphire silk bliaud, and the sleeves were fitted tightly to slender arms, the cuffs draping to the floor. She reminded him of a princess, ethereal and enchanting. Just looking at her made him feel unworthy. She appeared sweet-tempered, beautiful…and completely out of his reach.

The idea of invading a man's bedchamber would horrify the Lady Katherine. A jolt of remembrance shot into his groin at the memory of Honora. He imagined her body would be lean and sleek. Honora would never lie passively upon his bed. She would meet him, thrust for thrust, crying out with pleasure.

Damn. He blinked, forcing the vision away. He didn't care anything for Honora. The brief kiss he'd stolen had been a mistake. Nothing of any importance to either of them.

Ewan tried to envision kissing Katherine. Her kiss would be as gentle as her spirit. When she became his bride, he would have to be mindful of her virginal softness, tempting her slowly until she yielded to him. And she would marry him. He would find a way to coax her into accepting his suit.

The group of men gradually shifted until at last Ewan was standing before her. With a deep bow, he greeted her. 'Lady Katherine, it is good to see you again.' He set the basket down at her feet.

Katherine managed a smile, but her nose wrinkled, as though she were fighting a sneeze. Offering both hands to him in welcome, she smiled. 'Ewan MacEgan. It has been many years since I've seen you.'

'I've thought of you often, since my fostering ended.' He sent her a sincere smile, hoping she would look upon him with favour. 'And I've brought you a gift.' He uncovered the basket, revealing the grey-striped kitten. The animal perched its paws upon the edge of the basket, mewing softly.

Katherine's smile seemed forced. 'How…kind of you.' But she made no move to take the animal.

Ewan picked up the cat, holding it out to her. The feline nipped at his fingertips. Katherine's smile grew strained, but she reached out and stroked the animal's head. The kitten purred with delight, rubbing its head against her fingertips.

Her nose wrinkled again, and this time, she did sneeze. 'Thank you.' She gestured for a maid to take the cat away, and sneezed again.

A suspicion suddenly took root in his mind. Could Honora have played him false? As Katherine's eyes grew red, and she continued sneezing, it was apparent that he'd fallen neatly into her sister's trap.

'I didn't realise the animal would offend you,' he said, taking the basket back from the maid. 'I'll bring you a different gift.'

Katherine rubbed her eyes. 'No, it's all right. Truly. I like cats, but I seem to have trouble whenever I'm around them.' She tried to smile, but sneezed again.

No doubt Honora had known this. A slow fury built up inside him, anger that he'd believed her. He'd thought there was no harm in asking for help, never realising she would trick him so.

Honora would have much to answer for when he saw her again. He did not stay in the solar with Katherine for long, for he needed to bring her something else. Since his funds were limited, he could not buy expensive trinkets. Perhaps a ribbon to match her blue eyes.

He frowned, thinking. They were blue, weren't they?

It didn't matter. As long as his gift made her smile, that was enough. Ewan grimaced, not wanting to waste time with bargaining and purchasing. He needed to train for the tournament on the morrow, proving his abilities. He had no doubt he could best any man there.

The only men who had ever truly presented a challenge were his brothers. As the youngest MacEgan, they'd tormented him in every manner, never sparing him, even when he'd begged for mercy. Because of it, he'd gained strength beyond that of most men.

There was a bond among them, a knowledge that he could ask his brothers for anything, and they would be there for him.

Bevan would help him prepare for the tournament. And right now, Ewan needed the distraction of a fight to take his mind off his failed gift.

He searched the *donjon*, but his brother was nowhere to be found. Outside, the rain had increased, spattering against the mud so that training would be nigh impossible.

Ewan cursed, resting his hand upon his own sword hilt. The weapon held no jewels, nor was it as finely made as his brother Patrick's. Serviceable and simple, the blade was all he'd been able to afford. But it belonged entirely to him.

He noticed a door opening quietly, and a small figure slipped inside the armoury. His instincts went on alert, and he recognised Honora instantly.

His palm curved over his sword hilt, gripping the metal as though it were her neck. He wanted to throttle her for making him look like a fool before Katherine.

And a fool he was, for believing Honora's words. He had a few choice things to say to her. He threw open the door to the armoury, and found her standing alone, a sword in her palm.

Her veil was wet from the rain, her damp saffron bliaud silhouetting her slender form. She was taller than most women, her chin high enough to reach his shoulder.

'Nothing's changed, I see.' He let the door close behind him. A circle of torches lit the dim space, while above, the rain pounded upon the wooden roof. 'You're still borrowing your father's weapons.'

'What do you want, Ewan?'

'An apology, perhaps. Or revenge would be acceptable.' He unsheathed his sword, circling her.

Honora moved immediately into a defensive stance, never

taking her eyes from him. Though the bliaud and white veil were meant to emphasise her womanly shape, there was no mistaking the expert way she handled the sword.

'I'm amazed you can lift that,' he commented, keeping his footwork even and smooth. 'It's almost as heavy as you are.'

'Stop flattering me, MacEgan. I've been using a sword as long as you have.'

'Really?' He lunged, and the steel of his blade met hers. It was a test, to see if she remembered any of her earlier training.

Honora tore off her veil and slashed her sword towards his head. 'Really.'

Her sleeves moulded to her body, revealing the outline of muscle. Though her skirts should have hindered her movements, she took large strides that kept her from falling.

Her dark hair hung against the back of her neck, and the ends stuck out, as though she'd hacked them off with a knife. The effect made her face softer, his eyes drawn to that mouth again. Right now, her lips were tight as she concentrated on the fight. Her eyes weren't the same green as his own, but a softer shade, like new spring leaves.

As she struck blows against his blade, he parried each one without effort. Not once did he reveal the stiffness in his palms that made it difficult to grasp the hilt fully. The scarred skin was a permanent weakness that he fought to overcome.

'You lied to me about your sister.' He switched hands and struck back, forcing her to retreat. The sound of metal against metal reverberated in the stillness. 'She doesn't like cats at all. They make her sneeze.'

At least Honora had the grace to look guilty. But when he lowered his blade, she spun, slicing the sword at his throat.

He dived, tripping her legs with his own as he rolled upon the hard ground. Her weapon flew from her hands, and she struck the dirt. Within moments, he had her lying on her back, her wrists pinned.

'Admit your defeat, Honora.'

Chapter Three

She grimaced. 'If you'd paid attention while we were growing up, you'd have known that Katherine can't abide cats.'

'She was fourteen years old when I was fostered with the Earl of Longford. I rarely saw her.' He released her, sheathing his sword before he sat on the ground, resting his back against the wall. She retrieved her sword and cleaned it, before placing it back upon the wall. Afterwards, she sat down an arm's distance from him, her knees drawn up beneath her skirts.

'But you want to wed Katherine.'

'I do, yes.' He eyed her closely, the way a thin sheen of perspiration lined her brow, the hitch in her breathing from the sword fight. Her riotous black hair stuck out in every direction.

'Why?'

He hesitated in answering, for there were selfish reasons, as well as his own fascination with Katherine. He admitted to himself that were it not for her dowry and lands, he wouldn't be pursuing her. Honora would see the truth, regardless of what he said. Always had there been complete honesty between them.

'She is beautiful—' he began, but broke off as his gaze shifted over to Honora's features. She had changed in the years since he'd seen her. But unlike her strong, firm body, her face held a vulnerability. Soft, like the woman she tried to hide.

At his stare, she tried to smooth out the locks, which made her hair even worse. With a wry smile, she added, 'Beautiful, the way I am not.'

There was chagrin in her voice, a self-consciousness that he hadn't expected. Ewan reached out and touched the ends of her hair. 'You're fair enough, Honora. But in a different way from Katherine.' Like water and sand, the two sisters could not have been more opposite.

'You are a skilled fighter,' he commented. 'Better than some of your father's guards, I'd wager.'

'I'm not good enough, or I would have beaten you.'

The corner of his mouth turned up. 'You'll never beat me again, *a chara.*'

She rose to her feet, studying the blades mounted to the wall. 'Shall we find out?'

He mused upon it. It would do no harm to let her try. 'We'll have a wager, then. If I win this sparring match, you'll tell me truly what would win the heart of your sister.'

'You're not going to win.'

So sure of herself, wasn't she? He gestured towards the wall. 'Go on, then. Choose your sword.'

She selected the same blade, lightly slashing the air. Without warning, she aimed the blade towards his middle, and he blocked the thrust.

'And what did you want, if you win the wager?' he asked.

'Your heart on a pike, perhaps.' She gave a thin smile and struck again, releasing anger that appeared to be about something else, rather than the match she'd lost earlier.

'If you want to win my heart, there are nicer ways to go about it. A bit of land, perhaps. Or a new horse.'

'I'll buy you a ribbon for your hair,' she gritted out, her blade swinging in a vicious arc.

He let her tire herself out, but there was no question she

had skill better than most men. Her technique was flawless; if he hadn't been paying attention, there was a time or two when she genuinely could have won.

Her cheeks were flushed with exertion, her eyes narrowed with complete concentration. 'Why aren't you fighting me back?' she demanded. 'Stop defending my blows, and show me what you know.'

Her challenge made him quicken his assault. He attacked, forcing her towards the corner of a room. Using his full strength, he kept his sword moving, sending strikes against her weapon that surely would weaken her arm.

But still she kept meeting his force with her own blade. Her face was tight, exhaustion making her move slower.

When at last he had her trapped, he swung his sword, and she didn't block him. Catching himself at the last moment before he skewered her, he cursed and drove the blade into the wall.

Honora kicked his feet out from under him, and his head cracked against the ground. She sat upon him, holding the sword to his throat, one hand upon the hilt, the other on the flat side of the blade.

'Do you yield?' Her voice was throaty, as though he were her prisoner in bed sport. No longer did he care that he'd lost this match. Honora's skirts had ridden up, her thighs straddling his waist. Her firm backside rested upon his manhood, and instantly he hardened.

With the close contact, Honora reddened, suddenly aware of her effect on him. Ewan palmed her hips, intending to lift her aside. Instead, he felt the firm shape of her bottom, and Honora expelled a sharp breath.

Her face was bright with exertion, her hair damp with perspiration. She looked like a woman who had been made love to for hours. Gritting his teeth, Ewan tried to ignore his body's reaction.

'You play a dangerous game, Honora. I could have harmed you.'

'But I won, didn't I?'

His stomach muscles flexed as he took both of her hands. Ignoring the possibility of the sword slicing his palm, he pushed her backwards until he was seated upright. She had no choice but to loosen her grip on the weapon.

With his face so near to hers, he could conquer her in another way, their mouths mingling in a kiss like the one before. His desire flared with the need to possess her again. Honora tried to scramble off his lap, but he couldn't let go of her. Not yet. He might have lost this sparring match, but he wanted her to understand his displeasure.

'What is my forfeit?' He reached back and gripped her nape, winding his fingers in her shorn hair to trap her. Her breath caught, her shoulders rising as though she were suddenly afraid of him. The sword rested between them, and Honora moved it away.

'Let me up, MacEgan.'

'After you answer my question. You never said what you wanted, if I lost the match.'

She dug in her heels and tried to push backwards, but the motion sent her rocking back against his erection. He could almost imagine loosening his trews, raising up her skirts until he sank inside her.

Damn her. Whether it was intentional or not, she'd awakened a craving he wanted to satisfy. But he could not. Not if he wanted to wed Katherine. Lust was something he'd never expected with Honora, but it was easily avoided.

'I want...your help in capturing a thief.' Honora didn't sound fully convinced, and he wondered why she'd hesitated. She tried again to escape his grasp, and this time he allowed her to get up.

'What thief?'

She picked up the blade, cleaning it meticulously. 'Someone stole a wooden chest from the chapel, and I believe it's a member of the household.'

'Have you spoken with your father?'

'Yes, but he's found nothing.' Frustration tensed in her face. 'It could be one of Katherine's suitors.'

'But you don't think it's me.'

She rolled her eyes. 'I wouldn't be telling you all this if I believed that. And besides, I went looking for the chest in your room. It wasn't there.'

'What do you want me to do?'

'Listen to the other suitors. You always were good at slipping around without anyone seeing you. Let me know what you find out.'

'Why does it matter to you, Honora?' He leaned against the wall, noting that she was still uncomfortable. 'You live on your husband's estate now, do you not?'

'I am not ready to return. Not yet.'

The violent edge to her voice drew his curiosity. She was running away from something. Or someone. A dark thought occurred to him, as he recalled his brother's wife, Genevieve. She had been betrothed to a Norman knight who'd taken his fists to her. Thanks to Bevan, she'd escaped the marriage.

Was someone threatening Honora in the same way?

'Who has harmed you?' he asked, softening his tone.

She gripped the sword tightly, lifting the blade into a fighting stance. When he looked closer into her eyes, he saw fury, not fear. 'Do you think I would let any man hurt me?'

Her words were meant to push him away, to convince him to leave her alone. And yet, he didn't quite believe her. Something had happened, something that troubled her deeply.

'It's late,' Honora continued. 'Send word to me if you learn anything about the thief.'

He didn't ask her why she cared about a stolen chest. It was apparent she needed something to distract her. And though he didn't particularly want to get involved, he couldn't allow a thief among them, either.

Inclining his head, he agreed. 'I'll help you.'

* * *

The games began at dawn. Lord Ardennes had arranged several matches to test their skills, among them wrestling, foot races, archery and sword fighting. Ewan had selected wrestling as his first test of skill.

Before he approached the fighting arena, his brother Bevan offered a warning. 'They don't like Irishmen. Be prepared for treachery.'

'Don't interfere. This is my fight.'

'If they threaten your life, I'll interfere, tournament or not. You're my brother.'

His older brother still held little faith. But then, Bevan had been preoccupied, as of late. His wife, Genevieve, was expecting their fourth babe this summer, and Ewan knew Bevan would rather be at her side than here.

'I'm going to win,' he reassured Bevan quietly. And he would. There was no question in his mind that he would claim the victory. His brother looked unconvinced, but at last, Bevan relented and stepped back.

Ewan moved towards the dais, where Lord Ardennes waited with his two daughters. The other suitors were dressed in preparation for the fighting, most wearing chainmail armour. All were Norman, and each one held the title of knight or lord.

It made Ewan uncomfortably aware that he was the lowest ranked among them. And though the Baron had agreed to let him court Katherine, he suspected it was out of courtesy to his foster-father—not because Lord Ardennes had any intention of honouring a match between them.

Uneasily, he awaited his turn to greet Katherine. Both women wore their finest gowns: Katherine in a cream-coloured bliaud embroidered with gold, while Honora wore a dark blue gown. Their heads were veiled and crowned with silver bands.

Lord Ardennes was saying something that he couldn't hear, and Honora stared off into the distance, her cheeks flushed.

'What was that?' he asked the man beside him.

'The Baron is offering both daughters in marriage. His eldest daughter will wed before the younger.'

Honora was seeking a husband? Ewan tensed at the declaration. Now why hadn't she mentioned that? She'd said nothing about remarrying. And she was supposed to wed before Katherine could choose a suitor?

From the guilt written on her face, it must be true.

Suddenly, he began to wonder if their chance encounters were not so coincidental. She'd crept into his bedchamber, for God's sakes. As he drew closer to the dais to pay his respects, his irritation with Honora grew.

Of all the women in Christendom, Honora was the very last one he'd wed. Her stubborn nature clashed with his own, and he hadn't forgotten the way she'd tormented him as a lad. The man who took her to wife would need infinite patience.

He forced his anger away as he bowed before Katherine. 'Lady Katherine, you look lovely this morn.'

She smiled and offered him a white ribbon as a token. 'I shall enjoy watching you fight, MacEgan.'

From his periphery, he noticed Honora glaring at him. He ignored it, for she had no cause to be displeased.

'I owe you a gift still,' he continued, directing his full attention to Katherine. 'Is there aught you desire?'

She thought a moment. With a bright smile, she offered, 'I should like to spend an afternoon getting reacquainted. The last time I saw you was years ago.'

Satisfaction poured through him, reinforcing his confidence. So, he did have a chance at winning her hand. The pretty blush upon Katherine's cheeks made him feel like he could lift up a stone wall. 'If it means spending time with you, I would be glad of it.'

Honora kept her gaze firmly fixed upon the fighting arena, but he sensed she was rolling her eyes.

Katherine beamed. 'Excellent. We shall bring a meal with us, and Honora can come as well.'

Honora blinked at her sister, sending a fierce look in his direction as if to say, *not a good idea.*

He didn't think so either. He'd rather have time alone with Katherine. Likely Honora had no desire to be a chaperon, but neither of them could protest without raising suspicions. 'I will await you on the morrow.'

'At the stables, if you please. Just past terce.'

He bowed in agreement, and turned to Honora. Though she attempted a smile, it was strained around the edges. He lowered his voice. 'You didn't tell me you were planning to wed again.'

'No, I didn't.' From the tension lining her face, she was not pleased. Though she wore the outer finery of a lady, she appeared uninterested in finding a husband. Instead, she seemed to be counting down the hours until her escape.

'Is that what you want?'

Her discomfort seemed to intensify. 'I don't wish to talk about it now.'

Suspicions took root, but he held back the questions. Instead, as a gesture of peace, he offered, 'I wish you luck in finding a man who pleases you.'

'These men aren't here for me, Ewan,' she whispered, glancing down at her hands. 'They're here for Katherine. Yourself included.'

Misery lined her voice. He hadn't expected to feel sorry for her. Though he didn't know what, if anything, he could do, he supposed he could investigate the suitors. He'd promised to help her find the thief, after all.

'I'll find out what I can about the other men.' At least it was something. He bowed to her, tightening his fist around Katherine's ribbon.

As he turned to leave, she called out to him. 'Ewan, wait.'

'What is it?'

She seemed to weigh an invisible decision over in her mind before she leaned in. 'The tallest man, Sir Ademar of

Dolwyth, likes to fight with both hands. Watch him carefully when you face him with a blade.'

'I will.'

The ghost of a smile touched her lips. 'I bid you good luck. You'll need it.'

'He's handsome, isn't he?' Katherine cupped her chin in her hands, leaning forwards to watch the wrestling match about to begin.

'Who? Sir Ademar?'

'No, Ewan.' Her sister gave a dreamy smile, which chafed at Honora. For the love of heaven, Katherine barely knew him. Already, the very mention of Ewan MacEgan seemed to make her swoon.

Honora gripped her knife, and tried to keep the annoyance out of her voice. 'He has hardly any land of his own.'

'But his brother is a king. Surely that would make him a prince.'

'Patrick MacEgan is a petty king, of no higher rank than our own father. And Ewan is the youngest of five brothers.'

Her sister didn't seem to care. 'Father would not have invited him, were he not a suitable husband.'

Honora didn't point out that it was their father's best friend, the Earl of Longford, who had done the inviting. She glanced over at Longford, who was seated near their father. Stout, with grey hair and a grey beard, Longford's eyes were quick and shrewd. She'd always had a fondness for the Earl, when she'd spent nearly a year with their family. Her father had sent her away, as a punishment for her mischief.

It had turned out to be the greatest gift, for there she had secretly learned to wield a sword.

She caught the eye of Bevan MacEgan. From the way Bevan kept his eyes upon Ewan, even during his conversation with the Earl, Honora sensed his protective nature. The scars upon both cheeks emphasised a harsh face, making her uneasy. It would not be wise to make enemies of the MacEgan family.

The first wrestling match was about to begin, and Ewan was paired up against Gerald Elshire of Beaulais. Beaulais was a shorter man, with reddish hair and a stocky form. His family name was well known, and Honora leaned in to watch them fight.

Ewan had stripped off his outer clothing, save the pair of trews he wore. Katherine's white ribbon was tied around his upper arm, and in the morning light, the sun glinted off his dark blond hair. Heavy muscles outlined his chest, his body as honed as a sword. Though Honora had seen him unclothed before, it was as if he were an entirely different man.

He had one of the most magnificent forms she'd ever seen. His broad shoulders narrowed to ridged stomach muscles, and his trews strained against the tight outline of his hips. Honora's cheeks flushed at the sight, for she'd touched him that night, feeling his smooth skin still warm from sleep.

She shifted her thighs restlessly. Only yesterday, she'd inadvertently aroused him, and she well remembered the feeling of his body nestled against hers.

Don't think of him in that way. He doesn't want you.

Honora closed her eyes, trying to forget his heated mouth claiming her own. Even now, watching Ewan move against his opponent, her body grew uncomfortably sensitive.

Ewan locked his arm around Beaulais, his arm muscles flexing. Where had he come by such strength? Honora recalled him building stone walls, hefting large boulders when they'd grown up, but his muscles then had been lean and tight.

Now, they showed a massive strength she'd never known he possessed. No wonder he'd been able to lift her so easily. But despite his size, he'd been careful not to crush her when his body weight had rested atop her own.

She took a deep breath, trying to block out the other

memory, of the last time a naked man had lain atop her. Her wedding night had been painful, humiliating and empty. And enduring Ranulf's bed was something she'd loathed. Not once had she felt any desire for him, only the hope that he would be done with her quickly.

What would it be like to lie with a man who touched her with gentleness, kindling true desire? Her gaze shifted back to Ewan, and beneath her gown, goose bumps formed upon her skin.

No. She didn't want to take a lover, especially not now.

Beaulais threw a punch, and MacEgan's head snapped backwards. Blood trickled from his lip, but Ewan only smiled at his opponent. He didn't look at all bothered by the slight wound. He responded with a knee to Beaulais's stomach, moving in to wrap his right arm around the man's neck. His arm flexed, strangling his opponent.

Beaulais tried to escape his grasp, but Ewan snaked his foot around the man's leg and tripped him, sending him sprawling on his back. Within a few seconds more, the match was over.

Katherine clapped in delight. 'Wasn't he magnificent?'

Honora could only nod. *How* had he learned to fight like that? She found herself hoping Ewan would win, her attention focused completely upon him. Match after match he won, until he was declared champion of wrestling.

In archery, Beaulais bested him, while Ewan's arrow went slightly to the right of the centre.

In the foot race, Ewan barely edged out Sir Ademar of Dolwyth, claiming his second win. Last was the sword fight, and the men were allowed a short rest before the final test of skill.

Honora stood, hoping to walk a little, to diminish the nervous energy gathering in her stomach. Her path was blocked by her father, the Earl of Longford and Bevan MacEgan, who were engaged in conversation.

'By God, I knew I should have placed a wager on Ewan.' The Earl shot a pleased look at Bevan. 'Your brother has improved greatly since he was fostered here. I knew a bit of Norman training would help.'

'Irish training,' Bevan corrected.

Longford only smirked. 'Thought you'd say that. He's done well for himself, and I believe he'd make an excellent match with young Katherine here. Might as well get them married so you can return to Genevieve, eh?'

'If that is Ewan's wish.'

'Other suitors are competing for Katherine's hand,' Nicholas interrupted. 'However, he might consider my eldest daughter, Honora.'

Honora's cheeks flamed. Her father made it sound as though she were an afterthought, a woman taken as a consolation prize.

She reached out and clenched the pommel of her dagger. It shouldn't matter whether Ewan wed Katherine or not. Why should she be anything but happy for her sister? She certainly didn't want Ewan for herself.

More than ever, she wanted to leave behind this tournament, to hide in the armoury or in the stables. Her unsettled future made it impossible to do anything else but worry. She hadn't been able to concentrate on finding the thief, ever since her father's suggestion that she marry. And she couldn't shake the feeling that someone was watching her.

She made her excuses, claiming she needed a moment to take care of her personal needs.

'Return within a few minutes,' Nicholas warned. 'The sword fighting will be the last competition, and I expect you to be present.'

The glint in her father's eyes made it clear that he would brook no arguments. Sometimes she wondered if he secretly knew about her swordfighting skills. She'd been careful never to let him see, for he would not understand her need to excel in swordplay. But, nevertheless, there were times when his gaze appeared all too knowing.

She promised to return soon. Skirting the edge of the crowd, she came face to face with Sir Ademar.

'My lady,' he greeted her, bowing.

She leaned up to study the knight. Though exceptionally tall, his face was pleasing enough to look at. With light blond hair and dark blue eyes, he had a Norse look about him. Sir Ademar was one of the stronger fighters, and she'd seen him defeat many a man in combat. He was very quiet, however, and rarely spoke to anyone.

'Sir Ademar.' Honora nodded in greeting and tried to move around him.

'Might I—?' He stopped, as if gathering his thoughts. 'M-might I speak with you a moment, Lady Honora?'

His face coloured at his stammer, but he forced himself to continue. 'Your father tells me that…y-you are planning to remarry.'

Not really, she wanted to say. Instead, she responded, 'It is his wish, yes. I have not decided whether or not I will.'

'I would be most…most honoured if you would c-consider me as a potential husband.' Sir Ademar stared down at the grass, embarrassed at his awkward speech. Honora didn't know if it was nerves or whether he always had difficulty speaking. But this was the first time any man had openly declared an interest. She could not have been more startled.

'You flatter me,' she managed. 'But weren't you courting my sister?'

His face fell, turning morose. Venturing a chagrined smile, he managed, 'She…she would never consider a man like me.'

Wouldn't she? Honora wasn't so sure. But then, Katherine seemed taken with Ewan MacEgan, so possibly Sir Ademar was right. A touch of sympathy caught her by surprise.

Though she couldn't be certain why she did it, Honora untied a blue ribbon from her hair and gave it to him. 'Here. Take this when you go to fight.'

Sir Ademar tied it around his arm, the small bit of silk

contrasting against the chainmail armour he wore. A faint
smile perked at his mouth, as though he couldn't believe
what she'd just done.

Honora could hardly believe it herself. But his clumsy
offer had touched her somehow.

'God grant that I…may be victorious in this…next ch-
challenge.' The pride in his voice made her smile, and he
didn't seem quite so intimidating.

'I bid you good fortune.' And she was surprised to discover
she meant it.

A horn resounded, and Sir Ademar bowed, exiting towards
the fighting arena. Alone, she stood back while the men
readied themselves for the last challenge.

When she saw Sir Ademar's opponent, Honora's smile
fell. It was Ewan.

While the Norman knight wore chainmail, Ewan had
chosen a lightweight leather corselet to wear over his tunic.
Leather braces protected his arms, and he carried a heavy
wooden shield. He caught her glance and raised his shield in
a discreet salute.

He'd done that when they were children. Long ago, she'd
thought he was mocking her, because he was allowed to fight
while she could only watch. Now, she realised it was meant
to show respect.

Though there were a thousand reasons why she should not
care who won the tournament, a part of her remembered the
awkward boy Ewan had been. The boy who had been her
friend once, teaching her what he'd learned from the sword
masters, even though it was forbidden.

All of her earlier good wishes towards Ademar crumbled
away, for now her true wish was to see Ewan emerge as the
winner.

Honora hurried back to the dais, wanting a better seat to
watch the fight. As she passed by a small undergrowth of
shrubbery, she spied something brown and rectangular-shaped.

When she knelt down, she nearly caught her breath. For there, nearly hidden amid the weeds, lay the chest stolen from the family chapel.

Chapter Four

There were a few minutes before the match was due to begin. Ewan's entire body ached, and sweat mingled with blood upon his skin. After the last fight, he'd taken a slice across his upper arm. An irritant, nothing more, and it was worth the wound to secure the win. Now he had one remaining round.

Honora's warning reverberated in his mind. *Watch for a switch*. Though he could fight using either hand, he strongly favoured his right. Best to end this match quickly.

Ewan drained the cup of ale his brother held, regaining his strength. The cool drink didn't alleviate his thirst, but he took a few moments to calm his breathing and to focus on the upcoming match.

'You've done well this day,' Bevan remarked.

The rare compliment brightened his mood. His older brother found fault more often than he praised a fight. 'Good enough for now. But there's still this last fight.'

'Use your brain, not your arm. And for God's sakes, keep your eyes off your feet.'

Ewan hid a smile. He hadn't done that in years, but Bevan wouldn't let him live it down. 'The Baron says there will be a prize for the winner.'

'Whatever it is, give it back to his daughter in her honour.'

A sound idea, if the prize were gold or silver. 'I should go.' He handed the cup back to Bevan and moved towards his opponent. 'They're starting.'

Ewan glanced over at the dais. Katherine sat beside her father, an anxious smile upon her face, while Honora was missing.

It didn't sit well with him to see her gone. Was she all right? She'd been tense for most of the tournament, her smile strained. His gaze shifted through the crowd, accounting for each of the suitors. No one seemed to be missing, save her.

Why would she leave now, when the fighting was about to begin? Honora loved to watch swordplay. He started to back away from the ring to search for her, when suddenly she emerged from a small grove of trees. In her hands, she held a wooden chest.

Ewan stepped in front of her. 'Are you all right?'

Honora nearly stumbled, and he caught her arm. 'Yes, I am fine.'

His shoulders relaxed. He was about to excuse himself when she held out the chest.

'I found this in the underbrush over there. It's what I was searching for the other night.'

'The chest you thought was stolen.'

'It *was* stolen,' she insisted. 'Wooden chests don't grow legs and walk out into the trees.'

But if someone had taken it, why would they leave it behind? 'I've heard nothing, Honora. Most of the men speak of your sister and little else.'

'Keep your eyes open.' Her gaze snapped to the cut upon his arm. Gently, she examined it. 'What happened to you?'

'I let Beaulais cut me, in order to move in closer.'

Her hand stayed upon his shoulder a moment longer than it should have. Though her palm was callused from holding the sword, her touch warmed his skin.

'Honora, don't.'

'Don't what?' She drew back, her fingertips coated with his blood.

He chose his words with care, not wanting to offend her. 'I'm going to wed your sister.'

Embarrassment flooded her face. 'If she'll have you.' With another step backwards, she added, 'I did nothing except examine your wound. You've too high an opinion of yourself if you believe I wanted you.'

This was going badly. He tried to apologise. 'I didn't mean—'

'Your match is next.' She cut him off. 'Go and fight Sir Ademar. Perhaps he'll cut your other arm.'

With the chest tucked against her side, she strode off to the dais. Ewan stepped towards the ring, his annoyance rising.

Why did he always seem to fall into her trap whenever he was near her? And why, in God's name, did she provoke him so? He'd meant only to be polite, to see to her safety. But within a few moments in her presence, they were arguing.

He unsheathed his sword and prepared for the fight against Sir Ademar. The tall knight wore chainmail armour, his coif and aventail hiding all but his face. Ewan circled his opponent, waiting for the right opening. The weight of the armour would slow the knight down, and Ewan intended to take full advantage of the weakness.

Sir Ademar lunged forwards, and Ewan sidestepped, blocking the strike with his own sword. They exchanged a few blows, each trying to gain the other's measure.

Upon the knight's shoulder, Ewan spied a blue ribbon. Honora's token, he realised. As he parried another blow, he asked, 'Are you courting Honora?'

'I am. And I saw you…s-speaking with her just now.' Sir Ademar swung his sword full force, and Ewan barely blocked it with his shield. 'You made her angry.'

'I make her angry by breathing.' Ewan moved in, striking fast, forcing the knight to retreat. This was his chance to end the fight, and he used his full speed and agility, attacking without cease.

From the corner of his eye, he saw Katherine watching him, her hands pressed to her mouth. Honora's expression was intent, and her gaze locked with his. She lifted her left hand in a silent message.

The switch.

Ewan transferred his shield to the other arm, narrowly missing a slice to his flesh. Sir Ademar fought just as hard with his left hand, as with his right, and Ewan had to give his full concentration to the man's sword. Over and over, the knight struck, until the victory began to slip away from Ewan's fingertips.

Frustration at his weakness provoked a rage. He ignored technique, relying on brute strength. As a boy, too many times he'd been cut down, told he wasn't good enough. His brothers had tried to protect him, ordering him not to fight.

But he'd stubbornly refused to give up. And he wasn't about to lose this match now.

Sir Ademar's sword slashed towards his middle, and Ewan had no time to raise his shield. The blade sliced deeply into his arm, and he threw himself backwards, rolling away. Energy roared through him, his pulse pounding as he avoided another blow. His grip on the weapon loosened, but he managed to regain it.

Mud caked the right side of his face and shoulders, as he backed away from the knight, waiting for the right moment to attack. Sir Ademar sliced his sword downwards, but Ewan blocked the strike, using his legs to trip the man.

Around him, he heard the crowd shouting their approval, though most encouraged Sir Ademar. Blood flowed freely down Ewan's arm, but he felt none of the pain.

With all of his strength, Ewan raised his shield to deflect another blow, then he swung hard, ceasing at the edge of his opponent's undefended throat.

'Halt!' Lord Ardennes called.

Ewan kept his blade steady, but then he looked down and saw the knight's own sword positioned at his gut. He cursed, for he hadn't won the match.

The Norman knight smiled, stepping back to sheathe his sword. 'A draw, MacEgan.'

Ewan gave a brief nod, though he wasn't pleased. He'd intended to show his skills to Katherine, and though he hadn't lost, neither had he been victorious.

His mood was black when he approached the dais. Sir Ademar walked alongside him, his own armour also caked with mud.

'You fought well, Sir Ademar.' Katherine smiled, then offered the same praise to Ewan.

Lord Ardennes lifted a hand. 'It is time for the feasting. Since you held the victory in most of the contests, MacEgan, you may sit between my two daughters this day.'

It was not an offer of Katherine's hand, he noticed, though it was an honour. He should have been glad of it, but at the moment, he was filthy, his body ached and he was bleeding.

Ewan asked the Baron's permission to leave the fighting ring. He wanted a few moments alone to clear his head and to wipe off the mud.

When it was granted, he walked back to the grove of trees beyond the fighting ring, remembering a creek that he'd spied on their journey here.

The fight unsettled him, for he'd nearly lost. Ewan swiped at the blood on his arm, wincing at the depth of the cut. Sir Ademar was a worthy opponent, a man not easily defeated. Ewan would simply have to work harder to win. If it meant training an extra hour each day, so be it.

When he reached the icy water, Ewan stripped off his tunic and dunked his head beneath the surface. The cold chill slowed the bleeding from his arm slightly, but the wound needed to be stitched.

He waded into the water, still wearing his trews in the hopes of cleansing them. He wished he'd thought to bring a change of clothing with him.

A rustling noise caught his attention, and Ewan spun, startled by the intrusion. Gerald of Beaulais emerged from the trees. His hand rested upon his sword hilt.

'Your sword skills are lacking, Irishman.'

Críost. Hadn't he defeated the man already in the wrestling match? And here he was, half-naked, with his weapons lying upon the shore.

'But I defeated you.' He remained in the water, inching his way closer. He reached down into the water and closed his palm over a round stone. 'What is it you want, Beaulais? A lesson in hand-to-hand fighting?'

The nobleman reached for the dagger at his belt. 'Leave Ardennes. And abandon your courtship.'

A flash of metal caught the sun, and Ewan threw himself sideways. The blade sank below the water, and a second later, Beaulais collapsed. Behind him stood Honora, a stout limb in her hands. A line of blood trickled down Beaulais's forehead.

'What in the name of God do you think you're doing?' Ewan bellowed, striding from the water. 'Did you murder him, then?'

'He was about to murder you!'

'He threw the knife as a warning. I saw it coming and avoided it.' Ewan approached Beaulais's body and nudged it with his foot. Thanks be, a low groan resounded from the man's throat. 'I don't need you, or anyone else, to defend me.'

Honora's face transformed from pale white to furious red. 'Fine. Let the next man kill you, then. I'll stand back and do nothing.'

'Why are you even here?' Ewan demanded. 'You're supposed to be with your father, preparing for the feast. Or have you forgotten that you are meant to choose a suitor?'

'I haven't forgotten.' But she looked embarrassed, sud-

denly aware of what she'd done. Her gaze drifted down to the
ground, and she held the branch as though it were a sword
hilt. Her sleeves stretched against her arms, and he could see
the outline of her lean muscles.

Cold water from his swim dripped down his torso, down
to soaked trews. Honora's stare travelled from his feet, past
his thighs and stomach before she met his firm stare.

'Stop chasing after me, Honora,' he warned.

Her lips pressed tightly together, her green eyes flashing fire.
'I wasn't chasing. I was trying to save your ungrateful hide.'

Ungrateful? He hadn't needed her help. Did she still believe he was a spindly lad of sixteen, unable to defend himself? Not a chance of that.

Ewan took a step closer, but she raised the limb, as though
she were contemplating striking him.

'Do not even consider it.' Wrenching it from her hands,
Ewan cracked it over his knee and tossed the pieces aside. 'Go
back to your father, Honora. I'm not the man for you.'

'I wouldn't want you if you were the last man in England.'
Honora sent him a furious look before she picked up her
skirts and fled his presence.

Ewan picked up his fallen weapons and stepped past
Beaulais's unconscious form, his fury rising higher. Why had
she interfered? Beaulais might have retaliated before knowing
she stood behind him. She could have been hurt.

Damn her. Nothing had changed, not in five years. She lacked
faith in him, but he wasn't about to justify his fighting skills to
her. He had nothing to prove, especially not after today's victory.

He cast a glance at the unconscious man at his feet, his annoyance rising. And by the look of it, thanks to Honora, he'd
just made another enemy.

Ewan shared a trencher with Katherine, ensuring that she
had the choicest pieces of roasted pheasant and smoked
herring. The Baron had spared no expense in the feast, and

Ewan revelled in the food. His favourite dish of *blanc-manger* was the most exquisite he'd ever tasted. The chicken paste had a hint of almond milk, sugar, and the light crunch of fried almonds gave it texture. It made it easier to keep his mind off the pain of his arm.

But even as he ate, he was uneasy about what had happened with Beaulais. The man would not hesitate to retaliate. The only question was when.

'You haven't lost your appetite, I see,' Katherine remarked, in an attempt to make conversation.

'Would you care for more?' Ewan broke off a portion of gingered salmon, but she shook her head, declining.

Though he gave Katherine his full attention, he was well aware of Honora on his opposite side. He offered her the same courtesy, in order to maintain appearances, but he could see the shuttered anger in her expression.

Beaulais staggered into the hall some time later, his gaze livid. A piece of linen was wrapped around his forehead, and he joined the other suitors at the lower table. Conscious of the man's venomous glare, Ewan stared back, willing Beaulais to look away.

Instead, the nobleman drew a dagger, letting the blade flash in the torchlight. There was murder in his eyes, a visible threat.

Honora wouldn't be foolish enough to confess she'd brought Beaulais down, would she? The Norman lord wouldn't take kindly to being struck by a woman. And though Ewan was confident he could handle the man's anger, he wasn't so sure about Honora. She was far too reckless.

A harper played lively tunes, breaking the silence and redirecting the attention of the guests. Ewan ignored Beaulais and reached for a strawberry. Bringing it to Katherine's lips, he complimented her beauty. As she blushed and accepted the fruit, his elbow accidentally brushed against Honora's. She jerked away, her eyes narrowed.

'My pardon,' he apologised. From the way Honora shrank back, it was as if he'd struck her.

Then her expression changed, and she lowered her voice. 'You're bleeding.'

He glanced at his tunic sleeve, which had darkened in colour. 'It's nothing.'

'You need to tend the wound. It's deep.'

She acted as though his arm had been severed. Though the trickle of blood irritated him, it was hardly serious.

Ignoring her insistence, he offered her a piece of fruit. 'Would you care for a strawberry?'

She shook her head slowly. In her eyes, he saw worry. And though he wanted to make a lighthearted response, something to make her smile, he knew it wouldn't work. Honora had always been able to see past his teasing.

And he was still staring at her with a strawberry in his hand. He turned and fed the succulent fruit to Katherine. Honora stiffened, as though he'd hit her.

Was she jealous? He couldn't believe that to be true, for she'd claimed she wouldn't wed him if he were the last man in England.

He watched her speaking to Sir Ademar. A strand of dark hair came loose from her veil, hanging against her neck. The curve of her cheek was soft, unexpectedly delicate. When he reached for his tankard of ale, he caught her light fragrance, a hint of apples. She had tasted just as wild and tart as the fruit when he'd kissed her.

He drank deeply, trying to push the idle thoughts away. His reaction had been instinctive; it would have been the same with any woman. They had been friends once, but if he wasn't more careful, he'd make an enemy of Honora. He didn't want to cause any more awkwardness once he wed Katherine.

As the feasting wore on, the ale flowed more freely. Katherine excused herself to speak with the other ladies, and

Ewan went to watch several games of chance. He was weary from the day's fighting and leaned up against the wall after the trestle tables were pushed to the side. His brother Bevan was still talking to the Earl of Longford, but his expression was glazed as though he, too, wanted an escape.

Ewan reached out and touched the sleeve of his tunic, which was slick with blood. Damn it, Honora was right. His arm was growing numb from the bleeding, his body weakening.

'Whom did you pay to fight on your behalf?' a male voice interrupted from behind him. 'One of the maidservants, perhaps?'

It was Beaulais. Ewan sensed a blow coming and stepped sideways, causing the Norman's fist to strike the stone wall instead. Beaulais's face turned purple with rage, and he clutched his hand.

'Your fighting hasn't improved, I see,' Ewan commented. When another punch sliced towards his face, he blocked it, cracking his fist across Beaulais's jaw.

The Norman countered with a blow to his arm, and Ewan sucked in air, the pain rippling through him. He slammed the full force of his fist into Beaulais's stomach, but the man followed through with another hit to his mouth.

Ewan tasted blood and threw himself to the ground, knocking the nobleman off his feet. Rolling back up, he grasped Beaulais and lifted him up high. It was an act meant to demonstrate his strength and to humiliate his opponent. A gasp resounded through the crowd, to his satisfaction. With his muscles burning from the strain, he tossed Beaulais into the dirt.

Leaning down, he lowered his voice so only Beaulais could hear. 'Don't threaten me again, Norman. Or the next time, you'll be unable to rise without help.'

He stood, facing the crowd of people. Lord Ardennes appeared indifferent to the fight, while Katherine was horrified, her cheeks scarlet with embarrassment. Honora didn't spare a glance towards Beaulais, but the gleam in her green eyes revealed a hint of pride. It was quickly replaced with anger. Ewan suspected that if they were alone, she'd blister his ears.

To Katherine, he gritted out, 'Forgive me', and turned to leave. His eye was swelling up and blood ran down his arms.

He passed his brother on the way to the stairs, and Bevan sent him a warning look. The silent censure irritated his already-foul mood. He'd had enough of this night.

As he reached the bottom of the winding stairs, he heard the sound of quiet footsteps behind. Ewan spun and saw Honora standing behind him.

'You frightened my sister,' she said. There was no anger in her tone, only a resigned air. 'I'll send her to tend your wounds, and you can apologise in private.'

He hadn't expected that. His shoulders lowered, his anger softening. With a low voice, he added, 'I did not intend to offend her, or you, by fighting in your presence.'

She studied him, her clear green eyes discerning. 'It was my fault. I shouldn't have struck Beaulais when I did.' She rested her palm against the stone wall, her eyes revealing guilt.

'I can take care of myself, Honora,' he murmured softly. He reached out and tucked the wayward strand of hair back beneath her veil.

She gave an involuntary shiver at the touch. 'You'll have to watch your back. Beaulais won't stand for the insult.'

'I'm not afraid of him, Honora.'

'Perhaps you should be.' She took a step backwards, her gaze sweeping over him. Ewan became conscious of his damp trews and the dried mud from earlier. 'In the meantime, you should let Katherine help you.'

His forearm stung with the slickness of blood. She was right. 'Where shall I await your sister?'

'In the solar. I'll send her there within the hour.' With a nod from her as dismissal, he turned to leave. Raking his hand through his hair, he wondered exactly what he could say to Katherine to make amends.

'I can't tend his wounds,' Katherine protested, in the privacy of their chamber. 'I'm not good at healing.'

'He wants to speak with you,' Honora replied. When she'd watched Ewan fighting, a part of her had been fascinated at his massive strength. He'd picked up Beaulais and tossed him like a stick of kindling.

She'd been unable to tear her gaze from him, and when it had ended, her skin had prickled with awareness.

A bead of sweat had run down his neck, outlining the gleaming chest. He hadn't looked like that at sixteen, still a skinny lad not yet grown into manhood. But now…

Sweet Jesu, she'd wanted to touch him, to know that strength for herself. And though he drove her to madness with his stubborn arrogance, she couldn't deny what she felt when she was around him. The very air seemed charged with desire, every movement intensifying the startling ache inside her.

When she'd seen Beaulais attacking him earlier today, she'd struck out without thinking of Ewan's pride. He'd needed help, and she'd given it, nothing more. Any soldier would do the same for a friend. But he'd taken it as an insult, one she hadn't intended.

It was just as well that he'd renewed his dislike towards her. She was finding him more and more difficult to resist. Strong and bold, she couldn't help but admire the man he'd become.

He needed the softness of Katherine to balance his fierce demeanour. Not a woman like her, as quick to argue with him, unwilling to yield. If she wed a man like Ewan, they'd shred each other to pieces.

Or they'd set one another on fire.

She could envision fighting with him, and afterwards,

making up. Having tasted the warmth of his mouth and the flames that seemed to burn her up inside, she knew he was far too dangerous.

'I asked him to await you in the solar,' Honora told her sister. 'You needn't do anything but tend his cuts and let him apologise.'

Katherine blanched. 'Honora, it isn't a good idea. Really, I don't think—'

'It will be fine,' Honora interrupted. There was no question Ewan needed to be stitched up. And her sister would have to tend wounds from time to time, once they were wed. It was a good chance for them to have a moment alone. She changed her tactics. 'Didn't you say you thought he was handsome? He was the best fighter of any man there. You saw it for yourself.'

'Yes, but I don't like blood. It makes me faint.'

Honora rolled her eyes. 'Don't be a goose. It's nothing but a scratch. You'll bind it with linen, and that will be that.'

Katherine didn't look convinced. 'It looked bad. And…I'm nervous about being alone with him. Come with me, won't you, Honora?'

No, she didn't want that at all. She needed to remain right here, to remind herself of the thousand reasons why Ewan MacEgan was not a man she should desire.

'I'll send one of your maids, if it will make you feel better,' Honora offered.

Katherine stood and laid a hand upon her arm. 'I know you don't like him very much. But truly, you can sit in the corner and embroider something. Or—or mend a gown. I have one with a torn hem.'

Honora faltered. If it would convince Katherine to go, perhaps she could simply remain out of view, in the corner with a bit of sewing.

No, no, no. She shouldn't even consider accompanying her sister. What if Ewan tried to kiss Katherine? He wouldn't want her there, intruding upon a private moment. Her cheeks burned at the thought, for he was quite good at kissing.

'Say you'll come,' Katherine begged. 'For me.' She reached out, linking her pinkie finger with Honora's. It was a gesture they'd done as young girls, a sisterly promise that could not be broken.

'Please,' Katherine asked again.

It wasn't a good idea, but Honora decided as long as she stayed far away from them, it might go well enough. She could stare at the ceiling and count cobwebs, if need be.

She braved a smile and nodded. Katherine hugged her, murmuring thanks.

'Go on, then,' Honora bade her sister. 'I'll follow.'

Chapter Five

When they arrived in the solar, Ewan awaited them on a bench. He'd put on his tunic again, and the long sleeves covered the gash Honora had seen on his forearm. He rose in silent respect.

'I am sorry if I frightened you, Lady Katherine,' he began. 'I should not have fought Lord Beaulais in your presence.' Approaching both of them, he offered his hands to Katherine.

Honora slipped off into a corner, pretending to busy herself with the embroidery on a gown. Though she tried not to listen to their conversation, she could not help herself.

'Honora told me you were wounded in the fighting earlier,' Katherine remarked. She bade him sit down, and added, 'I'll see if the basin of water and herbs have been prepared.' She left the chamber, and the door closed behind her.

Ewan shot Honora a frown. 'Why are you here?'

'It was Katherine's request.' Honora lifted up the embroidery. 'She was afraid to be alone with you.' Grimacing at the awkward situation, she offered, 'Forget I am here.'

A strange expression flashed upon his face. 'You aren't easily forgettable, Honora.'

She didn't know what he meant by that. There was a look in his eyes that she'd never seen before, a searching gaze. The planes of his face were narrow, casting shadows upon his cheeks. Despite the bruising, he was still the most handsome man she'd ever seen. Her gaze fastened upon his mouth, swollen from the punch he'd suffered.

She was not going to think about Ewan sitting so close, nor was she going to think about his kiss. He was going to wed her sister.

She ripped the seam of the gown, taking satisfaction in the act of destruction. Taking a deep breath, she threaded her bone needle and tried to pretend she was alone. She pierced the linen fabric, trying to calm her mind with the rhythm of even stitches.

Praise the Virgin, Katherine returned at last with the basin and herbs. Her sister chatted lightly about mundane topics, of the crops and household doings. Honora risked a glance and saw the grey pallor upon Katherine's face as she dabbed at the cut upon Ewan's lip.

But she did not raise the sleeve of his tunic to inspect the true wound. Ewan answered Katherine's questions, a warm smile upon his lips as he spoke to her. Even so, the timbre of his voice was unsteady, as though he were in pain.

Why didn't he raise his sleeve? Or have Katherine examine his ribs? Honora had seen the blows he'd suffered earlier in the tournament. He might have cracked a bone. Yet her sister appeared oblivious, forcing a smile and tending minor wounds.

When Honora lifted her gaze once more, Ewan was watching her over Katherine's shoulders. His deep green eyes stared into hers in a silent message. He needed help. And Katherine's nerves were beginning to show as she talked faster and faster.

Honora jerked her attention back to her sewing, not knowing what to do. Would Ewan want her to intervene? He might not trust her to tend the wound.

After a time, he rose and thanked Katherine, bidding her a good eventide. He kissed her hand, his fingers lingering upon her wrist. Honora stabbed the bone needle into her embroidery, tossing it in the basket.

'My lady, if you would not mind…?' Ewan sent Katherine a chagrined smile. 'I would like to have a word with your sister.'

Katherine shook her head. 'Not at all. I will see you on the morrow, Ewan. Remember—near the stables, past terce.'

He bowed his head. 'I look forward to it, my lady.'

When the door closed, Honora studied him. 'Do you want me to look at your arm?'

He nodded, wincing as he tried to lift up the sleeve of his tunic. The caked blood made it impossible.

'I'll work quickly,' she promised, because being alone with him was not wise. She needed to escape his presence, to sort out the strange longings she shouldn't feel.

'Your sister looked about to faint. I didn't want to offend her with my blood.'

Clearly, he felt no such compunctions with her. She resisted the urge to ask what he would do when he married Katherine. Her younger sister was softhearted and loathed blood. 'I'll do what I can. What about your ribs?'

She lifted the tunic away, being careful of his wounds. Upon his upper arm, the angry gash seeped blood. 'This will need stitching, I think.'

'My ribs aren't broken. Bruised, perhaps, but it's nothing.'

'I can bind them for you, if you like.' Without waiting for a reply, she went to fetch the needle and thread from her basket.

She was relieved that her voice sounded so calm, as though he were any other man. He'd never guess how much it unnerved her, seeing his bare skin once again. She could think of nothing else but the first night she'd seen him naked, and the way his warm body had felt pressed up against hers.

When she reached his side, she examined the wound. Dirt and dried blood edged the gash. 'I need to wash your skin or else the blood may become poisoned.' She spied an ewer of wine and poured it on to the cut, sponging it clean. Ewan let out a hiss of pain.

The skin was torn open, the edges refusing to mend. 'You'll have a scar from this.'

'I know it.' He didn't flinch when she pricked the needle into his flesh. 'But scars are the mark of honour.'

'Or the mark of a man who didn't move quickly enough.'

'Have you any scars, Honora?'

'None that I'll show to you.'

His mouth curved upwards in a smile, turning intimate. 'Every warrior has scars.' With his free hand, he reached out and touched her shoulder. 'Even ones you cannot see.'

Especially those, Honora thought. She concentrated on sewing the wound with tight, even stitches. She wasn't going to think about the closeness between them, or the way she was standing between his thighs. He smelled good, a masculine scent of earth and rain. In the firelight, his green eyes watched her.

'Why did you cut your hair?' he asked.

Honora nearly stabbed herself with the needle. An innocent question, but one she didn't want to answer. She managed to keep stitching, fumbling for a better response. 'It makes it easier to wear a helm.'

It was the truth, but not the real reason.

'Sometimes I train with the other soldiers,' she continued. 'They don't know who I am.'

'The armour is heavy.'

It was, but she'd trained for several years to accustom herself to its weight. Enough that she could stand it for short intervals.

'I can't wear it for very long before I tire,' she admitted. 'But it's the only way I can fight against the other men, without them knowing who I am. I'd lose my skills otherwise.'

'Why is it important to you? Why should it matter, whether or not you can fight?'

She didn't know what to say. He would never understand. 'It matters to me.'

'You're a woman.' His voice was deep, like a caress. Honora shivered at the sound of it.

'I am a warrior. Even if no one knows it.'

She could see the dissent in his eyes, but to his credit, he said nothing. Honora knew full well that she wasn't the sort of woman her sister was. Katherine was the fresh-faced beauty, the virginal woman who knew everything about tending a household.

She had known nothing, a fact that Ranulf had never failed to remind her. Despite her best efforts, she had given her husband no pleasure in his home, nor in his bed. Had she fallen ill and died, she doubted if he would have noticed.

'Why do you fight?' Ewan asked again, staring as if he could see the answers in her profile.

'Fighting is something I can do well,' was her answer. It was the only thing she could do with any sort of expertise, save the embroidery. And even that, she'd only learned because it was necessary when tending wounded men. Blood had never bothered her, and she'd sewn up countless wounds.

After she tied off the thread, she packed the wound with comfrey and crushed garlic that Katherine had left behind. There were no cobwebs to help the wound bind, but with a tight bandage, it might do well enough. She wound his arm firmly with the clean linen. 'Do you want me to wrap your ribs now?'

Against her desires, she found herself staring at his mouth. The heat of the room grew stifling, and perspiration rose up on her skin.

'That won't be necessary.' His hand reached out to hers, and she grew self-conscious of the rough calluses upon her palm.

'The cut will be better in a sennight or two,' she remarked. 'But try to keep it covered when you fight.' Taking a step backwards, she drew her hand away and waited for him to leave.

Ewan didn't take the pointed hint. Instead, he moved in until she was cornered against a wall. 'Don't ever take a risk like that again. Beaulais might have harmed you.' He rested his hand against the wall behind her. Once again, the familiar scent of him seemed to pull at her senses.

Honora tried to keep her breathing steady, to ignore the rapid pulsing of her heart. 'I could have blocked him, had he tried to strike me.'

'You take too many chances,' he argued. 'And while I am glad you can defend yourself, there's no reason to seek trouble.' He cupped her chin. 'You find it well enough on your own.'

'Don't patronise me.' Her face felt as though it were on fire, and he was far too close. The gentle pressure of his fingertips against her chin made her hands tremble. 'And don't touch me.'

He lifted his hands up and stepped away. 'As you wish. But let there be peace between us, Honora.'

'Why does it matter?'

'If I'm going to wed your sister, I would like for us to be friends.'

Friends. Had they ever been just that to one another? She had followed him around far more than was proper. If the truth be known, years ago she'd held a secret admiration of him, wishing that he would fall in love with her.

But he hadn't. He'd been kind enough, but most times he'd tried to avoid her. Looking back, she understood the reason. It was difficult for any man to love a woman who had attempted to skewer him with a sword.

'Friends,' she repeated. 'I suppose there's no harm in it.' She offered him her hand, as though it meant nothing. But the light grip of his hand upon hers sent a wild heat blazing through her. 'As your friend, I'll warn you not to do anything foolish again, like you did tonight.'

The corner of his mouth turned up. 'Why would you say that?'

Tilting her head, she remarked, 'Fighting a man when you've been bleeding for hours, Ewan? Now was that wise?'

'I won, didn't I?'

She shook her head. 'I had to sew you up again afterwards.'

He sent her his most charming smile and released her hand. 'Just a scratch, Honora.' Turning serious, he changed the subject. 'Did you ever learn anything more about your thief?'

'No. Nothing.'

'Most of the men speak of Katherine or their own estates. I've heard not a single mention of the chest. But at least it was recovered.'

'It isn't only the chest,' she admitted. 'A cross and a chalice were also stolen.'

'And were they found?'

She shook her head. 'Not yet. But that isn't what bothers me most. Neither were valuable. They were made of wood, not silver. I can't understand why anyone would want them.'

'I don't know. But I'll try to find out anything I can.' Ewan raised his bandaged arm. 'I owe you for this.'

'It was no trouble.' Honora forced herself to walk calmly to the door, bidding him goodnight, when what she'd really wanted to do was flee back to her room, hiding her burning cheeks beneath the coverlet.

Friends, he'd said. She didn't know how that would ever be possible.

Ewan waited near the stables, the mid-morning sun casting beams amid the clouds. His brother Bevan had left at dawn to visit with his father-in-law, the Earl of Longford. No doubt the Earl would pressure Bevan to return to Erin, to be at Genevieve's side for the new birth. Ewan hoped he could convince Katherine to wed him sooner and thereby grant Bevan his wish.

In the meantime, he'd been given a chance to spend time with Katherine. None of the other suitors had done so, to his knowledge, and it boded well for his chances of winning her hand.

Katherine had done her best to tend his wounds last night, though she couldn't have endured sewing up the gash, the way her sister had. Honora didn't cringe at the sight of blood or injuries, having sewn up a fair number of them over the years. He could easily see her doing the same for half-a-dozen sons, were she fortunate to bear children.

The thought pricked him. Honora didn't want to wed, and though he suspected part of it was her reluctance to let a man hold dominion over her, he sensed a shadow from her former marriage. Something had happened, something she would never admit. It bothered him, to think of Honora falling victim to a man, even her husband.

At that moment, Katherine arrived. Her emerald bliaud contrasted against her fair skin and white veil, making her blue eyes appear more vivid.

'Ewan,' she greeted him with a smile. Behind her stood Honora, holding a basket. He recalled that Katherine had asked her to accompany them. Once again, Honora appeared desperately uncomfortable, and Ewan hardly blamed her.

'I hope you are feeling better after yesterday,' Katherine continued. She drew closer, studying the cut upon his lip.

In truth, his arm still ached, but Ewan said nothing about it. 'I am, yes.'

'Good. Then let us ride out. I am weary of these walls.'

Within a few minutes, they were mounted and travelling outside the castle gates. Katherine led the way, while Ewan followed. Honora remained behind at first, but a few moments later, she brought her horse alongside his. She wore a serviceable grey bliaud, her hair hidden by a veil. Only a slim golden girdle around her waist gave any colour. Ill at ease, she offered, 'I tried to convince her to go alone.'

Her comment was an apology, but he appreciated the effort

nonetheless. He shrugged. 'There are worse places to be than in the company of two beautiful women.'

'I am not beautiful, and both of us know it. Don't mock me.' The words were spoken calmly, not in anger, but by a woman who believed them. Urging her horse forward, Honora joined her sister.

Not beautiful? Did she truly think that? No, she didn't have the soft beauty of her sister. But the wildness of her and the shorn hair gave Honora an exotic appearance, one that most men did not perceive from the veil she wore.

She had changed, more than he'd realised. Though Honora had always had an intensity to her demeanour, fighting hard and arguing harder, never had he said anything against her looks. Who had convinced her that she was unattractive? Her husband? If that were true, then it was a good thing the bastard was dead.

Katherine drew her mare to a stop near an open clearing. Honora joined her and took the two horses to let them graze. In the distance, shadowed mountains stretched up, covered with green trees. Grey skies dotted with heavy clouds foretold an afternoon rain.

Ewan dismounted, and Honora took the animal from him without asking. By tending the horses, she avoided both of them, giving him and Katherine time to speak alone.

Katherine chose a large rock to sit upon, green grass spearing up amid the dead growth from last winter. Honora remained closer to the hillside, and she rubbed one of the horses down while studying their surroundings. The wind blew against her veil, revealing a hint of dark hair against her slender neck.

She looked pensive, worry creasing her face. He didn't know what troubled her, but he suspected it was more than the thief. Her reluctance to confide in him made it seem far worse.

She lifted her eyes to his, and he tried to reassure her

without words. Shaking her head, Honora turned away in silent rebuke.

She was right. He had no business interfering in her life, and it wasn't any of his concern.

'Ewan, could you help me with this?'

Katherine struggled to lift down a basket of food. His stomach was raging, though it was not nearly time for a meal. He offered a friendly smile and asked, 'What did you bring with you?'

'I thought we could enjoy our noon meal out of doors.'

Praise be to the saints. Ewan sent her a hopeful look. 'Must we truly wait that long?'

'Not if you are hungry now.' A laugh escaped her, and she opened the basket. While he helped himself to a cold leg of roasted chicken, Honora was still lagging behind.

'Are you going to join us?' he asked.

'What?' Honora glanced up and saw the food. 'No, I'm not hungry.'

He sat with Katherine, wondering what to say to her. This was his first opportunity to demonstrate that he would be an excellent husband for her. And yet, he couldn't think of a single thing to say, beyond a simple thanks for the food.

Katherine stared down at her hands, but she didn't attempt a conversation either. Honora was walking through the long grasses, her hand shielding her eyes in the sunlight.

'Do you think she'll marry?' he asked Katherine, nodding towards her sister. The topic of Honora's future was a safe one.

'I hope so.' Katherine studied a piece of cheese as if she intended to hold it, rather than eat it. 'She deserves to be happy, after what she endured at Ceredys.'

'And what was that?'

Katherine rubbed her arms, as though it had grown cold. 'She won't tell me. But I know she's angry about what happened there. She doesn't sleep well at night.' Lowering her voice, she added, 'Also, someone has been searching her belongings. I don't know why, but I've found her gowns spread out, as though they were looking for something.'

The thief again. Ewan frowned, for Honora had never mentioned a threat to herself.

'Does she know about it?'

Katherine shrugged. 'I've tried to keep it from her. She has enough worries. But I've alerted Father's soldiers to keep our chamber guarded at all times.'

'Good.'

She ventured a conspiratorial smile at him, and Ewan reached out to take her hand. The smooth skin was cool, completely unlike Honora's roughened palm. Katherine allowed him to hold her hand for a few moments, but when his thumb grazed her palm, she pulled her hand back.

'What is the matter?' he asked.

She gripped her hands together, staring off into the distance. 'It's my foolishness. And I'm feeling angry at myself for what happened last night. I was weak, when I should have tended the cut on your arm.'

It was the last thing he'd expected her to say. 'It's all right.'

'No, it wasn't. My sister helped you, when it should have been me.' Katherine lowered her gaze, as though ashamed of herself. And when she stared at Honora, there was envy in her eyes.

He understood what it meant to compare herself to a sibling. All his life, he'd lived in the shadow of his brothers. But now, he was finally seizing control of his fate. With Katherine as his bride, he could at last be master of his own lands.

To lighten her mood, Ewan suggested, 'If I slice my arm open again, I'll call upon you to sew it up.'

Her lips tilted. 'And as soon as you start to bleed, I'll likely faint. You'd be better off with a healer.' She shook her head and sighed. 'Honora has far more courage than I.'

He didn't deny it, but neither did he expect Katherine to

be the same as her sister. To change the subject, he asked, 'Is there anyone she might wed?'

'Sir Ademar asked her to consider him,' Katherine admitted. Her colour deepened, though Ewan didn't understand why. 'He told me last night.'

He'd known that Honora had given Ademar a token, a ribbon. Yet she'd said nothing about him as a possible husband.

Ewan reached into the basket and tore another chicken leg off the roasted fowl. No. Sir Ademar was not at all suitable for Honora. Off the battlefield, the man was far too quiet. Honora would run over him, dominating every aspect of their marriage. She could only live with a man who had the personality to equal her own.

'Will she accept him as her husband, do you think?' He kept his question casual, as though he weren't interested in whether or not Honora intended to marry.

'Perhaps.' Katherine broke off another piece of cheese and leaned closer to him. 'He has been kind to her.' Raising up the food, she looked directly into his eyes. 'He's handsome, too.'

When she placed the cheese in his mouth, Ewan captured her fingertips, kissing them. It was expected of him. But her fingers felt cold beneath his mouth. Katherine's face turned scarlet, but she did not pull away.

Before he could pursue things further, a noise interrupted them. Horses were approaching at a steady speed.

Ewan broke away and unsheathed his sword. From this distance, he could not see the men, but he would take no chances with their safety. Katherine made a small sound, and he pushed her behind him. From his periphery, he spied Honora clenching her dagger, poised in a fighting stance.

It was three men, armed, but carrying no shields. Ewan at last recognised two of the suitors, Sir Ademar and Beaulais. The third man he hadn't seen before.

Honora had gone white. She moved beside him, and her fear unnerved him. Nothing and no one had ever frightened Honora.

But this man did.

Chapter Six

Ewan moved beside Honora, keeping Katherine behind them. 'Who is he?'

'John St Leger of Ceredys. My husband's son and the new Baron.' There was no tremble in her voice, but Honora looked as though she were about to be sick.

Ewan sheathed his sword, but rested his hand upon the hilt. The men drew their horses to a stop, but did not immediately dismount. He wasn't surprised; it allowed them the physical height advantage.

Katherine stepped forwards to greet them, but Ewan halted her. 'Wait.'

'Why are they here?' she murmured. She glanced at her sister, whose face was the colour of snow.

Honora did not move. Her hands locked around her waist, as though she craved a sword and scabbard. In a low whisper so her sister couldn't hear, she murmured, 'Keep him away from me, Ewan.'

He almost wondered if he'd imagined the words. What had this man done to her? But he gave a slight nod, letting her know he'd heard.

Lord Beaulais was the first to dismount, and he sent a false smile towards Katherine. Ewan's grip tightened on the sword hilt. If Beaulais dared to offend the women, he'd find himself with a few missing limbs.

'We saw you leaving with the women, MacEgan.' The nobleman smirked and added, 'You didn't think we'd let you have both of them all to yourself, now did you?'

Ewan folded his arms and regarded Beaulais. 'I don't recall Lady Katherine inviting any of you.'

'Her father invited all of us,' Beaulais corrected.

Sir Ademar cast a fleeting glance at Katherine. He didn't speak to her, nor smile, but something provoked Ewan's suspicions. There was an uneasiness in the knight's demeanour, as though he had come to prevent the other two from an attack.

But right now, his greater concern was Honora. Ewan took a step closer to her, even as Sir Ademar dismounted.

The knight approached them, though his gaze flickered back to the men. 'I am glad to see you this morn, m-my Lady Honora. You look…' he struggled to find the right words '…very fine. That is, I mean…your face is like a…'

'A diamond. A pearl. Just choose a damned jewel and be done with it,' Beaulais shot back.

Katherine glared at the nobleman, and nodded for Ademar to continue. The knight knelt before them, his face crimson. Ewan almost pitied the man.

Certainly Honora did, for she accepted the knight's hand and nodded for him to rise. 'Thank you for your kindness, Sir Ademar.'

The softness on her face caught Ewan by surprise. He was accustomed to seeing her in fierce concentration, as though she were facing an enemy. But at this moment, she became gentle, reminding him that she was female and desirable.

Ewan didn't like the way she was looking at the knight, even if the man's intentions were honourable. Honora smiled at Ademar, and Ewan wanted to tear her hand away from his. It was an irrational thought, for what did it matter if she chose to wed the knight? It was one less suitor competing for Katherine's hand. But it bothered him more than it should have.

A moment later, after she drew back, he felt the soft touch of Honora's hand upon his spine. What was she doing? He nearly jerked away, so startled was he to feel her hand upon him. She moved her palm towards the dagger sheathed at his side.

She had her own weapon…why the need for a second blade? Then again, he didn't trust Beaulais not to start a fight.

Katherine exchanged a glance with Sir Ademar and offered an excuse. 'We were about to return to Ardennes, weren't we? If you'd like to accompany us back—'

'I fear we interrupted your meal.' Beaulais gestured to the basket of provisions with a rueful smile. 'There's no need to return so soon.'

To her credit, Katherine did not invite the men to join them. 'I'm afraid there isn't really enough.' She offered an apologetic smile. 'I had packed provisions for only three of us. If we return to the castle, I would be pleased to offer a more fitting meal there, for you and the others. You must allow me to do so, as your hostess.'

Despite the gracious offer, Ewan was glad to see that Katherine's smile seemed to be hiding annoyance. Good. He didn't want her pairing up with any of these men.

John of Ceredys walked towards Honora, his hands out-stretched in greeting. Honora didn't move, keeping her grip upon the blade at his side. The simple touch made him aware of her, of her sudden reliance upon him. He made a silent vow to keep her safe.

He'd never seen Honora this agitated, and he couldn't quite tell whether it was fear or rage. Either way, it was best if Ceredys kept his distance.

'Lady Honora. I have missed the pleasure of your company at Ceredys.' The Baron tried to step around him to greet her, but Ewan remained fixed in his position.

'I don't believe the Lady Honora wishes to speak with you.' Ewan drew his sword slightly, in a silent threat.

'And what does the lady say for herself?' John demanded.

'Lord Ceredys.' Her voice was clear and steady, showing no fear. 'You've made a long journey.'

Her body tensed, as though she were about to attack the man. Ewan had never seen her this way, as though she wanted to murder Ceredys. Why? What had the Baron done?

Katherine intervened again. 'I really do want to return.' She began packing up the basket, and looked at Ewan in a plea for help.

'We'll go, as you wish,' he acceded.

But as she moved towards her horse, Ewan made it clear to every man there that he would not let any harm come to the women. He didn't miss the anger kindled in Lord Ceredys's eyes.

Nor the rage that Honora tried to hold back.

John had followed her.

Honora clenched her fist around the grip of her dagger, wishing to God that it wasn't a mortal sin to kill a man. Just having him near made her skin crawl.

She'd remained close to Ewan and Katherine for the rest of the day, though she felt badly for interfering with their courtship. John was not to be trusted, even with a castle full of servants and guards.

After the evening meal, she rose and followed Katherine to their chamber. As she passed the men seated at the trestle tables, her senses went on alert. It took a great deal of composure not to draw her weapon. Especially when John's hungry eyes locked upon her.

It wasn't right, his forbidden desire. She hated everything about him, from the gleaming golden hair to his dark brown eyes. As she passed him, he smiled, raising his goblet in salute. She didn't acknowledge the gesture.

He was to blame for what had happened to the people of Ceredys. All of it lay upon his shoulders.

And hers.

Her father was right. She'd been hiding here, creating excuses for not going back. How could she dare to make a life for herself when so many were suffering? Her skin grew cold, and she barely saw her surroundings, as though she looked through a mask.

Ewan waited for her to pass in front of him, and his hand brushed against the small of her back, warming her skin. He made her feel safer, for he would not allow John to follow.

Katherine bade him goodnight, and Ewan kissed her hand. Honora was about to continue up the spiral stone stairs, but Ewan called her back. 'Why do you fear John of Ceredys? Did he harm you at your husband's estate?'

She paused her hand upon the wall, choosing her words carefully. 'I don't fear him.' She hated him. The very thought of the man made her want to carve out his heart. 'But he threatens his own people. And I want him gone.'

She said nothing of the personal threat to herself. John's eyes had rested upon her at every moment, as though he were trying to strip away her clothing. And after what he'd done to the maidservant—

She closed her eyes, as though it could make the nightmare go away. Without thinking, she fingered the ends of her hair.

Ewan touched the edge of her chin, to meet his gaze. His green eyes watched her, as if trying to discern the truth. 'Did he force you?'

Honora shivered, not wanting to remember it. 'No. I...I defended myself against him.' After her husband's death, with the help of Marie St Leger, she'd hidden weapons in every chamber. Without her mother-in-law's assistance, she might have fallen prey to John's unnatural desire.

Ewan sensed what she hadn't told him, and a rage darkened his face. 'Do you want me to get rid of him? I'll speak to your father.'

Honora shook her head. 'No. He's here because my father asked him to come.' And because John's approval was expected before she could remarry.

Not that it mattered, for she had no intention of doing so. Praise God, John could never wed her himself, according to the consanguinity laws of the Church. As her son-in-law, he was now related by blood. But she wasn't naïve enough to think it would stop him from forcing his body upon her.

'You don't look well,' Ewan remarked.

Was it that evident? She felt as though she were about to be sick, just thinking of John.

He reached out, resting his palm upon her nape. The simple touch gave her comfort she hadn't expected. His thumb stroked the exposed part of her neck, sending an unexpected ripple of gooseflesh.

What was he doing, touching her like this? She knew she should move forward, to escape the warmth of his hand. But for a moment, it felt good to pretend that he would protect her. That she could feel safe.

Reluctantly, she took a step up the stone staircase, and his hand fell away. 'I must go. Katherine will be waiting.'

'Be sure to bar the door,' Ewan warned. 'And I'll keep watch over John of Ceredys. He won't harm you.'

Honora paused on the stairs, looking back at Ewan. His dark blond hair framed a strong face that made her heartbeat quicken. For a moment, she wished he would pull her into his arms and hold her close. She wanted the comfort of a man's embrace, to lose herself in it.

She ascended the stairs, wondering why she was having these sudden, unexpected thoughts about Ewan. She had no right to think of him in that way.

Put it aside, Honora. Let him go. He wants Katherine, not you.

She tried to convince herself that she didn't want him either. She'd had her chance at marriage, and it had been a miserable failure of her own making. Not only that, but she was avoiding her responsibilities at Ceredys. She couldn't stop thinking about the people, wondering what they were enduring in her absence.

What to do, what to do…

She rested her palms against the stone. Her father's suggestion, that she wed a man for his army, began to metamorphose. She needed a strong enough warrior, a man with influence enough to subdue John. Sir Ademar had not come into his full inheritance yet, and Ewan did not possess nearly enough to hire the men she needed. The only suitor with enough wealth was Gerald of Beaulais.

She couldn't even consider it. Beaulais and John were like brothers in their way of thinking, cold and calculating. And the other suitors had not the funds, nor the strength, to fight against John.

She needed to hire men of good reputation, men who could be trusted. But it would require a king's treasure.

An unexpected smile faltered at her lips. A pity she could not find the legendary treasure of Ceredys. Marie St Leger had spoken of gold and thousands of silver coins, enough to buy a kingdom. She claimed that the ruby she wore about her neck had come from the original treasure before it was buried again, in the midst of a siege.

Had she not seen the jewel for herself, Honora would have believed it to be a child's tale. But Marie had kept the ruby until Ranulf died. Then it had disappeared, but her mother would not say where.

Norse treasure would be enough to hire a band of soldiers. If it could be found…

Honora shook the idle thoughts away. They were foolish and impractical.

She reached for the dagger at her side, her palm tracing the rounded pommel. If she truly wanted to help her people, she should wed again, putting aside her own feelings. And still, the thought made her insides twist into knots of worry.

When she reached their chamber, Katherine had already gone to sleep. Honora undressed, and when she stood in her shift, she pulled the heavy wooden bar across the door. The cool spring air chilled her skin, and she burrowed beneath the coverlet, huddling her knees up for warmth.

Outside, the wind rattled the wooden shutters in a rhythmic thumping noise. Over and over, the sound jarred her consciousness.

She tried to shut the noise out of her ears, but it continued, battering her senses. Dark memories invaded, despite her efforts to avoid them

John was here, within these walls now. And though she told herself not to fear him, she retrieved her blade and hid it beneath the mattress. If he dared to invade their chamber, she would be ready.

It wouldn't be the first time he'd done so.

She'd sensed him that night at Ceredys, heard the door quietly open. Her hand had reached for a dagger she'd kept hidden beneath the covers.

When she felt his cold hand touch her shoulder, she'd sliced the blade against his chest, shoving the bedclothes aside. He'd roared with anger, but she'd forced him down upon the bed, holding the blade to his heart.

'I should kill you,' she'd whispered. 'Here and now, for what you've done.'

His breathing quickened, and whether it was out of fear or excitement, she couldn't be certain.

'Leave the women alone,' she demanded.

Like a rutting dog, John had forced many of the young maidens against their will. Their fathers and husbands were enraged at his actions, but the few who had sought revenge had lost a hand or their lives.

'They wanted me,' he argued. *Against her palms, she felt the warmth of his blood, and it was all she could do not to finish this.*

'The only thing they want is your death,' she said, inching the blade towards the hollow of his throat. *'And were I you, I should be careful of my actions. You might happen upon an accident.'*

'Do you dare to threaten me?'

What she'd hoped was to frighten him. Let him feel the same fear he'd spawned upon the people of Ceredys. 'Be assured of it. The next woman you touch, the next bag of grain you steal from them, will be your last.'

Honora touched the ragged ends of her hair. She should have killed him that night. It would have been better for everyone. But she'd foolishly let him go.

Within hours, she'd been taken prisoner within her own home, locked up in a storage cellar. She'd gone for a day without food or water until the blacksmith had found her. He'd set her free, giving her a bundle containing her possessions.

'The Lady of Ceredys bid me give this to you,' he said.

'Thank you.' She took the bundle, her heart heavy. 'I will find a way to repay you for what you've done.'

The older man had lowered his head. 'God speed, my lady.'

As a final farewell, she'd sliced off her heavy braid, leaving it behind. No longer would she be enslaved by a man. Relieved of the burden, she'd donned the armour and helm of a soldier, slipping away at last.

It had been too long. She didn't know what had become of the blacksmith, or anyone. The people were suffering under John's rule, and she'd found no means of helping them. An appeal to the king would do nothing; a man could treat his serfs however he wished, so long as he paid his taxes and offered his fealty.

There had to be a way to stop him.

Honora gripped her arms so hard, there would be bruises

come the morn. Her skin was freezing, but she let the discomfort pass through her. Steeling herself, Honora put on a brave front. John of Ceredys would not touch her. Nor would any man.

Chapter Seven

The chapel was empty, save the soft glow of torches lighting the whitewashed stone walls. After Mass that morning, Ewan had spent the past quarter of an hour in quiet contemplation.

Honora had returned the wooden chest, and it rested behind the altar, against the back wall. Made of yew, it reminded him of a chest his grandfather Kieran had carved. The surface contained a simple design, of scrolls and slanted lines. He touched the outside band, feeling as though the pattern had a meaning he could not quite grasp.

He rubbed his eyes, feeling suddenly weary. Something wasn't right about this thief. For the chest to reappear with nothing amiss, suggested that the man hadn't intended to steal it.

When he'd spoken with Honora, she'd claimed that the man had used a sword, that he'd attacked her in the chapel. Possibly two men.

Likely one had taken the chest, while the other fought her. Anger slid over him at the thought of her coming to harm. She took too many risks, forgetting herself when it came to a fight.

He reached out and turned the chest over. Sometimes a skilled carver could hide something within a secret opening.

But as he studied every inch of the wood, he could see nothing.

Ewan left the chapel and ventured outside onto the battlements. Rain clouds swept over the skies, and he stopped to look over the castle grounds. For a moment, he studied the defences, contemplating the way his own fortress would appear, once he built it.

He'd dreamed of this. And he sensed it was so close now, almost within his grasp. His own estate and a wife at his side to help him tend it.

A hand touched his shoulder, and he whipped around, his blade unsheathed. Honora's forearm blocked his knife from her throat.

Shaken, Ewan lowered the blade. 'My apologies.'

'I didn't mean to startle you.'

He offered a wry grin. 'I'm the youngest of five brothers. Used to be six, when Liam was alive. If I didn't move quickly, I paid the price.'

'Tormented you, did they?'

'Every day of my life.'

She ventured a smile, and it warmed him. His attention focused on the curve of her cheek and the brightness of her green eyes. Her veil hid her dark hair completely, and he suspected he was one of only a few who knew about her shorn length. It should have been unattractive and mannish. Instead, the harsh cut enhanced her beauty, emphasising a soft jaw and full lips.

He shouldn't be thinking of her in such a way. It troubled him, for he'd come here to win the hand of Katherine of Ardennes. And he was spending entirely too much time with Honora.

'What brings you outside in this fine weather?' he asked. The dark clouds were shifting, a light mist of rain beginning to fall.

'Avoiding John.' She crossed her arms, as if to ward off an evil spirit.

He gripped his sword hilt, the metal biting into his scarred palm. 'What did he do to you, Honora?' He kept his voice soft, though underneath, he held back the rising apprehension.

'It's nothing.'

She refused to look at him, and it blackened his temper, his imagination conjuring up all the reasons why a woman would fear a man.

'I don't believe you.'

'Believe whatever you want, MacEgan. My reasons for avoiding John are my own.' She turned away from him, staring back at the wooden door.

Her silence only made him suspect the worst. 'Did he hurt you?'

She shook her head. 'Not me, no.' The rush of colour in her face made her pull her hand back, and she covered her cheeks.

Then John had hurt someone else. And from the look of it, Honora felt responsible.

She took another step backwards, and he realised he was inadvertently cornering her. He forced himself to let her go. 'You asked me to keep him away from you. Do you still want that?'

Her shoulders lowered. 'It isn't fair of me, I know. You cannot stay with me at every moment. I suppose it's time I faced my fears.'

But she looked far from eager to do so. She left the battlements, closing the door behind her. He didn't follow, though he wanted to.

Honora deserved happiness after her first marriage. And if she decided to wed, Ewan wanted her to choose a man who would care for her. After being fostered together, he knew Honora as well as a sister.

A shot of guilt pooled inside. His thoughts towards her recently were not of the brotherly nature. Especially since he'd felt her body pressed up close to his. The soft sounds she'd uttered in her throat when he'd kissed her, driving him beyond reason, made her dangerous.

It was lust, that was all. He could curb those feelings easily enough. It was best to put her from his mind, concentrating on the woman whose heart he truly wanted.

Two more days passed, and Honora hadn't seen John. She knew better than to believe he would leave her alone. No, he would wait for her to let down her guard, before making his move.

Her sister felt no such uneasiness. This morning, Katherine's eyes were bright with excitement.

'He's taking me out riding,' she confessed while she dressed, pulling her bliaud over her head.

'Who is?'

'Ewan, of course.' Katherine raised her arms so her maid could finish helping her dress. 'You're not to tell anyone,' her sister warned. 'Especially Father. He's far too protective of me.'

'And with reason.' Honora didn't like this idea at all. Her sister was young, too naïve about the ways of men. 'You shouldn't go alone.'

'Ewan wants to know me better, so he said. And I—I think I'm going to accept him for a husband, Honora. Don't you think a bride should have time alone with her betrothed?'

You're not betrothed yet, Honora thought. She closed her eyes, counting to three. Of course Katherine would want to be alone with Ewan. But what if MacEgan tried to seduce her sister? What if he touched her in the manner of a lover?

The way he'd touched her.

Honora fisted the edges of her own gown, wishing she'd never allowed it. She didn't want to know what Ewan's mouth tasted like, what his body felt like.

And she didn't want Katherine to know it either. Her sister was far too innocent to be alone with a man. If Ewan dared to lay a finger on Katherine, Honora would cut off his hands and feed them to the dogs.

'Where are you going?' Honora kept her tone casual, as if she didn't care. The more she thought about them together, the more she worried about her sister.

'To the old abbey. The ruins are romantic, don't you think?'

'I think they'll crumble and bury you alive if you get too close.'

Her sister rolled her eyes. 'I should have known better than to ask you.'

'Well, it's true. Go there, if you want, but don't let him kiss you.'

'And why not? He looks like a man who knows how to kiss.'

He certainly does, Honora thought, but it wasn't a good idea to say so.

'You're so young, Katherine.'

'I am nineteen years old. Many women wed at the age of thirteen.'

'And thank the Blessed Virgin you weren't one of them.'

Katherine sat down upon the bed, her hands folded across one knee. 'I never asked you…what it was like between a man and a woman. But, Honora, I want to know. You were married. What's it like when a man touches you?'

Oh, Jesu. Her cheeks flamed. How was she supposed to answer that? Honora knew nothing of the way it was meant to be. Ranulf had been unspeakably cruel, and it had been her fault. If she'd kept her fighting skills hidden from him, he'd never have been the wiser. A good wife was not expected to fight off her husband on their wedding night. Nor was she supposed to wound and defeat him.

Ranulf had not forgiven her for it, and he'd thrown her dagger into the fire, forbidding her to ever touch a weapon again. He'd ordered his men to hold her down and beat her for disobedience.

And later, when she'd lain upon their bed, bruised and bleeding, he'd taken her innocence. Honora had wept, wishing to God she were dead. But he'd enjoyed humiliating her.

'I don't know what to say.' Honora stared down at the floor. Never could she admit the truth to her sister. 'I can only hope that your marriage is better than mine was.'

Katherine's smile vanished. 'I'm sorry. I shouldn't have brought it up.'

A sour knot formed in her stomach. 'Perhaps things will be different for you. I hope so.' She helped Katherine adjust her veil, then stepped back to look at her. Her sister wore a deep violet bliaud made of wool and embroidered with silver thread. Close-fitting, the horizontal tucks emphasised her small waist and slender arms. Her sleeves draped down to the floor while a corded girdle hung at the top of her hips.

Honora rubbed her own arms, the tight muscles not at all delicate and soft like her sister's.

'I'll be back by sundown,' Katherine promised. 'If Father asks—'

'I'll say you're not feeling well, and you're keeping to your chamber.' Honora reached out to her sister. 'I'll ask the servants to prepare a basket of food, for Ewan likes to eat. And do not be late, or I *will* come after you.'

Katherine's smile returned. 'Thank you, Honora.' She hugged her and fairly flew from the room.

Honora stared at the wooden door for so long, her eyesight blurred. Her sister was going to be alone with Ewan MacEgan. He was going to court her, using every tactic he had to win her heart. He needed Katherine's land in Erin, the dowry that would help him establish a foothold. Like any strategist, he would use his strengths to his advantage.

Damn, damn, damn. Worry needled her protective nature, eating away at her stomach. It wasn't jealousy. No, that had nothing to do with it.

Should she follow them and remain in hiding, in case Katherine needed her? Neither of them needed to know she was there.

Her conscience told her that this was not at all a good idea.

Katherine deserved privacy, not her older sister spying on her as though she were a child.

But therein lay the truth. They were sisters. And Honora would allow no one to hurt Katherine. Not even a man she trusted.

She changed her gown into a brown wool bliaud that would help her blend into the trees near the abbey ruins. In order to arrive before them, she would have to leave immediately.

Honora hid her hair with a veil, but she planned to remove it as soon as she arrived. The scrap of white fabric would easily give her position away. At her waist, she felt for the dagger, ensuring that it was still there.

Finally, she left the chamber. Within a quarter of an hour, she was on her way to the ruined abbey.

Ewan helped Katherine dismount, tethering her mare to a nearby tree. She looked as lovely as a rose, her pale skin contrasting against the rich purple of her gown. He let his hands linger upon her waist, waiting to feel the same rush of need he'd felt with Honora.

But there was nothing.

He pushed aside the sense of restlessness. It would take time to know Katherine, and he was certain he would feel something towards her, eventually.

'I am glad you asked me to ride with you today,' Katherine said, smiling. Her cheeks had a light flush to them, as though she were nervous about being near him.

'We've never spent time alone, have we?' Ewan took her hand and led her towards the ruined abbey. As a sixteen-year-old lad, he'd sometimes visited this spot, so near to the Earl of Longford's lands. He'd practised his fighting skills here, imagining that the abbey was his own castle.

Honora had been his opponent, more often than not. They had spent hours together, battling with swords. And though she'd driven him half-mad, following him everywhere, she'd also provoked him into becoming a better fighter, a better man. Because of her taunts, he'd spent weeks lifting heavy stones, building up his strength until he could best any man at wrestling or hand-fighting.

Why was he thinking of her so often? It made little sense, for they were barely friends. And yet, never had he felt such mind-stealing lust, the need to be with a woman. Kissing Honora had been a mistake, one he wouldn't repeat.

Katherine sat down upon the grass, spreading her skirts out. It was an invitation to sit beside her, and yet Ewan felt uneasy about it. Like a predator invited to dine upon succulent lamb.

'It's a nice day,' she offered.

'It is, yes.'

Damn it all, was he still sixteen? He'd never had this much difficulty talking to women before. Quite the opposite.

'Would you like some food?' Katherine suggested. 'Honora reminded me to pack some provisions.'

She was about to stand, but Ewan took her hand. 'No. Not yet.'

He needed to know if a spark could be kindled between them. Surely kissing one woman was the same as any other. The need to know, to see if he could expel Honora from his mind, made him cast aside courtesy. He reached out and caught Katherine by the nape.

Her eyes widened, her lips parting with surprise. Without asking, Ewan leaned in and kissed her. He put everything into the kiss, hoping to coax the same desire he'd felt with Honora.

But there was nothing. He felt like an older brother, kissing a woman who didn't want to be kissed. Breaking away from her, he saw her cheeks flush. She touched her hand to her lips, then flushed. 'I was hoping you would do that.'

And he, in turn, wished he hadn't. Somehow, he mustered a smile he didn't feel.

A loud rustling noise caught his attention. There, in the

grove of trees near the ruins, he saw a branch moving. No wind was present, and he moved his hand to his sword.

'Stay here. There's someone in the trees.' He pressed her back towards the ruins. 'Climb up until I come for you.'

Katherine obeyed, and Ewan saw the branches move again. He darted forward, running in the direction of the sound. His weapon drawn, he rushed to find out exactly who was hidden in the underbrush.

When he cleared the trees, he saw Honora gripping a dagger, her gaze furious.

Ewan groaned. 'Now why am I not surprised to see you?'

She shot him a withering look. 'I was looking after my sister, to ensure that you didn't try to ravish her.'

He reached for her wrist to keep the knife at bay. 'You should know me better than that, Honora.'

'You seem to have a habit of kissing women. First me, and now her. I say you aren't trustworthy.'

The edge in her voice caught him by surprise. Was she jealous? He'd never imagined it was possible, but there was no doubt Honora was upset about his courtship.

Ewan turned her wrist, forcing her to drop the blade. 'I doubt if your sister would appreciate your efforts.'

At that, she looked down at the ground. 'I'm not sorry for it. If it were any of the other suitors, I'd have done the same.'

Likely that was true. 'Now that you're here, you may as well join us.' He started to pull her towards the clearing.

'No!' Honora tried to break free of his grasp, her voice panicked. 'Do not tell her of this.'

Ewan ignored her, lifting her up and over his shoulder. The incongruous position was meant to shame her for her spying, and he ignored her pleas to let her go.

He would, of course. As soon as he revealed the spying to her sister.

'I've found our intruder,' he called out to Katherine. The maiden was perched atop one of the taller stones, and as he'd expected, fury darkened her face. When he reached the abbey ruins, he set Honora down.

'What are you doing here?' Katherine demanded, climbing over the ruins until she stood before her sister.

Honora's face turned crimson. 'Just—ensuring that you were all right. You've—you've been gone awhile.'

'I've been gone for only a few minutes.'

Ewan stepped back, beginning to enjoy himself. He'd never had any sisters, and at the moment Katherine looked ready to tear Honora's eyes out.

'You were spying on us.'

'I was protecting you.'

'I say spying.' Curling her hand into a fist, Katherine punched her sister on the shoulder. 'Go back and find your own suitor. This one isn't yours.'

In spite of himself, Ewan couldn't stop his smile. He'd never had women fighting over him. It was an experience he rather enjoyed. Settling back beside the basket, he opened it and chose a piece of mutton, preparing to watch the war unfold.

Honora dodged another blow. 'I've already told you, I don't want to wed again. If you'd open your eyes, you'd see that I'm only going along with what Father wants. For you, so that you can marry a man of your choosing.'

Katherine pulled back to deliver another punch, but Honora caught her hand. 'Enough. We'll go home, and put this behind us.'

'Did you think you would take him away from me?' Katherine reached out and tripped her sister, rolling Honora onto the grass.

Ewan took another bite, resting his arm upon a knee. A pity Bevan couldn't see this. Or his other brothers. He'd never been so entertained.

Honora fought hard, and used her full strength to pin Katherine to the ground. Her sister struggled, but could do nothing to free herself.

'I'm going to let go of you now. Don't try to fight me again, or I'll only embarrass you more. Do you think Ewan wants to see you behaving in such a manner?'

Actually, yes, but he couldn't say that.

Katherine let out a foul curse, but stopped struggling. Honora released her, and she sat up, rubbing her wrists.

'Ewan, I am sorry for this,' Honora apologised. 'Please bring my sister home.' With a dark look, she added, 'And if you aren't back within an hour, I will hunt both of you down.' With that, she started walking back to the forest.

It occurred to Ewan that she'd come without an escort. Not wise at all, given the animosity she felt toward John of Ceredys.

He was about to suggest that they all return together, but the ire upon Katherine's face made it clear that she would not welcome such an idea. Her face was smeared with dirt, her hair coming loose from her veil. She looked ready to murder her sister.

'You've quite a fist, for such a lady,' Ewan ventured.

Katherine let out a huff, wiping at the dirt upon her gown. 'There is more to me than you might think.'

So it seemed.

Chapter Eight

Honora went to her old trunk in the corner of the room. She'd left it behind when she'd married Ranulf, believing she'd never need it.

But now, she wanted a few hours to escape her worries. The morning had gone badly, and she deeply regretted what she'd done. She had only intended to protect Katherine, to ensure her safety.

But when she'd seen Ewan kissing her sister, something inside had snapped. She'd deliberately rustled the trees, wanting him to keep his hands off of Katherine. And it had worked.

She was a terrible sister for feeling this way. There was nothing wrong with MacEgan. Certainly, Ewan would make Katherine a good husband, even if his fortunes were less than other men.

Honora sat down upon the floor, resting her hands on the wooden surface of the trunk. Once, she had been as carefree as her sister, believing that her wedding would be a moment of joy. She'd been so hopeful, believing that Ranulf was a man as kindly as her father. But she'd been wrong.

A heavy sigh escaped her. She couldn't ruin her sister's happiness. No doubt if Katherine wed Ewan, her union would be different. Ewan was a steady man and would take care of her younger sister.

Why, then, was she feeling so morose? She didn't want Ewan for herself. She wasn't the sort of woman who could make any man a good wife. Ranulf had made that clear.

And now, it seemed she wasn't a good sister either. Katherine was right to despise her for spying. For that was what she'd done, no matter what her intentions had been.

She needed a distraction, a means of distancing herself from her problems and letting out her frustration. Her hands were positively itching for another sword fight.

But when she opened her trunk, her clothing was no longer in neat folded piles. Instead, bliauds and shifts were tangled up with veils, and it was clear someone had searched the chest. For what purpose? She didn't like the idea of anyone going through her belongings, whether friend or enemy.

She doubted if her sister had touched it, for Katherine had more gowns than most women would ever need. There was nothing of value within it, except…

Her throat nearly closed up as she reached to unlatch the false bottom. Still there. Thank the Blessed Virgin. Honora sighed with relief as she lifted up the suit of heavy chainmail armour, along with a pair of men's chausses, braies and a tunic.

Though she loathed the armour, it was necessary for concealing her identity. She could move among her father's soldiers, and none would be the wiser. She'd stolen it from a dead soldier, after a Welsh lord had tried to conquer their lands a few years ago.

She set the armour aside and busied herself, folding up the rest of the gowns. More than ever, she sensed that someone was watching her. Possibly John or one of the other suitors.

She removed her gown, stripping down and replacing it with the men's clothing. She lifted the chainmail shirt over the tunic. The byrnie hung down over her torso, straining her shoulders under the weight. The skullcap and coif hid her shorn hair, and it made her neck ache just to wear it. Last, she donned a conical helm. She wore no further armour, unable to tolerate the heaviness.

Only for a short time, she promised herself. Then she would return and no one would know.

Right now, she needed to test the weight of a sword, to feel the rush of blood pumping through her veins. And though she could wear the armour for only an hour at best, it would help her to forget about this disastrous afternoon.

Katherine would confront her about Ewan, and she still didn't know how to respond. She doubted if an apology would mean anything to her sister.

Honora struggled to walk at first, regaining her balance. But as she exited her bedchamber, her muscles remembered the feel of the weight, the sensation of cold metal links against her cheeks and hair. With each step forward, she felt herself regaining a sense of power.

No one questioned her when she slipped inside the armoury. Nor did anyone notice when she emerged, a lightweight sword strapped to her waist. She'd forgone any gloves, preferring a stronger grip by fighting bare-handed. The gauntlets were too large for her hands, anyhow.

Honora stepped outside, striding through the bailey towards the practice grounds. The men had already begun sparring, and she had to stop herself from smiling at the familiar sound of steel clashing. Several of Katherine's suitors were training alongside her father's men.

'Looking for a match?' a familiar voice asked. She spun and saw John of Ceredys. At the sight of him, her skin grew cold, her palms sweaty.

Fear convulsed in her stomach, making her take an involuntary step backwards. A coldness built up within her, a need to avenge the women he'd defiled. And without thinking of the true consequences, she heard herself saying, 'I accept your challenge.'

* * *

After he returned Katherine safely to the *donjon*, Ewan found his brother Bevan inside their shared chamber. 'How was your visit with Longford?'

Bevan grimaced. 'The Earl is a good enough sort. He enjoyed the poteen I brought him. But Genevieve's mother—' He shook his head.

'Took your head off for leaving Genevieve behind, did she?'

'I wasn't about to drag her across the sea when she's going to give birth soon, now was I?' Bevan rubbed his ear, as though Lady Longford had boxed it. 'But Helen thought I should have brought some of the children. She misses them.'

'You could have, you know. I'm certain Duncan would have thought it a wonderful adventure.' Ewan had a fondness for Bevan's eldest son. The lad was only seven years of age, but he reminded Ewan of himself as a child.

'If I'd brought him, Lady Longford would have fed him sweets from dawn until dusk.'

'I see nothing wrong with that.' Ewan stretched, even as his brother glowered.

'Wait until you have children of your own, and you'll think differently.' Bevan shook his head. 'And by the way, how is it with Lady Katherine? Have you settled on a betrothal?'

'I believe I've gained her favour. No thanks to her sister.' He explained Honora's antics from that morning. She'd claimed she was only ensuring that her sister was protected. But it reminded him of how she'd followed him, years ago. Always there, always hanging on to him when he didn't want her there.

Strangely, he found it less of an annoyance. She'd been furious with him for kissing Katherine, and wasn't that interesting? Like a jealous woman, she'd practically shaken the branches off the tree to gain his notice.

It should have irritated him. Instead, it intrigued him.

'Did you learn anything while you were visiting the Earl?' Ewan asked.

'Only that I'm grateful there's a sea between us.' Bevan

shuddered. 'Otherwise, they would already be arranging betrothals for the children.'

'I mean about…other matters. Did you hear anything about Honora's former husband, Ranulf St Leger?'

Bevan rubbed the stubble of beard upon his cheeks. 'Now why would I be wanting to know anything about him?'

Ewan shrugged, trying to behave as though the answer didn't matter. 'I would know why Honora loathes the idea of remarrying.'

'Why don't you ask her that yourself?'

'I have. And she won't tell me anything.'

Bevan's eyes turned contemplative. 'It bothers you, her former marriage.' Before he could deny it, his brother continued. 'Have you asked yourself why you're asking such a question? Would you rather court her instead of Katherine?'

'No. Honora is too—' He struggled to find the right words. Too vivid, too passionate.

'Too troubled,' he finished. 'And Katherine has dowry lands in Éireann, south of Dubh Linn. Honora's lands are bound to John St Leger, Ranulf's son. I want no part of that.'

'Then stop asking about Honora, and concern yourself with Katherine.'

It was sound advice, and he knew he should obey. Yet, with each passing moment, he wondered why he couldn't seem to cast her forth from his thoughts.

'You should return home, Bevan,' Ewan suggested. 'There's no reason for you to linger any more.'

'I came to witness your wedding.' Though his brother's tone was gruff, Ewan knew that Bevan missed his wife.

'There is no need. The Earl of Longford will act as witness.' With a pointed look, he added, 'Genevieve will not be pleased if she gives birth early and you are not with her.'

'The babe will not be here until late summer.'

'And they all come when they are expected, do they?' Ewan saw his brother's look of discomfort, for their youngest son, Cavan, had taken them all by surprise. It was only by the grace of God that the child had lived.

'Return home to your wife and the children,' Ewan urged. 'I will be well enough. And I'll bring my bride to meet our family, once we are wed.'

Though Bevan appeared uneasy about it, he did not argue. 'Don't linger here, then. We'll expect you home by Midsummer's Eve.'

The summer feast was one Ewan particularly enjoyed, and he nodded in agreement. 'I will be there.'

'Good. In the meantime, I'll speak to the Baron and find out what I can about a betrothal for you.' Bevan reached out and gripped his hand.

Ewan returned the squeeze and met his brother's gaze. 'I'm going to win the land, Bevan.'

'I do not doubt it. But I'm not certain that a sweet, fair lady is quite what you want.'

His brother's words resonated in his mind. Why would he want anything less? Katherine was perfect for him.

'Have a safe journey.'

His older brother gripped him in an embrace, slapping him upon the shoulders. 'I'll send Connor back in my place. He'll escort you home.'

'I'd rather spend the journey alone with my bride.'

Bevan's scarred face cracked a smile. 'I can understand that. But don't do anything foolish. Like wed the wrong woman.'

As if there were any chance of that. Honora and he could not be any more ill-suited.

After his brother departed, Ewan reached for his scabbard and sword. A hard fight was what he needed now, a chance to push himself beyond the limits.

Perhaps then he could get Honora out of his mind.

John tossed her a shield, and Honora caught it, raising the wood to meet his first blow. He wasted no time in attacking, hammering blows against her blade that numbed her shoulders.

But she continued her defence, remaining steady on her feet.

'Not much of a fighter, are you, lad?' John moved in closer, forcing her to raise her shield to block his strike.

He was toying with her, making it difficult to judge his skills. He could defeat her if she didn't concentrate.

Honora watched carefully for an opening, then used her full strength to arc the blade towards his ribs. At the last moment, John used his shield to deflect the slice, knocking her arm backwards at the force.

She'd never fought him directly. Her earlier victory against him, that night when she'd used her knife, had been with the advantage of surprise. His strength and cunning undermined her confidence, and she was starting to question the wisdom of this match.

He continued to best her, forcing her to retreat. Then her blade slipped free, and she nicked his arm, drawing blood.

John roared with anger, charging at her. Honora didn't think, couldn't move. At the last possible moment, she raised her wooden shield, stunned when John knocked it aside. Without it, she had only her blade to block his attack now.

The others moved in, watching the sparring match. Sir Ademar, along with Beaulais, stood among them.

Honora struggled to keep her sword upright to defend herself, knowing that she'd chosen poorly for her opponent. John didn't fight fair, and the flat of his blade caught her across the chest.

The breath knocked out of her lungs as she hit the ground, back first. Honora raised her arm over her face, unable to sit up from the heavy armour. Then another male voice spoke.

'You've won the match, Ceredys. Let the lad go and tend his humiliation in private.'

It was Ewan. Oh, heaven, she prayed he wouldn't recognise her. Not after she'd been defeated so soundly.

Honora rolled sideways, struggling to sit up. The chain-mail byrnie made it nearly impossible. Her back ached, her chest burned, but if she hadn't worn the armour, no doubt she would be dead.

Slowly, she rose to her feet, her head hanging down. It was the worst fight she'd ever endured. What had happened to her courage, her fighting skills? Everything had dissolved when she'd faced John's blade.

The others let her go, but she heard footsteps following behind. With a glance over her shoulders, she saw it was Ewan. Now what did he want?

Let him go away, she prayed. She needed to rid herself of this armour and tend to her wounds in private.

When she entered the *donjon*, he caught up to her. His voice remained just above a whisper. 'I know what you're doing, Honora. And I want to talk with you. Now.'

He knew. How? She'd revealed none of her hair, none of her female form. Nothing should have given her away.

She sent him an infuriated look. Keeping her voice low-pitched, she demanded, 'And just what am I doing?'

'You'd best be in my chamber within the next two minutes,' he ground out in a voice just above a whisper, 'or I'll be having a few words with your father.'

'This armour...' she protested.

'Get rid of it, then,' he acceded. 'But make no mistake, be there, or I will drag you inside.'

She strode up the stairs, her thighs burning with exertion by the time she reached the chamber she shared with Katherine. Opening the door slightly, she cursed inwardly when she saw her sister sitting there.

Jesu. She couldn't enter, not without revealing herself. Silently, she closed the door and retraced her steps back to Ewan's chamber. Knocking slightly, she nearly fell forwards when the door jerked open.

Ewan closed the door behind her, barring it. Then he

reached up and removed the helm and coif from her head. 'I thought you were going to change back into your gown.'

'Katherine was inside our chamber,' she admitted. 'I couldn't let her see.'

Ewan's face tightened, his anger exploding. 'And yet you paraded among the men as though you were one of them? Why? Why would you seek out danger in that way?'

'I wanted to train. I'm losing my skills, and I need to—'

'You've no need to wield a sword.' He helped her lift away the chainmail byrnie, setting the armour shirt aside. 'Damn it, Ceredys could have hurt you.'

He did, she wanted to say, but her stubborn tongue fell silent.

Clad in only the tunic, braies and chausses, Honora sat down. She rested her elbows upon her knees, leaning forward to hide herself. The tunic stretched across her breasts, and she grew uncomfortably aware of the wound she'd suffered from John's blade. Though the mail had protected her from being cut, the armour had bruised her skin. Her body ached, and her arms were exhausted. She longed to sink into a hot bath, letting the water soothe her tired muscles.

'You're in pain. Let me see.' He didn't ask permission, but moved closer, kneeling before her. He loosened the ties of the tunic, and she didn't stop him. Baring the flesh above her breasts, he revealed the reddened skin.

His fingertips grazed the surface, gently examining it. 'You shouldn't have fought him.'

'I know that now.' But she had foolishly believed herself capable of defeating John. She'd wanted revenge for all that he'd done. And she'd failed.

Hot tears sprang to her eyes, but she blinked them away. Embarrassed at her loss, she didn't know what else to say.

The touch of Ewan's hands loosened her hold upon her thoughts. His fingers rested upon her shoulders, the gentle warmth inviting. Without thinking, she put her hands upon his.

She wanted him to kiss her again. Shame filled her, for that could never be.

To cover her thoughts, she traced the scars on his palms. 'These have healed well.' When he'd first come to the Longford estate to be fostered, she'd seen the angry red slashes, the result of torture he'd endured.

'Did it hurt, when they cut you?' she asked softly.

'It hurt worse, knowing I had betrayed my brother. If I hadn't confessed where they were hiding, Marstowe wouldn't have found them.'

'But Bevan forgave you.'

Ewan nodded. He pulled his hands away, resting them upon her waist. 'It took longer to forgive myself.'

She needed to pull away from him, but his hands trapped her in place. What was he doing? Why was he remaining so close to her?

Swallowing hard, she said, 'I am sorry for following you and Katherine. It was wrong of me.'

He studied her, his stare penetrating. Those heated green eyes captured her own, watching her with open desire. 'Why did you?'

'I told you, I wanted to protect her.'

'From kissing a man like me.'

'Yes,' she whispered.

His hands slid under the folds of the tunic, pressing back the fabric to study her skin, reddened by the armour. The unexpected sensation of his hands upon her sent a spiral of heat up her spine.

'Ewan, don't.' It was a lover's touch, not the touch of a man inspecting a wound.

'You should never have challenged him,' Ewan insisted. 'You aren't strong enough to defeat him.'

Her pride flared up. 'My skills are good enough. Strength doesn't matter.'

'It does. And you should have known your limitations.'

'I can best any man among them, MacEgan. Including you.' She tried to push his hand away, but he held her shoulders, granting no reprieve. In a silent war, she fought against his unyielding strength.

'You won't best me, Honora. Not ever.'

His voice was deep with the undertones of sexual frustration. When she looked into his eyes, she saw that their battle had shifted into something else. He wanted her. And he didn't like it at all.

He relaxed his hold, allowing her the chance to escape. But Honora didn't move. She wasn't sure she could, for right now, her skin was covered in goose flesh, her blood turning hot. Without thinking, she rested her palms upon his tunic, trying to still her racing heart.

'You need to leave, Honora.' Even as he spoke, his hands cupped her shorn hair, sliding through the softness. He massaged her temples, and Honora closed her eyes, drinking in his touch.

'Why do you make me feel like this?' she whispered. 'It was never this way with Ranulf.'

She'd been misused by her husband. Ewan was sure of it. He wanted to tell her that no man should ever mistreat his wife, that it wasn't her fault. He wanted her to know how desirable she was, that any man would want her.

The way he wanted her.

Her mouth, sensual and full, was slightly open. And he could no longer deny himself this craving for her. His mouth descended upon hers, for he needed to know if the last time had been accidental lust.

It wasn't.

Quite simply, Honora's kiss took him apart. Though he'd never understand what it was about her that enslaved him, he wasn't about to release her sweet mouth. Not yet. His tongue slid inside, in the imitation of what he wanted to do to her.

No brotherly thoughts, this time. He wanted to lift her

atop the bed and drive himself deep inside her body until she cried out in ecstasy. His manhood ached, its hardness straining against his trews. He wanted her wet, to drive her into the same frenzy he felt.

The sounds she made while he kissed her, the throaty moans, aroused him to the point of pain. He lifted her leg around his hip, lowering her to the floor.

She kissed him back, as lost as he was. He ran his mouth down the softness of her throat while his hands caressed her back. Loosening the tunic even more, he revealed the swollen redness above her breasts, kissing the spot with his mouth.

He brought his hands up her smooth stomach, resting his palms to cup her bare breasts. He let the heavy weight of them sink into his palms, and he wanted his mouth on her tight nipples.

Damn her for taking such chances with her life. Seeing her struck down had driven him past the brink. The idea of any man hurting her, whether intentional or not, kindled an undeniable fury.

With his thumbs, he grazed the erect nipples, growling when he heard her sharp intake of breath. He lifted her up to straddle him, sliding his hard erection between her thighs. She was shaking, as though caught between fear and need.

Through the men's braies she wore, Ewan cupped her bottom, kneading the tight flesh as he lifted her against his shaft. *Críost*, he wanted to take her right then. He wanted to rip the fabric apart, plunging his body inside hers.

Honora clasped his head between her palms, pleading, 'Ewan, no.' In a broken voice, she whispered, 'This is wrong.'

His brain was clouded, unable to gather a clear thought. Honora pushed away from him, and he released her immediately.

God above, what had he done? He'd never meant to lay a hand upon her, much less allow things to go this far. He released her immediately, sitting back with his knees drawn up. 'You're right. I'm sorry.' Resting his forehead on his palm, he now understood his brother's warning.

He'd let himself fall prey to her spell, seduced by this unexpected fire between them. He didn't like himself at all, nor what he'd done.

'It won't happen again,' he swore.

Honora righted her clothing, but he saw her trembling fingers. She gripped the bedpost until her knuckles whitened. 'Do not speak of this to Katherine. Promise me.'

He gave a curt nod. If Katherine learned of it, his courtship chances were over.

'You'd better go,' he said.

She nodded, looking miserable. After she'd fled the chamber, Ewan expelled a curse.

Desire meant nothing. Though he might have lost his head, acting upon lust instead of logic, he knew he could never wed Honora. Not only would they argue with each other from dusk until dawn, but she lacked the land he needed.

She would only control her portion of Ceredys during her lifetime. Afterwards, it reverted back to John and his heirs. Any children she bore would never see an acre of the land.

No, it was better for Honora to wed a man with his own holdings, his own estate. A man like Sir Ademar of Dolwyth, who stood to inherit his own fortune.

Ewan tried to ignore the surge of rage that blackened his mood at the thought of another man touching Honora. She wasn't his, and never would be.

It was better for both of them that way.

Chapter Nine

When she entered their shared bedchamber, Katherine kept her back turned, without acknowledging Honora's greeting. Her sister was furious, and rightfully so.

And though Katherine knew nothing about what had just happened, Honora felt as though her sins were emblazoned across her face.

Her guilt and self-loathing trebled, making it difficult to find the right words. There was nothing she could do except apologise and vow to herself that she'd not succumb to temptation again.

'I'm sorry,' Honora began. 'I didn't mean to pry earlier, only to watch over you.'

Katherine stiffened, and when at last she turned around, she frowned. 'Why are you wearing a man's clothing?' Her tone was so startled, it was as if Honora had walked naked into their chamber.

'My—other clothes were soiled,' Honora lied.

Though her sister didn't appear to fully believe her, Katherine reached for a fresh gown from Honora's trunk. Her movements were stiff, as though she were fulfilling an obligation. 'Here.'

Honora took the garment but did not put it on yet. 'You're

my only sister,' she said, continuing the apology. And regardless of what had happened with Ewan, she'd allow nothing to threaten their bond. 'I don't want anything to happen to you.'

'I am not fourteen years old any more,' Katherine argued. 'I don't need a keeper.'

'You're right,' Honora admitted. 'But it's hard to let go of old habits.' With a heavy sigh, she added, 'I behaved badly.'

'Yes, you did,' her sister agreed. 'You had no right to follow us.'

'I deserved this.' Honora touched her cheek, where Katherine had struck her earlier. The flesh was tender and would bruise later, she knew.

Katherine looked uncomfortable at the reminder. 'No. I shouldn't have struck you.'

You would do more than strike me, if you knew what I've done, Honora thought. But she shook her head. 'I deserved it.'

Loosening the ties of the tunic, she lifted it over her head and started to put on the gown.

When she saw the red welt across her chest, Katherine stopped her. 'What happened to you? I didn't do that, did I?'

'No. It was my own clumsiness.' Another lie, added to those she'd already told. But thankfully, Katherine did not ask further questions.

Instead, her sister offered, 'Do you want me to tend it? I'm not as good as you at healing, but it must pain you.'

Honora's throat grew dry. The peace offering was so undeserved, she hardly knew what to say. 'I'll tend it later, after I've bathed.'

Katherine helped her arrange the bliaud, strangely quiet. 'I know about the armour,' she said suddenly. 'And your fighting.'

Honora froze, and an argument sprang to her lips.

'Don't deny it.' Katherine lifted a hand, shaking her head. 'I've known about it for years.'

It was the last thing she'd expected Katherine to say. 'When did you find out?'

'When you came back from Longford.' Her sister sat down upon the bed, her hands folded in her lap. 'Though I don't understand your desire to fight, I won't tell Father.'

'I don't understand it myself sometimes,' Honora admitted. It was true. When she donned the armour, it weighed down upon her, the burden of both the chainmail and the forbidden need to fight.

'I used to think—it was our brother's spirit,' Honora continued. 'It's as though a part of him lives on in me. Is it foolish, wanting to fight as he would have?'

'It is.' Katherine folded her hands in her lap. 'I fear for you, Honora. You could be killed if you don't cease this. You haven't the strength of the other men.'

Normally, she would have argued with her sister, for she had won numerous matches. But both she and Ewan were right. Today had been different, for she'd allowed her concentration to slip. Her fear of John had dominated the fight.

Katherine's arms slipped around her in an embrace. Honora hugged her back. 'I didn't mean to worry you.'

'Just stop,' Katherine pleaded. 'You have nothing more to prove.'

Only to myself, Honora thought, but did not say it. When they broke apart, Katherine passed her a veil to hide her hair. Honora donned it while her sister adjusted her own appearance, studying herself in a mirror of polished steel.

'I think I'm going to wed Ewan,' Katherine confessed.

Honora squeezed the pommel of her knife so tightly, she wondered it didn't break off. 'Really?' Anger thrust through her mind, coupled with a touch of fear.

Katherine spun around, hugging her waist. Her cheeks burned with hope. 'I—I think I could learn to love him, Honora. He is the right choice for me. I'm going to speak to Father tonight.'

Honora tried to manage a smile, but could not. Hurt caught up in her throat, but she quelled it. 'Are you certain?' The words tumbled out of her mouth, as though she were trying to change Katherine's mind. 'There are other men who might suit you better.'

'None so handsome as him.' Katherine adjusted her hair, tucking the long braid behind her veil.

Honora ceased her arguments, for what was the point? Ewan deserved a wife like Katherine. Gentle and industrious, her sister would make him happy.

She wouldn't allow this cold feeling to spread and grow within her. She had no claim upon Ewan, even if his kiss still tingled upon her mouth.

What she had done to Katherine was wrong. Unforgivably so. The guilt made it hard to face her sister, and she despised herself.

'I wish you well with him.' Honora squeezed her sister's hand, praying Katherine would never learn of the betrayal.

'What about you?' Katherine asked. 'Is there a man whom you wish to wed? Sir Ademar, perhaps?'

There was a curious flush to Katherine's face, but Honora reassured her, 'Don't trouble yourself on my account.' She had no intention of marrying anyone. 'I'll see to it that you get the man you want.'

She crossed the room to stare outside the window. This awful feeling inside was guilt, nothing more. Ewan was her friend, and they had agreed not to let anything happen again. She trusted him to keep that vow.

There was no other choice.

John St Leger sat across from Nicholas of Ardennes. Although they held an equal rank and now a kinship tie through Honora, the younger Baron envied Nicholas. The fine castle, with nearly all the wood converted into stone, was far superior to his own inheritance.

He wanted more. He coveted the gleaming gold, the comfortable scents of good food and ale. The castle left to him by his father was debt-ridden, a crumbling fortress with not nearly enough funds to let him live in the style he wished.

He blamed the women. His grandmother, Marie St Leger, had known where the family's treasure was hidden. Jewels and gold, spoils from a Norse raid, had kept the estate in fine form while his grandfather was alive. There was supposed to be more, but only Marie knew where it was hidden.

And now she was dead, damn her. He'd done everything to get the information out of her, but even with her dying breath, the bitch had refused to tell him.

Now Marie's ruby had gone missing. It rightfully belonged to him, along with the rest of the treasure. He suspected Honora had stolen the gemstone, and it was possible Marie had given her the secrets of the treasure. He'd seen them together too often.

He'd never met any woman like Honora. Powerful, bold and defiant. His groin ached, just thinking of her. Even when she'd threatened him with her knife, he could not deny the way she aroused him. She should have married *him*, not his father. Ranulf had stolen her, against his wishes.

He had every intention of getting her back. Not as a bride, but as a lover perhaps. He wanted to taste that fine skin, to subdue her flesh beneath his. He wanted her to fight him, for he'd enjoy punishing her. And then, when he'd broken her, he would force her to confess the location of the ruby and the treasure.

But first, he had to bring her back to Ceredys. And that meant gaining the support of her father.

'Lady Honora has been gone for some time,' John began, sipping his ale as though it were a casual matter. 'Has she been well?'

Nicholas shrugged. 'Well enough, I suppose. Though she's neglecting her responsibilities at Ceredys.'

And the little thief had taken what belonged to him. But

John took pains to keep his expression calm. 'I've come to ask her to return. The people miss their lady.'

'She will, soon enough.' Nicholas steepled his hands upon the wooden table. His gaze was dark, and John wondered what Honora had revealed about her sudden departure.

'I understand you are pressuring Honora to remarry,' John began.

'*Suggesting*, yes.' Lord Ardennes looked displeased. 'She has no children and was widowed at a young age.'

'Most would not wish her to remarry. It would be a sin for a man to succumb to the temptation of a widow. The Church does not condone it.'

'The Church can be convinced of anything, so long as their coffers are kept full.' Lord Ardennes frowned. 'I believe it would be in Honora's best interests. Sir Ademar has already offered for her.' The Baron refilled his own goblet, but did not grant John the same courtesy.

John pretended not to notice the slight, but it was an invisible slice upon his pride. The quality of the drink far surpassed the ale at Ceredys, and he blamed Honora for it. Was it not her responsibility to oversee the brewers?

His frustration mounted higher. She needed to return, to assume her responsibilities and see to it that the estate was put to rights. For several months, she had shirked the needs of Ceredys. It would stop. She could no longer avoid her role as Lady, and if that meant convincing Lord Ardennes that he would deny any marriage offers, so be it.

'We both want what is best for Lady Honora,' John admitted. He had to tread carefully, for Lord Ardennes would not take well to threats. 'And though Sir Ademar may have offered, we must decide whether or not the match would be in her best interests.'

Ardennes reached out for a fig, drenched in honey. John had never tasted such a delicacy, but he'd not lower himself to ask the Baron for such favours.

'True.' Honora's father ate the fig, licking his fingertips. 'I almost considered Ewan MacEgan for her. There seemed to be an interest, but she denied it. He has voiced his interest in Katherine instead.'

'The Irishman has virtually no property. I am surprised you would consider him at all.'

'I had a conversation with his older brother, Bevan MacEgan, not long ago,' Ardennes remarked. 'It seems that the King of Laochre has offered a gift on Ewan's behalf, a bridal price for whichever daughter he chooses.'

John hid his displeasure, feigning interest. 'Gold?'

'Horses.' Ardennes beamed. 'Brought over from the Holy Land, I understand. Finest animals one could hope for.'

He hadn't known about the Baron's weakness for horse-flesh, but it was the clear the man was positively gloating over the prospect.

John set his empty goblet aside. 'Let MacEgan wed your younger daughter. Honora is needed at Ceredys. Since I have no wife, her presence is sorely missed.'

Ardennes rubbed his chin. 'I will suggest it to her once more. But Honora has said to me that she has no wish to return.' His gaze sharpened, and John didn't care for the sudden threat he sensed.

'My daughter is not, nor has ever been, the cowardly sort,' the Baron remarked. 'Why would she flee your protection?'

The pointed question held a note of warning, but John would not give Lord Ardennes any cause for concern. With a light smile of apology, he said, 'There was a man who held an unwanted interest in Honora. One of my retainers. Once I discovered it, I had the man sent away. She can return without fear of him.'

Ardennes relaxed his shoulders, believing the tale he'd spun. 'Good. I am glad you've corrected the matter. I would hate to think that you'd allowed anything to happen to my daughter within the safety of her own home.'

John veiled his irritation, but at least Honora had not told her father the true reason for her departure. Her silence made it easier to bring her back again.

'Where is the Lady Honora?' he asked with a smile. 'I have not had the opportunity to speak with her at length. She must be wanting to hear the news from Ceredys.'

'She is outside in the gardens, I am told.' The Baron waved his hand in dismissal. 'You may go and seek her out, if it pleases you.'

'I shall.' John gave a curt nod, itching to see Honora. He would bring her back to Ceredys, where he could look upon her face each morn, watching her move about her tasks.

As he walked towards the gardens, he thought of exactly what he would say to her.

Honora knelt down beside a bed of herbs, her fingers wrenching out a weed. If only she could tear out her guilt as easily. The entire morning, Katherine had been chattering about Ewan this and Ewan that. Finally, Honora had made her excuses, needing any form of escape.

She rubbed at her shoulders, for her arms ached after the fight from yesterday. The raw sore above her breasts was a blatant reminder of her failure.

She wasn't ready to fight John—that much was clear. But she could learn.

Thinking back on her mistakes, she realised that she'd expected him to fight fairly. John had seized every advantage, using her weaknesses against her. In that moment, she had become his victim, unable to defend herself.

It wouldn't happen again. If she were to fight against him in combat again, she would win. Even if it meant taking his life.

She sobered at the thought, for she'd never killed anyone. And yet, it was what warriors did when necessary. They protected their people at all costs.

Warriors did not cower at the idea of killing an enemy. And

that was what John was. An enemy who was hurting innocent people. As Lady of Ceredys, it fell to her to guard them.

Honora was so caught up in the idea, she didn't notice Ewan's approach until his shadow fell over her. Her pulse quickened at the sight of him. His face was haggard, as though he hadn't slept well. She supposed he mirrored her own discontent.

'I came to apologise for what I did yesterday.' In his hand, he carried a grey-and-white-striped kitten. The tiny feline let out a tiny mew, and Ewan passed it to her. 'And I thought you might want to give this lad a home, since your sister cannot care for him.'

Honora reached out to touch the silky fur, and the kitten mewed again, arching its head against her hand. Her heart softened at the sight of the creature.

'I accept your apology. It was my fault as much as yours,' she admitted.

He didn't meet her gaze, but his shoulders relaxed slightly. He sat back, his wrist resting upon his raised knee. Neither spoke, and Honora played with the kitten, not wanting to risk the tentative truce.

The animal began climbing up her bliaud, sinking its baby claws into the blue fabric of her gown. Honora lifted it into her hands and finally asked the question she feared most. 'Have you spoken to my sister?'

'No. I've not seen her since our visit to the ruins.'

Ewan grew solemn, his eyes turning troubled. 'But I am going to wed her.'

Honora ran her fingers over the garden dirt, pretending his words didn't matter. They shouldn't, not at all. She knew Ewan needed Katherine's dowry lands in Ireland. His decision was a practical one, and he would be kind to her sister.

'It will be a good match,' she managed, though her throat seemed swollen with so many other things she wanted to say. 'I hope you both find happiness together.'

He stared at her, his eyes seeing past her shield. 'You're lying to me.'

'And what if I am?' Honora shot back. 'Does it matter? My sister has everything you want. She has the land, the beauty, and she will have no difficulty caring for the estates.'

Unlike me. Irrational, unreasonable tears were filling up her eyes, and Honora wrenched another weed out of the soil, trying to force her anger onto the plant.

Their mother had died when she was just a girl, and there had been no one to show her how to manage. In time, Katherine had taken command of the household with the help of the seneschal. Her sister had taught her a little about the estates, but it wasn't nearly enough.

'Katherine doesn't have everything I want,' Ewan said quietly. 'But it will have to be enough.'

The words were not a comfort. Instead, they pierced her as surely as a blade through her heart. Honora dried her eyes on the sleeve of her gown. 'Don't say it.'

'It was like kissing a little sister,' he continued. 'Nothing like what it was between us.'

'Why are you telling me this?' Was he trying to hurt her more? Ewan had been her friend for so long, she couldn't let that ground shift from beneath her.

'If circumstances were different—'

'They aren't.' Honora knew better than to let herself believe he might have chosen her. 'My lands are tied up with John's. I can't give you the land you need. And I couldn't be the sort of wife you'd want.'

'I don't know what your husband did to you to make you believe that.' He took her hand in his, the large palm covering her fingers. 'You're a desirable woman, Honora.'

Now Ewan was the one who was lying. Ranulf had chastised her for being a cold wife, a woman incapable of giving him comfort. She'd been as useless in the marriage bed as she'd been in their home.

No, marriage was a prison, nothing more.

Her hand closed over an oak seedling, and she yanked the wayward tree out of the herbal bed. 'Go to my sister.'

Ewan took her palm and raised it to his lips, in a gesture of farewell. The touch of his mouth on her skin sent a ripple of warmth through her body. 'I don't want to lose your friendship, Honora. In spite of what happened.'

She didn't answer, though she felt like weeping. Instead, she spent the next few minutes weeding the garden, letting her thoughts stray.

Her father expected her to remarry. She would have to choose from among the remaining suitors, as soon as Katherine arranged the betrothal with Ewan.

Right now, she wanted to flee Ardennes, to protect her fragile freedom. But she couldn't, for if she did, Nicholas would not allow Katherine to wed Ewan. Her father was just stubborn enough to carry out his threat.

Honora no longer knew what to do.

Lord, please, no, she prayed. Her only hope was to plead with her father. There had to be a way to change his mind.

When the last weed was gone, Honora rose to her feet and turned to leave. She nearly stumbled at the sight of John approaching.

Fair-haired, with a burgundy tunic and dun chausses, he wore a silver chain to denote his rank.

How many serfs had starved to give him that chain? she wondered. Anger bled through her veins, and she was tempted to draw her blade. But the thin smile upon John's face made her question why he was here.

'My lord.' She greeted him with a stiff curtsy, while her hand rested upon the grip of her dagger. Bloodthirsty thoughts, of carving out his heart, raged through her mind.

'Will you not offer me an embrace of welcome, Lady Honora? Or should I call you Mother?'

She refused to let his taunt pass. 'I am not your mother.'

Although they now had a kinship bond through marriage, she'd never acknowledge it.

When Honora tried to walk past him, John blocked her way. A patronising smile spread over his face. 'True. I have never thought of you as a mother. I thought of you as the bride I was supposed to have. He took you from me, you know.'

She didn't know what madness he was speaking about. 'I was always betrothed to Ranulf.'

'But it was supposed to be me that you wed. My father promised, and then he broke his word.'

And thank heaven for that. Her marriage to Ranulf had been a nightmare, but it would have been far worse had she married John.

'Marie spoke of you before she died,' he said.

At the mention of his grandmother, Honora faltered. Marie had been the only ally she'd had at Ceredys, a steadfast friend. 'What did she say?'

He ignored the question. 'You saw her often, didn't you?'

'She was kind to me.'

'Then you must have seen the ruby she wore around her neck. And she must have told you about the Ceredys treasure.'

It was then that she understood why he was here. He coveted Marie's belongings. The glint in his eyes spoke of a man desperate.

'I saw the ruby on a few occasions.' She glared at him. 'But she never spoke of the treasure.'

'It belongs to me. But it's gone, along with the ruby.' He drew closer, his gaze menacing. 'I think you took it when you left. And I think you know exactly where my inheritance lies.'

His hand tried to slip towards her waist, but Honora unsheathed her knife. 'I know nothing.'

'I don't believe you.'

'Believe what you like. But if you touch me, I will cut off your fingers.'

He laughed, raising his hands in mock surrender. 'So abrasive. And do you treat all of your suitors in this way?'

'I have no suitors.'

'That isn't what your father tells me.' John circled around her, and Honora kept her grip firm on the knife.

From the nonchalant expression on his face, he didn't feel at all intimidated by her weapon. It deepened her anger, and she wanted to prove to him that she was a threat. Aye, she'd lost the sparring match, but it didn't make her helpless.

'Which man will you choose? Sir Ademar, perhaps?' John continued circling, edging her closer to the herbal bed. Honora took a step backwards, her foot brushing against the prickly rosemary.

Damn him for making her afraid. She was halfway cowering amid the plants, just to escape him. And he was gloating about it.

'Or will you take another man into your bed?' His voice was silky, hinting at his own forbidden desires. 'A man who knows how to conquer you.'

Her common sense snapped. Who was he to threaten her in this way? How dare he corner her, behaving as though he were her master?

Without thinking, she darted forward, slicing her knife at his face. The tip of her blade caught his cheek, and blood welled up. His grip caught her wrist, and he squeezed until she thought he would break her wrist. 'That was a mistake, Lady Honora.'

She bit her lip hard to keep from crying out. He stared at her, letting her know with his eyes what he wanted to do to her. And the coldness there, the utter ruthlessness of his gaze, terrified her.

At last, he let go, and she nearly sank to her knees from the pain. John stepped past her, as though she were something to be discarded. After he'd gone, she released the tears, hot tears of rage against her helplessness.

She'd always taken comfort in her fighting skills, but he'd stripped that away. He'd made her aware of her weaknesses, and with that knowledge, her confidence withered.

Had she really thought she could raise up men against him?

Shaken, Honora rose to her feet, still clutching her injured wrist. With her other hand, she reached down to pick up the fallen knife.

Aye, she had made a mistake in cutting John. And now, she had no doubt he would retaliate. As she returned to the *donjon*, she felt her anger building even higher.

She needed to train harder. She needed to anticipate his moves, never letting herself become his victim.

And next time, she would win.

Chapter Ten

'What happened to your wrist?' Katherine asked when Honora returned to their shared chamber.

Honora couldn't hide the reddened skin, and she didn't know whether to confess the truth to Katherine or not. A lie would be easy, but then again, she didn't want Katherine to trust John.

'The Baron of Ceredys and I had a disagreement in the garden,' she admitted. 'He did not take kindly to it.'

'He hurt you.' Katherine's tone sharpened. 'And Father needs to know about it.'

'I will tell him,' Honora replied, though she had no intention of doing so. Nicholas would hardly believe her, and even if he did, John could claim that he'd defended himself when she'd tried to stab him. Which was the truth.

No, her father would only take John's side and order her punished for the injury. Best to say nothing.

'You still treat me as though I am a child,' Katherine said softly. 'I know something terrible happened to you when you dwelled at Ceredys. But you never speak of it.'

'If I speak of it, it is like living it all over again,' Honora admitted.

'Don't return there,' Katherine cautioned her. 'If John did this to you, I don't think it would be wise to live with him.'

Her sister took her uninjured hand, squeezing it lightly. 'You worry about me so often, but this time it's different. Father gave you a choice, and you should think of yourself. Marry the man *you* want.'

'I can't,' Honora said softly. At her sister's questioning look, she added, 'I don't want to wed any man at all. Not after my first marriage.' She drew Katherine into a soft embrace. 'But don't worry. I'll find a way to change our father's mind. He'll let you wed MacEgan without forcing me to remarry.'

'I think you're giving up too soon,' her sister said. 'Sir Ademar offered for you. He would be glad to have you as his bride.'

Honora shook her head. There was no man who would ever accept her for who she was. Not her father, not Ranulf. Both of them wanted her to be a meek, subservient woman who obeyed their commands. But she was a warrior at heart, even if she could never reveal it to anyone.

'Go and have the healer look at your wrist.' Katherine pushed her towards the door. 'I'll speak to our father about John.'

'No, it's not necessary.' Honora didn't want Katherine tangled up in her war with John. 'Right now, I'm going out for a ride near the river. I want some time to think.' And time to make her plans.

In the past few days, there had been no sign of the chapel thief. Possibly the man had found what he sought, or he'd given up.

'Don't go alone,' her sister warned. 'Take a guard with you.'

Honora nodded, though she had no wish for an escort. Right now she wanted to be alone, away from everyone else, while she practised with a sword. Though it was dangerous, she felt the need for solitude.

Katherine embraced her again, her expression wary. 'Be back by sundown.'

Honora sent her sister an exasperated smile. 'Yes, Mother.'

* * *

The river cut through the Ardennes lands, narrowing to a stream that fed the castle's water supply. From the past few days of rain, it had swollen above the banks, spilling into the grasses.

Ewan studied the horizon, searching for any hidden threats to the lone figure resting beside the river. It seemed Honora was still alone.

Katherine had come to him, warning of her sister's intent to go riding. 'She says she'll take a guard, but I know she won't. And after what John did to her wrist—'

She explained the rest, and Ewan's temper flared. Knowing that the bastard had hurt her again, only moments after he'd left Honora's side, made him want to ensure that Ceredys never raised a hand against a woman ever again.

Katherine had pleaded with him to follow Honora and to protect her. 'I trust you to take care of her,' she'd said.

Her consummate faith was a harsh blow to Ewan's conscience. He didn't deserve her trust, not after what he'd done. But neither did he want Honora to be alone and vulnerable to attack.

The silvery reflection of the river glinted in the distance, and he slowed his horse. Honora was standing beside her mount, looking into the distance.

Her blue bliaud was rumpled, her veil askew upon her head. In her left hand, she held a sword, moving through a few practice swings. Her slender form moved with grace, the sword a natural extension of her arm.

Like the blade, she held a power of her own, cool and deadly. And despite the face she put on before others, he'd seen beneath her steel façade.

Instinct warned him to stay away from Honora, despite his promise to her sister. Something had shifted between them, and it unsettled him. He'd come here planning to wed Lady Katherine. She held the key to everything he wanted, land of his own and a wife at his side.

And yet, he found himself daydreaming of Honora. Even

last night, he'd awoken in a cool sweat, his body deeply aroused. He'd imagined her naked body twined around his, her warm skin beside him. He wanted to watch her face shift into ecstasy when he pleasured her. To taste her, to make her scream his name when he filled her body with his own flesh.

He wanted her more than anything he'd ever wanted in his life. And it had become a fierce torment, knowing that he would never have her.

Marriages were meant for alliances and increasing wealth, not personal desires. He couldn't give up everything, the ambitions that he'd dreamed of his entire life, for one woman. It wasn't fair to Honora either, for he had nothing to offer her in return.

The light gleamed against her sword before she sheathed it once more. Honora rested her face against the horse's saddle, her shoulders slumped. She gripped her right wrist, as though she were fighting back against the pain.

Ewan couldn't stay behind any longer. He brought his horse closer, knowing he was intruding upon a private moment.

'I know you're there,' Honora called out. 'Katherine sent you, didn't she?'

Ewan gave no answer, but tethered his horse at a nearby tree. She turned to face him, her expression guarded. 'What is it you want?'

'Your sister told me what happened. And that you came here alone.'

'I've a right to be alone, if I wish.' She kept her attention upon her horse, patting the mare's flanks. 'Especially if I need to train.'

'No. You're not going to fight Ceredys again.'

Trouble brewed in her eyes, and she sent him a furious glare. 'You aren't my master, MacEgan. Ceredys will meet my blade. I won't be his victim.'

'You're right,' he said softly. 'Because he will meet my

blade. And when I'm finished with him, Ceredys won't touch a woman ever again.'

To underscore his point, he lifted up her right wrist to study it. The skin surrounding her wrist was scarlet and starting to bruise. Gently, he touched the injury, his fingertips lightly skimming the surface.

'Tell me what happened.'

Honora looked uneasy. 'John cornered me, and I cut him with my dagger to escape. He grabbed my wrist and nearly broke it.'

She explained the rest, but Ewan hardly heard a word of it. He was going to tear Ceredys apart the next time he set eyes upon the man. 'I don't want you near him again. Stay close to your father, if need be.'

'I don't have a choice, Ewan.' She shifted her gaze back to the river. 'If I return to Ceredys, I cannot avoid him.'

'You can't even think of going back to live with a man like Ceredys.' Rigid anger tightened in his fists. 'It isn't safe.'

'If someone threatened your tribesmen, you would go back to defend them, regardless of the danger.' She unsheathed her sword with her left hand. 'There's no one else to protect the people from John. It is my duty.'

'You haven't the means.'

'No, but I'll find a way. I'll get an army of my own.'

She lunged with her blade against an invisible enemy. Her motions were charged with anger, as though she raged against her own weakness.

Ewan withdrew his own weapon, watching her. Though she poured her efforts into it, her fighting skills were noticeably weaker with her left hand.

Honora stopped for a moment, her sides heaving with exertion. 'My father wants me to wed a man with an army. Perhaps I should.'

Jealousy blasted through him, though he knew it was unreasonable. A husband would help Honora appeal to the king on behalf of her people. He could also ensure her safety.

But the idea of another man laying claim to her bed, touching her intimately, made Ewan clench his sword hilt. 'I thought you had no desire to wed.'

'I don't.' She touched her weapon to his. 'But my father won't let Katherine wed until I do.'

He hadn't known about that condition. Honora lifted a hand in dismissal. 'Don't fear. I'll find a way to change his mind.' With a shrug, she added, 'But I wouldn't make any man a good wife. Ranulf was right about that.'

'Honora—'

'No, it's true. Tell me honestly—if I had Katherine's dowry, would you wed a woman like me? A woman more comfortable with a sword than a spindle?'

Ewan studied her vivid green eyes, the shorn dark hair. Upon her face, he saw the self-doubts, the belief she held that she was undesirable. 'I would wed you in a moment, if you had your sister's dowry.'

Uncertainty and panic swept over her face. 'You're lying.'

He'd made her uncomfortable with the admission, which hadn't been his intent. To alleviate her panic, he added, 'And I'd likely murder you the next day.'

She seemed to relax at that. 'I might murder you first.' Circling him, she tapped her sword against his. 'Care to spar with me? Unless you're afraid I'll win.'

He wasn't, but he didn't want to injure her further. 'Can you fight with your left hand?'

'Somewhat.' With a slight smile on her face, she made the first strike. Ewan blocked it easily, and she grimaced. 'I haven't practised much.'

He waited for her to make the next move, keeping on the defensive.

'Don't you dare let me win,' Honora ordered.

'Have I ever?' He parried another strike, moving easily as she tried again to find a weakness.

'No,' she admitted. Venturing a smile, she added, 'It's why I've always liked fighting with you.'

He made no comment, though he'd enjoyed their sparring as well. But now, the fight had taken on a different cast, one he hadn't expected. As she wielded the sword, he noticed the flush of excitement on her face, the fullness of her mouth. His awareness of her grew more intense, and he had to remind himself of all the reasons why he needed to end this fight and bring her back to Ardennes.

He quickened his speed, slashing his blade towards hers while releasing his own frustration. But Honora met him, blow for blow.

He wasn't sure how she'd managed it. A trace of pride lined her cheeks. Her green eyes warmed with the challenge, even as he spied a faint perspiration upon her brow.

'I was grateful for your training, years ago.' She lunged forwards, and he parried the blow. 'No one else would teach me.'

'You were as good as many of the others.' He tried again to loosen the weapon by striking hard against her blade. Once more, she kept it steady.

'Sometimes better than you,' she teased.

He struck again, using his strength against her. Honora grunted as he slashed the blade, and when her grip faltered, he sent the weapon spinning into the grass. 'Not this time.'

She bent to pick up the sword, but Ewan stopped her. 'Leave it. Rest for a moment.' He walked beside her, towards the river. Honora bent down and scooped a handful of water to drink. The droplets trickled down her throat down into her bodice.

Ewan couldn't have torn his gaze away if he'd tried. The blue fabric clung to her skin, outlining firm breasts that he'd caressed in his hands only last night. He wanted to run his mouth over the water, peeling back her gown to expose her body. In his mind, he imagined pouring cold water over her nipples, watching them bloom. He'd warm them with his tongue and his mouth, suckling her until she grew wet.

She tempted him in a way no woman ever had. Everything about her—not only her fiery temperament, but the softness of her face, the way she moved. The way he'd always been able to talk to her.

Enough. This was a path to madness. The sooner he wed Katherine, the sooner he could be away from Honora.

'Do you want to start again?' she asked.

Aye, he did. But not a sword fight. He turned away so she wouldn't see his reaction to her. 'It's late. We should go back.'

'Go back if you wish. I intend to keep training.' She wiped her mouth with her palm.

'Not here, you won't. You're going back to your father's castle. It's not safe for a woman to be alone.' He wasn't about to leave her behind, no matter how she might protest.

'I don't need your protection. I can handle myself.'

He shot a glance at her bruises. 'Of course you can.'

'Stop mocking me.'

'You cannot defeat John of Ceredys, and you know this.'

Honora stormed towards him and reached for the sword at his waist. She unsheathed it, her face determined. 'I can, and I will.'

A second later, the weapon fell from her hands, and she clenched her wrist. Her face went white with agony. 'Wrong hand.' She winced.

Ewan led her to a flat stone and guided her to sit down. 'Breathe through the pain. It will pass.' He soaked her fallen veil in the cold river water and wrung it out, wrapping the icy linen around her wrist.

'I have to go back to Ceredys, Ewan,' Honora insisted. 'I can't let John win.'

The pain etched on her face was about more than her wrist, he realised. Even if he wed Katherine and left Honora behind, she wouldn't give up her quest to defend her people.

'He doesn't fight fair,' Ewan reminded her. 'And you're used to fighting by the rules.'

'I can learn to fight differently,' she insisted. 'Show me how.'

'You're hurt.'

'Please, Ewan.' She held the linen against her wrist, rising up on to her knees. There was such earnestness in her eyes, he didn't want to deny her. 'You're the only man who will help me.'

He didn't want to. She didn't truly understand what a man like John was capable of. She could lose her life, if she attempted an attack.

'It's too dangerous.'

She drew closer to him, resting her hands upon his shoulders. 'I won't forget what he did to the women of Ceredys. And whether or not you believe I should face him again, I intend to.'

The fearless vengeance upon her face made him aware that she would not hesitate to give up her own life in this battle. Without question.

And he wasn't about to have her death upon his conscience.

He picked up his fallen sword and held it up. 'You lost your fight against John as soon as you lost your sword.'

'I won't lose it, next time.'

He didn't want there to be a next time. But Honora wasn't the sort of woman to admit any weakness. Perhaps there was no harm in showing her a few methods of hand-to-hand fighting. At least she could protect herself, if she no longer had a weapon.

He took her left hand in his. 'You should learn what to do, in case you have no weapon.'

From the guilty look upon her face, he supposed she was reliving her earlier failures. Exerting pressure on her left hand, Ewan murmured, 'Take control of my blade. Don't let me overpower you.'

She gripped his wrist with her left hand, waiting for his next move. 'Now what?'

The light touch of her hands upon him shook his concentration. Her leg rested against his, braced in a fighting stance. The hem of her gown had ridden up, baring her calf.

'Use one of your legs to kick my feet from under me,' he instructed. 'The way you did before.'

'I only managed because your sword was caught in the wall.'

'Do it.'

Perhaps she'd bash some sense into his head when he struck the ground. Perhaps then he'd remember the woman he was going to marry, and not the woman he desired.

Honora kicked her leg towards him, but only struck the back of his calves. The blow did nothing to his balance, though he'd get another bruise from it.

'Is that the best you can do?' he teased.

She kicked again, but he didn't budge. 'I'm not strong enough.'

Gripping her elbows, he forced all of her weight to the side. 'Pull your enemy's weight on to one leg. Then take him down.'

While she was off-balance, he lightly tapped the back of her leg. Before she could drop to the grass, he caught her. Despite her strength, she weighed little to him. He meant to set her back upon her feet, but instead, he kept her in his arms, just holding her.

'What are you doing, Ewan?' she whispered.

He didn't answer for a moment. His eyes searched hers, and in them he saw the same confusion. He touched her hair, bringing his hand to her nape. 'I don't know.'

But he knew exactly what he'd been doing. He'd used this chance to hold her in his embrace, though it was wrong. Gently, he raised her back to a standing position.

Honora ventured a sad smile when he sheathed his sword. She fumbled with the linen upon her wrist, saying at last, 'Thank you for the lesson.'

'You did well, *a chara*, in spite of your wrist.'

She sobered at the endearment, her eyes turning serious.

'Am I your friend? After all of this difficulty with my sister, will I still be that to you?'

Though he nodded, inwardly he wasn't sure that could be true. And from the way she was looking at him now, he sensed that she wasn't immune to him either.

She gripped her wrists, her lower lip caught between her teeth like a guilty child.

'Stay here,' he said suddenly. 'I'm going for a swim.' He needed the icy water to drown the painful desire he wouldn't act upon. By God, he wasn't going to lay a finger upon her, no matter how badly he wanted to.

Ewan lifted his tunic over his head, unbuckling his sword belt. She sat beside the bank, watching him while he undressed.

'You'd best hurry up, or your clothes won't have time to dry,' she warned. 'You wouldn't want to return to my sister with soaked trews.'

There was an unspoken dare within the words, her green eyes full of amusement.

He didn't shy away from her challenge. 'That won't be a problem, Honora. For I won't be wearing clothes.'

Before she could voice a protest, he dropped his trews and walked into the water, completely naked.

Chapter Eleven

Honora didn't flinch, but looked her fill. By the blessed saints, the man had a beautiful body. All lean lines and pure muscle. She'd felt it pressed close to her, and it had stirred her senses. Though it was terribly wicked, she wanted to touch him again, to fill her hands with his toned flesh.

Ewan swam long strokes through the water, crossing the narrow river to the opposite side and back again. Like the prow of a boat, he cut through the current, his golden skin sleek in the water.

Honora sat on the hillside watching, her hands resting against her cheeks. She really ought to feel guilty, but instead she marvelled at how much Ewan had changed.

The afternoon sun was growing hotter, and her hair clung to the back of her neck. Her gown was sticking to her skin, and the water looked far more inviting than it should have.

What if she waded in to her knees? Surely she couldn't drown in twelve inches of water, could she? And if a fish happened to swim close, she could run back to the shore. Though she knew it was ridiculous to be frightened of a fish, the idea of something cold and slimy, sneaking up to nibble her skin, made her want to yelp.

'Are you going to join me?' Ewan asked, slicking his hair back. Droplets of water glistened upon his chest. 'It's not as cold as it looks.'

'I was thinking of wetting my feet,' she admitted. 'But that's all.'

'Go on, then. No harm in it.'

She squinted at him, as if deciding whether or not he was telling the truth. The water did look refreshing. She took her shoes off, dropping them on the embankment.

'Are you afraid?' he asked.

'No,' she lied. Gingerly, she took a step forwards. The sandy river bottom shifted against her feet in a silken caress. And the water, oh, the water was heavenly. Lightly cool with a hint of warmth. She took a few steps forwards until it lapped against her knees. Holding her skirts up to her thighs, she managed to protect her bliaud.

Ewan started to walk towards her, and as the water grew lower, past his chest to his waist, she held up her hands. 'You stay there.' She could almost see his hip bones, and, God forgive her, she already knew what lay beneath the surface.

He raised his hands up, as though in surrender. 'As you command.' He studied her, and asked, 'Are you still unable to swim?'

'I can,' she argued. 'But I'm not very good.'

'I'll carry you, if you want to cool off.' He backed away, lowering himself deeper into the water. As his shoulders disappeared beneath the rippled surface, he added, 'But you might get wet.'

The deep huskiness of his voice touched her like a physical caress. Without warning, her nipples grew erect, the heavy cloth confining them. She felt herself responding to him, her body rising up to a silent call.

Ewan disappeared under the water, and she stared at the spot where he'd just been.

What was he doing? When he didn't resurface, she began

to get nervous. The murky water made it difficult to see past waist-deep. Was he all right?

She sloshed into the deeper water, trying to see. The water was calm, with only a slight disturbance caused by the wind.

'MacEgan, stop this. Come out of the water!'

Nothing. Honora leaned down and splashed at the surface. She studied the water, hoping to glimpse him. Oh Jesu, it had been far too long. Did he need her help?

Something grazed against her knees, and she shrieked, splashing at the creature.

Ewan surfaced seconds later, catching hold of her waist. He roared a mock battle cry, tossing her up in the air. A screech slipped from her lips as she grabbed him on the way down.

'Damn you, Ewan. Don't let go of me.'

He gripped her tightly, moving into deeper water.

'Wh-what are you doing?'

'Making sure you don't let go.' He brought her into the water, still holding her in his arms. The lower half of her gown was soaked, the heavy fabric weighing her down.

'Take me back to the shore. I don't like this.' She gripped his neck harder, trying to lift every part of her body out of the river.

'In a moment,' he promised. His green eyes were almost the colour of moss, dark and forbidding. A single lift of her mouth, and she would kiss him. His skin was cool, completely at odds with the burning fire that licked at her insides.

He slid a damp lock of hair from her cheek, and the touch made her skin unbearably sensitive.

'Ewan,' she whispered. She needed him so badly, it hurt. Her fingers shook as she reached up to touch his strong jaw.

Without another word, he strode through the water and brought her back to the shoreline. Setting her bare feet upon the grass, he continued towards his fallen clothing. When he was fully dressed, he turned to her.

'Put on your shoes, and I'll take you back.'

She sat down, the breeze making her sodden gown chilly against her skin. It wasn't the only thing that had turned cold. She'd never seen Ewan this way, so distant. It was as if he couldn't wait to be rid of her. And it hurt in a way she'd never expected. After she put on her shoes, he helped her onto her horse.

She brought the animal up beside him, unsure of what she'd done to make him so angry. 'Ewan, what is the matter?'

'It's best if you stay away from me right now, Honora.' The hardened edge to his voice sounded predatory.

'And why is that?'

Without warning, he hauled her off the horse and dragged her mouth to his. The kiss ravaged her, tearing apart her arguments and forcing her to regret all the things she'd said. His heated embrace was carnal, and when his tongue touched hers, it ignited a fire inside her.

Wet and sensual, she could barely hold on to him as he kissed her. His tongue warred with hers, stirring up feelings she tried to keep buried.

For so long, he'd been her friend. He'd been the one to console her, when a sword fight had gone wrong. He'd bandaged her cuts, helped her with the lies to her father and to the Earl of Longford.

And, God help her, she didn't want to lose him. Not even to her sister.

She rested her palm upon his cheek, watching the rise and fall of his breath. Then she found herself leaning in and kissing him again. Lightly, the barest hint of mouths merging, she gave him a part of herself. No longer did he kiss her with the aching lust, but instead he restrained the storm, letting her take the lead.

She traced his mouth with her tongue, and his eyes darkened with a merciless desire. He wanted her, and she could feel his desire rising to meet hers.

After today, she would have no choice but to leave him forever. Like removing a part of herself, she'd do what was necessary to push him into Katherine's arms.

But for now, and only this moment, there was this. His mouth slid over her cheek, down to her throat. When Ewan stopped kissing her, she saw the raw apprehension in his eyes.

Like a man who hated himself for what he'd just done.

Ewan avoided both Katherine and Honora for the remainder of the afternoon. Guilt weighed down his thoughts, and he contemplated the right course of action. He didn't deserve to be here, much less wed Katherine of Ardennes. The kiss he'd shared with Honora had been the final blow to his honour.

He should leave Ardennes, turning his attention back to his ambitions. There were other heiresses, or better yet, other ways of gaining the land. Being alone was no less than he deserved.

He trudged into the Great Hall, taking a seat among the other suitors, next to Sir Ademar. The knight's face appeared grim, his knuckles white as he clenched his fists.

'What is amiss?' Ewan asked.

'Lady Katherine has made her choice of a h-husband. It will be announced this night.'

The unexpected news caught him without warning. Had she chosen a different suitor? Glancing around, he saw that Gerald of Beaulais was no longer among them.

'Where is Beaulais?' he asked Sir Ademar.

'Gone. He…he left since the Lady Katherine did not choose him.'

Ewan wouldn't miss the hot-headed Norman and was glad he'd gone. But he still saw tension on the knight's face. 'Whom did the Lady Katherine choose?'

Before Ademar could answer, the Baron of Ardennes stood from his chair upon the dais.

'My daughters have chosen from among the suitors,' the

Baron of Ardennes began, rising from his chair upon the dais. 'I am happy to announce their betrothals. Lady Honora has selected Sir Ademar of Dolwyth to become her husband.'

Sir Ademar glanced in his direction, an incredulous look upon his face. It was clear that Honora had not told him of her intentions, but the knight did not seem displeased.

Ewan's hands dug into the wooden table, caught up in disbelief. Honora had said she had no desire to wed. Had she changed her mind after what they'd done this afternoon?

He tried to catch her gaze, but Honora refused to look at him. Instead, she reached over and squeezed her sister's hand. Katherine's smile was radiant, her eyes searching the crowd.

And then he knew. Honora had agreed to a betrothal for her sister's sake. She smiled at Ademar when he approached the dais, but her heart wasn't in it.

Would she go through with the marriage? Though he knew it would be a good match, the simple fact was, he didn't want her to wed another man.

But the Baron hadn't finished. He stood, holding Katherine's hand, as he raised his goblet in a toast. 'My younger daughter has selected Ewan MacEgan as her husband.'

He was hardly aware of the words of congratulations spoken by those around him. Words failed him as he half-rose from his seat.

Honora stared straight at him, giving a faint nod. There was no happiness in her expression, only resignation. She believed this was what he'd wanted. And after this afternoon, after he'd broken his vow not to touch her again, she had taken it upon herself to bring Katherine back into his grasp.

He tried not to stare at Honora, but beneath her masked smile, he saw misery.

Ewan wasn't sure how he managed to walk to the dais, for each step made it feel like a snare had tightened around his neck.

And when Katherine flew into his embrace, he saw the sheen of tears in Honora's eyes.

* * *

That night, in the privacy of their shared bedchamber, Katherine whispered, 'Ewan hasn't said a word to me, Honora. Was I wrong to choose him?'

'Of course not,' she lied. 'It was a surprise, that's all. He was expecting to talk with our father first, I imagine.'

Honora's stomach wrenched at the thought of what she'd done. The stunned look in Ewan's eyes had made her want to weep. She had spoken to her father out of desperation, knowing that Ewan had too much honour to refuse the match. He would accept Katherine as his bride and gain the land he'd always wanted.

In turn, she would slip away quietly before her own wedding could take place. Though she disliked the idea of hurting Sir Ademar, there was nothing she could do.

'He hasn't spoken to me,' Katherine continued. 'And he looked so angry.'

'He wasn't angry with you. He was simply surprised that our father chose to announce it in that way.'

'And you're going to wed Sir Ademar.' Katherine's face flushed with excitement. 'He seems like a good man.'

'He is.' A kind, humble man, who didn't deserve to be used like this. Honora buried her face in the coverlet, wishing she could just run away right now.

Could she talk to Sir Ademar? Persuade him to go along with the deception in order to see Katherine safely wed? Perhaps she could grant him something in return, such as rents from her dower portion.

But, no. The knight had too much pride for that.

The night hours wore on, and Honora still couldn't sleep. When her sister's shoulders rose and fell in deep slumber, she donned a cloak and tiptoed out of bed. She hardly knew where she was going, or what she planned to do, but restlessness plagued her.

Most of the household was abed, and, except for the

guards, she saw no one else. She continued down the stair-case until she saw the familiar glow of candles inside the chapel.

As she drew near, she went to study the wooden chest. Why had it been stolen in the first place? The dim glow of candlelight cast a soft light upon the wood, but she could see nothing that made it different from any other carved chest.

She'd nearly forgotten about the thief, she'd been so caught up in worrying about John. Now she wondered if there was a connection between them.

He wanted the ruby Marie St Leger had worn, along with the legendary treasure. The funds never seemed to be enough, no matter how much he possessed.

The door opened, and her stomach sank when John entered the chapel, crossing himself as he did so. The gesture was almost a mockery, for surely he was a demon in the flesh.

'Come to pray for your sins, Lady Honora?' he murmured.

The red gash upon his cheek caught her notice, and she reached for her knife. It wasn't there. She'd forgotten to bring it, thinking there was no need, so late at night.

'What do you want, John?'

He moved closer, and Honora circled until her back was towards the door. She'd not let him imprison her again. Her mind spun with thoughts of how to escape him, should he threaten her.

'You're not going to wed Sir Ademar.' His gaze lingered upon her breasts, his eyes hot. 'You're going to come back to Ceredys where you belong.'

Honora clutched the edges of her cloak to hide her shift from John's eyes. 'That is my choice to make, not yours.'

'You're wrong,' he said smoothly. 'As the heir, I must approve any man you bring into the family. These were my father's lands, after all.'

'And you don't intend to approve any of the suitors,' she predicted. 'Do you?'

His thin smile was the only answer she needed. She turned to leave, but John stepped in front of her, nearly causing her to stumble.

'That isn't all, Lady Honora. There is still the matter of the ruby you stole,' he said. 'I know Marie St Leger gave it to you before you left.'

'She gave me nothing. How could she, when I escaped your capture?' She glanced backwards at the door.

'She set you free, didn't she? Not without aid, but I know she was responsible. And the jewel isn't at Ceredys any more.' He crossed behind her, blocking her escape. 'You know the punishment for theft.' He reached out and took hold of her wrist. 'I would hate for you to lose this hand.' His thumb caressed her pulse point, and she ripped it away.

'Don't threaten me.'

He ignored her. 'Return the ruby, and I'll say nothing to your father about this.' He pointed to the cut upon his face.

'How can I return something I do not have?'

John reached out and seized her wounded wrist. A hot pain shot through her, and she bit her lip against the searing agony. 'I've had enough of your defiance.'

Honora tried to force the pain away, using Ewan's technique to bring John down. But she couldn't centre her weight upon his, and her efforts met with no response.

'It was you,' she accused. 'You sent one of your men to steal from the chapel and search my belongings. You were looking for Marie's ruby, weren't you?'

John leaned in, staring into her eyes. He didn't deny it. 'I'm going to find it, Honora.'

Her eyes blurred with the torment of her wrist. Saints, help her, she had to break free of him. More footsteps sounded from behind her. She heard a male growl, and then she blinked as Ewan appeared in the doorway.

When he saw them, he attacked John with no warning. John released her, and Honora sank to the stone floor, cradling her wrist. She heard the crunch of fists against flesh, both men grappling with one another. When she scrambled towards the open door, she caught a glimpse of Ewan's face.

His expression was deadly. 'I'm going to kill him for touching you.'

Chapter Twelve

Honora sat back, her feet tucked beneath her skirts. Dear God, she'd never seen Ewan like this. Enraged, as though he'd lost control of his temper.

Blood poured from John's nose, and Ewan tripped him, knocking his head against the stone. John roared, reaching with his fingers to gouge Ewan's eyes.

Horrified, Honora stood up, searching for something to use as a weapon. Anything to end this. But save the wooden chest and candles, there was nothing.

John rolled over, his hand reaching for the sword at his belt. Honora stepped on it, and John sent her sprawling.

At that, Ewan became a man possessed. His fist snapped John's head backwards, and he closed both hands around the man's neck.

Oh, Jesu. He truly was going to kill John. Though she wanted to see the Baron gone, Ewan could face execution if he murdered a nobleman. The king would not stand for it.

'Ewan, don't!' Her voice seemed to break through the haze of battle rage, and Ewan loosened his grip on John's throat.

His fist ploughed into John's rib cage, and Honora leapt to her feet, racing to Ewan's side. Dodging another fist, she reached out to stop him. 'He's not worth it,' she pleaded. 'You've done enough.'

John lay unconscious, blood pooling into his tunic.

Ewan was out of breath, his face burning with fury. His tunic hung open; beneath it, his chest gleamed with sweat. Tight muscles were tense as he waited for John to get up.

'We're going to go now,' she murmured, taking him by the hand.

Though she was grateful he'd stepped in, she now worried that he shouldn't have. Her heart pounded at the sight of John's body. For the first time, she prayed the Baron would live.

Leading Ewan away, she alerted the guards and ordered them to send the healer to the chapel. In the meantime, she wanted to talk to Ewan, to soothe his temper. She sensed that his anger was not only directed at John.

She brought him outside, into the small garden inside the inner bailey. The darkness was only broken up by a few torches, the stark flames bright against the night sky.

'Thank you for coming to my aid,' she said gently. Touching his shoulder, she was conscious of his strength. 'But you didn't need to beat him that soundly.'

Ewan raked a hand through his hair, and as he steadied himself, his demeanour grew colder. 'I wasn't going to let him escape justice this time.'

'He thought I had his grandmother's ruby,' she explained. 'But I don't. It was a misunderstanding.'

'That isn't all John wanted.' His hand cradled her face, his thumb brushing her temple. 'I've seen him watching you.'

Honora closed her eyes, drinking in the sensation of his hands. God in heaven help her, she wanted so badly to be held by him, to be comforted in his arms.

'Why did you announce a betrothal?' he asked, his hand falling away.

She pulled away from him, moving towards the stone wall surrounding the garden. The night air was warm, and she let her cloak fall open to cool her skin. 'Katherine is the woman you want. And I thought it would…make it easier.'

'Easier to do what?'

She couldn't find the right words, for she didn't know what she was feeling. All she knew was that she wanted Ewan to be happy. And it was the best way to let him go.

He forced her to look at him, his hand resting on her nape. 'I can't wed your sister, Honora. Not any more.'

She didn't speak, too afraid of what she might say. She was as guilty as he for what she'd done to Katherine. She sat down on the grass, holding her bruised wrist, feeling as though her heart were just as battered.

Ewan sat beside her, unfastening her cloak until it lay upon the ground. Wearing only her shift, she drew her knees up.

He rested his hands on either side of her, leaning down. 'Do you want me to take you back to your chamber?'

All she had to do was say yes. A single word, and he wouldn't touch her at all. But the very thought of leaving him was unbearable.

She reached up to his shoulder, sliding her hand beneath his tunic. 'Don't go.'

Ewan lowered his mouth to hers, kissing her gently, softly. She grew pliant in his arms, the warmth melting over her like heat against ice. The touch of his kiss healed the buried hurts and fears.

'Don't wed Ademar,' he commanded, before his mouth came down upon hers again. 'Let no other man touch you.'

This time, he kissed her with a savage hunger, and she was overwhelmed by the forbidden feelings coursing through her.

She wanted to forget the bad memories, of a husband who didn't want her. Of the sister she was betraying.

For now, there was only Ewan, and this moment together. In the darkness, no one would see them. The temptation to surrender was heady, impossible to resist.

He laid her down upon the soft grass, his mouth moving down the column of her throat. She reached beneath his tunic with her uninjured hand to touch the hot, male skin.

The answering growl told her that Ewan liked her touch. She grew bolder, exploring his ribs, moving across his heartbeat. Never had she been given the chance to touch a man, to know the hard planes of his body.

Ewan lifted her bruised wrist, tenderly kissing the skin. His mouth moved over it, as if trying to heal it with his touch. Her body arched closer, her womanhood aching with need for him. His hand pushed up the hem of her shift, baring her legs until he lifted the fabric to her waist.

She was naked now, and the hush of the night air against her skin was both terrifying and arousing. She shifted her legs, moaning when his hand slid between her thighs. It shocked her to realise that she'd grown wet. What was happening to her?

The dizzying feelings built up inside, making her burn for something she couldn't understand. He teased the cleft, dipping his fingers inside her warmth. With his fingertips, he nudged at the swollen nub.

She grasped his hair, both fighting the erotic sensations and needing more. Never had she been touched like this. Never had she felt such a need, a raw craving to be filled.

Jesu, this was wrong. She needed to push him away, to gather her wayward thoughts.

But then Ewan lowered her gown to her waist, taking her breast into his mouth. She cried out, unable to break free of the mindless need for him. And when he continued to caress her folds, teasing and tempting the part of her that ached for him, she couldn't stop shaking.

'It would be like this, if I became your lover,' he said huskily. 'Every single night. I'd touch you here.' His hand stroked her sensitive flesh, finding a torturous rhythm. Her hands slid over his spine, guiding him closer until she felt his hot length resting between her legs. He was still clothed, but she yearned to remove the barrier between them.

'I'd taste your skin. Like this.' His mouth moved across the healing welts above her breasts. Lower, still, until he kissed each nipple. His tongue darted over the hardened tips, his warm breath sending shivers through her.

'I'd fill your body with mine. Like this.'

He slid two fingers inside her, and she responded with another surge of wetness. He mimicked the sensation of love-making, tantalising her with the promise of more.

Her body ached, reaching for something she couldn't explain. But as he moved his fingers, she arched higher, straining against him.

More. She needed him to intensify the pace, to ease the torment. But instead, he slowed down, his thumb spiralling against her while his fingers entered and retreated.

'Ewan,' she pleaded, grasping his head. Her muscles tightened, straining hard. She didn't understand what was happening to her, the raw sensations that were tearing her asunder.

And then, without warning, his mouth ground on top of hers, his hand rubbing her so hard she came apart, a blinding frenzy of tremors filling her up inside.

Oh, God above. She could hardly move, her body shivering with unfamiliar aftershocks.

Honora gripped him hard around the neck, wanting so badly for him to claim her. His eyes darkened with passion, and he took her hand and brought it to his trews.

The hard thickness of him reminded her of what would happen next. If she let him continue, he would thrust inside her. Like before, she would have to endure the pain, waiting for him to finish. He would pound against her while she lay still, and when it was over, he would leave.

All of her desire seemed to shrivel up and die.

Her heartbeat trebled, and she found herself unable to move or speak. This…all of it was never meant to happen.

She'd let him get too close, forgetting herself in his arms. The brutality of her husband came back, rushing over her until she couldn't help the tears. 'I need you to stop.'

Ewan misunderstood and sat up, pulling her into his arms. 'Hush, *a stór*. I'm sorry. I shouldn't have done that.'

She clung to him, unable to close off the memories. 'I can't. I never should have come here with you.'

He laced his fingers with hers. 'I would die before hurting you, *a ghrá*.'

'I have to go.' She straightened her clothing and stood. Without looking back, she fled to her chamber.

Ewan followed Honora silently. This time he wanted to be sure that no one bothered her.

He kept far enough away that she wouldn't see him, but close enough to shadow her. He didn't regret what he'd done to John of Ceredys. Not at all. He only wished he'd arrived sooner.

Easily, he could have killed the man. Not only for seeing the bastard gripping her wrist, but for the other times John had hurt her. The primal urge to protect Honora drove out all sense of reason.

It was only at her insistence that he'd stopped. And no doubt there would be consequences. He didn't care. Honora's father might be angry, but he wouldn't condone any threats toward his daughter.

Were it not so late, Ewan would confront Ardennes now. The Baron needed to understand the danger Honora faced from Ceredys and ensure that she never returned. It meant giving up her third of the land, but there was no alternative.

As Honora continued up the winding stairs, he watched until she disappeared from view behind her chamber door. Ewan waited several moments, to be sure she was safe.

He stood at the bottom of the stairs for some time, needing a distraction. Anything to take his mind off the restlessness filling up inside, along with the frustration Honora had caused.

He wandered down to the kitchens and coaxed a sleepy-eyed serving wench into bringing him an assortment of bread, cheese and leftover beef from the previous meal, along with a pot of ale. He found a corner in the hall amid the sleeping soldiers and suitors, and dug into the food. Though it satisfied his physical hunger, it didn't assuage his discontent.

He'd gone too far this night. It hadn't been intentional, but he'd been caught up with need for Honora. His body craved hers even now, chafing with an unfulfilled aching. He'd frightened her without meaning to, but she'd driven him past reason.

He'd listened to his carnal desires instead of his head, and now he'd lost everything. The land, and likely his friendship with Honora. With the way he'd behaved this night, it was no wonder she'd fled him.

And now he would have to leave Ardennes. There was no reason to remain here, especially not after he'd led Honora's sister astray. No longer could he take Katherine as his wife. And the idea of wedding a different heiress soured his mood.

Better to build his kingdom on his own, without a marriage dowry to secure the lands. He'd have to hire out his sword, the way Bevan and Connor had, to earn the funds. It would take years, however.

A hollow feeling spread throughout his body, coupled with the sense of loss. He didn't want to leave Honora behind, but what other choice was there? He had nothing in Erin to offer her. Best for her to remain under her father's protection.

He stood, exhaustion suddenly coming down upon him. It was only a few hours before dawn, but he doubted if he'd find any sleep this night. Footsteps resounded in the stillness, and a shadow crossed over him.

When he looked up, he stared into the face of Nicholas de Montford. Two soldiers stood at his side, dressed in chain-mail armour and conical helms.

'Take him,' the Baron ordered.

* * *

Honora didn't see Ewan all morning. With each hour that passed, her anxiety doubled. The entire castle was buzzing about John of Ceredys. According to the healer, Ewan had broken his nose and John's face was badly bruised. Anyone who looked upon him would know what Ewan had done.

'Lady Honora,' a voice interrupted. 'May I speak with… with you?'

It was Sir Ademar. The knight offered a tentative smile, a man behaving as if he could hardly believe she'd agreed to wed him. Oh, Jesu. She'd completely forgotten about her impulsive offer.

'Of course,' she responded.

Ademar bent down to atone for his exceptional height. Dark blue eyes warmed to look at her, but she saw the struggle as he tried to speak clearly. 'You s-surprised me last eventide when you…chose me.' He offered her his arm, and she took it, her mood plummeting even further.

'I should have spoken to you first,' she admitted.

It wasn't fair. He didn't deserve to be used like this. She couldn't go through with a deception like this, not when there were alternatives.

Honora took him by the hand and led him to a quieter part of the inner bailey. 'Sir Ademar, forgive me. I haven't been honest with you.'

His handsome face stiffened, as if he knew what she was about to say. She took a deep breath. As if that would make it any easier. As if she could somehow go back and undo the mistakes she'd made.

His expression grew tighter. 'You don't intend…to wed me, do you?'

She squeezed his palm. 'You are a fine man. And if I were to wed again, you would make an excellent husband.' Lowering her voice even more, she admitted, 'It was my father's wish that I remarry, not mine. He swore he would not allow Katherine to choose a husband until I agreed to wed.'

His cheeks reddened, and there was no denying the anger when he pulled his hand away from hers. 'And you…thought to use me.'

Honora nodded slowly, feeling like the most terrible woman in the world. 'I only wanted my sister's happiness. Not to embarrass you.'

He pulled his hand away, a flash of irritation in his eyes. 'Were you…planning to refuse me, before…the priest?'

'I wasn't going to let it go that far.'

'And if your father h-had asked us…to speak vows first…b-before your sister? Would you have wed me then?' No longer did the Norman knight appear quite so obliging. Instead, his mouth hardened, his eyes angry. She remembered that, despite his awkwardness, he was an excellent fighter.

She'd violated his sense of honour, simply by taking this course. Meeting his gaze directly, she apologised. 'It was wrong of me to consider it. I will speak to my father.'

'He is with MacEgan. There will be…justice after what he d-did to Ceredys.'

'Justice?' What was her father planning to do to Ewan? Nicholas wasn't known for leniency, and without her there to defend him, he would believe Ewan had attacked John without cause.

The ground on which she'd been standing seemed to crumble. 'I need to speak with my father.'

Now. Before Nicholas did something unthinkable.

Sir Ademar caught her arm. 'Why?'

She almost forced his hand away, but stopped herself. 'He did nothing but defend me. I don't want to see him punished for no reason.'

Ademar softened his grip. Knowing eyes stared into hers, as though he suspected the secret truth. Without questioning her further, he let her go.

'There will be…no betrothal between us,' he said quietly. 'I will…speak to your father.'

It was a matter of salvaging his pride, she realised. 'I am sorry for what I did.'

'Go to him.' Ademar gestured towards the hall. 'The man you truly want.'

Honora didn't bother arguing, but picked up her skirts to hurry. Inside, a soldier barred her path, preventing her from entering her father's private chamber.

'Let me pass,' she ordered.

'Lord Ardennes has forbidden it.' The guard kept his hand upon his sword hilt, though she knew he would never use it against her. He expected her to be intimidated by him, to walk away meekly.

She eyed him closely, judging his weight and girth. Slowly, she turned, as if to walk away. She visualised her opponent in her mind, remembering exactly the position of his sword and knife blade.

Swiftly, she turned and ran at the guard, pulling his weight off-centre and kicking his legs out from underneath. He crashed to the ground and she stumbled over him, throwing open the door to her father's chamber.

Conversation halted when she intruded. John sat before the Baron. His face was heavily swollen, his nose at an awkward angle.

Good. He deserved every blow and worse for what he'd done, both to her and the people of Ceredys.

Her father's grim expression turned furious. 'Honora, you were not asked to be a part of this.'

'Did John tell you that he attacked me while I was in the chapel last night? Ewan came to my defence.'

'So MacEgan said.' Nicholas glanced over at Ewan, who was standing with his arms bound behind him. 'But John also told me that you cut him with your own blade. And that you took jewels that rightfully belonged to him.'

Her hand tightened upon the dagger at her waist. 'There were no jewels.'

John regarded her with a cool expression. The menace behind his eyes made her want to step further away, but she held her ground.

'Marie St Leger told me, before she died, that she gave them to you.' John crossed his arms.

'Then they would be mine, wouldn't they?'

'They were not hers to give,' John argued. 'Return them to me, and I will forgive your act of violence.' His voice softened, as though she were a wayward child.

He had no idea just what acts of violence she was imagining at the moment.

She turned to Nicholas. 'Father, let Ewan go. He did nothing more than defend me.'

'We have already reached an agreement.' Ewan did not direct the comment towards her, but instead towards her father. 'I will leave Ardennes.'

Leave? But he couldn't leave. Her heart thudded as though it had dropped through an abyss.

'As I told your father,' Ewan said tightly, 'I no longer wish to wed Katherine. It was her request, not mine.' His dark green eyes bore into her with unspoken words. 'There is no other reason for me to stay.'

Her lips parted, but Honora said nothing. What had she expected? That he would want to marry her instead? That he would give up his desire for land, for her?

No. He would return to his life, and she to hers. It was better this way.

Why, then, did it hurt so much to think of him leaving?

Ewan cast a frigid stare at John. 'The horse is yours. As compensation for your injuries.' With a glance back at Ardennes, he added, 'The matter is now finished.'

When Ewan was dismissed from the chamber, Honora followed him. She sensed that more had happened, more that he wasn't telling her. But he never broke his stride, never slowed to speak to her. She had to run to catch up with him, and even then, she felt that he wanted nothing to do with her. What had changed?

'Ewan, what are you going to do?' She put her hand upon his shoulder.

The effect upon him was immediate. He placed his hand upon the small of her back and guided her towards the garden. He wanted privacy, she suddenly understood.

When they stood alone, he rested his hand upon the stone wall surrounding the garden of herbs. 'I'm returning home to Erin.'

He reached out and took her bruised wrist, smoothing over the injured skin with his thumb. Her heartbeat quickened, and his gentle touch seemed to soothe the abrasion.

'Have you told Katherine?' Her sister would be devastated to find out that Ewan was abandoning her.

'Aye. She knows.' The tight muscles of Ewan's forearm flexed against his weight. 'I'm leaving at dawn.'

Honora wanted to beg him to stay, though she knew he wouldn't. 'This is my fault,' she whispered. 'If I could go back and change it, I would.'

'It was my choice.' Ewan studied her closely, and bent forwards. 'I could never wed Katherine and be fair to her. Not when I wanted you instead.'

He leaned in and kissed her softly, the kiss of a man who meant everything to her.

But it was a kiss goodbye.

Chapter Thirteen

'You wanted to see me.' Honora joined her father once more in his private chamber. The afternoon sun cast beams of light upon her father's chair, in contrast to her sunken spirits. She had sought out Katherine, only to find that her sister was avoiding her.

Nicholas laced his fingers together upon the scarred wooden table, his posture stiff. 'I am sending you back to Ceredys. John will escort you home.'

No. He wouldn't force her to leave, not with the man who had injured her. Would he?

'I won't go with him,' she insisted. If her father truly cared for her welfare, he'd have ordered John to leave, not Ewan. But now she understood that the anger and frustration on his face was directed at her. 'Last night in the chapel, John attacked me. Does that not matter to you?' Honora extended her wrist and showed him the dark bruises encircling it.

But her father paid the injury no heed. 'I am disappointed in you, Honora,' he said. 'You shouldn't have provoked Ceredys.'

'How can you come to John's defence? He nearly broke my wrist!' She could hardly believe what she was hearing. Nicholas behaved as though the injury was her fault.

'Did you take the ruby?' he asked. 'The one he spoke of?'

Outraged arguments filled up inside her, but what did it matter if she denied it? Her father believed the lies of a man who had harmed her.

'I took nothing.' The words were swollen inside her throat. 'I swear to you.'

Nicholas let go of her wrist, shaking his head. 'I don't know whether you speak the truth or not.' He stared at her, his face grim. 'I had hoped that Sir Ademar would take you off my hands. But now even that possibility is lost.'

'Take me off your—' Her words broke off, the fury building up so much that it was hard to breathe. 'Am I a burden to you? Your own daughter?'

'Honora, you have a home. You have lands of your own, lands that you're neglecting, I might add. I didn't mind that you came to visit, but I never expected you to run away from your responsibilities.'

Honora's throat closed up, and she fought the urge to throw something. She clenched her knife, struggling to keep her temper still. 'I will return to Ceredys,' she said, her voice tight and drawn. 'When I am ready. You can be assured of that.'

And when she did, she would see to it that John never again raised his hand against the people.

Her father was already shaking his head. 'For your sister's sake, I want you to leave Ardennes now.' He lifted his hand in dismissal. 'It matters not to me where you go. But you'll not interfere in Katherine's marriage prospects again.'

Honora stilled, for she wasn't ready to go. Not yet. She hadn't made any plans, nor had she thought beyond the next sennight. 'You're casting the blame upon me. And I don't know why.' The ill feeling in her stomach worsened.

'You are to blame,' he said softly. 'Katherine accepted MacEgan's suit, and that very night she saw you embracing him.'

The blood seemed to cease within her body, for she hadn't

known it. She hadn't stopped to think who might have seen them, she was so caught up in the moment. And the truth was, she should have pushed Ewan away. She'd allowed him to kiss her, allowed him to touch her in ways she never should have permitted.

'I'm sorry,' she murmured. Idly, she rubbed at her aching wrist, wishing she could somehow wipe out everything that had happened. Her life was falling into pieces all around her, and she could do nothing to stop it.

She was about to leave when her father stepped in front of her. Nicholas reached to her side and withdrew her dagger from its sheath. Tilting it in the light, it cast shadows upon her face.

'Heed my words, Honora. A true lady would never strike out at a man. She would be obedient and dutiful. That is the only way you will ever find happiness. Never try to exert your will upon a man's.' With a flick of his hand, he cast the blade against the stone wall. The pommel struck hard and shattered from the impact, breaking free of the blade.

Her father closed the door behind him, leaving her alone. Honora stared at the broken weapon, feeling as though it were herself that was scattered across the floor. Once again, her dagger had been destroyed. It was as if her father had cast her aside, the same as the weapon. She bit back the swell of tears, staring at the pieces.

The grip and blade were separated, and she knelt down to pick them up. She doubted if it could be repaired this time. The tang of the knife blade was honed down so thin, it was no wonder it had shattered at the blow.

When she retrieved the pommel, the decorative handle felt awkward in her hand, the balance awry. It had been this way ever since she'd left Ceredys. But when she tilted it forwards, she realised it was hollow. Something small and round rolled on to the stone floor.

Honora caught her breath when she spied Marie St Leger's

ruby. Jesu. The oval-shaped gem was slightly narrower than her thumb. She felt uncertain of what to do now. She'd never liked the decoration when the blacksmith had added it, but now she realised Marie had made the pommel as a hiding place for the gemstone. The blacksmith must have wedged the stone inside the hollowed pommel, sealing it to the dagger grip. No one else could have reattached the blade with such skill.

Why had Marie done this? It was clear she had given the gem to Honora for a purpose, knowing how much the blade had meant to her. It was a gift, and Honora felt unworthy of it.

Kneeling upon the floor, she said a silent prayer for the woman's soul, the ruby clenched in her palm.

Marie St Leger had been an extraordinary woman, a lady who eschewed tradition for the way she believed things ought to be done. She had been delighted to learn of Honora's skills with a sword and had asked her to demonstrate, sneaking weapons of every sort into the chamber, though Ranulf had forbidden it. Swords, daggers…even a spiked mace at one interval.

But it was the sword Honora knew best, and Marie never tired of watching.

'Show me what you know,' the older woman had urged. She'd bribed one of the soldiers to join them one afternoon.

The poor man hadn't known what to do at first, when Honora had challenged him to a sword match. But when he began losing the fight, he was forced to intensify his efforts, using strength Honora lacked. But blow for blow, Honora struck back until the soldier's blade went flying out of his hand.

Marie had laughed with delight and handed the embarrassed soldier a bag of coins, ordering him to leave. After he'd gone, she embraced Honora.

'How I wish I could have learned to fight like you.' She smiled, tucking Honora's hand into hers. The wrinkled fingers were frail, but the strength beneath them was undeniable.

'*My son Ranulf might be a fool, but his wife is not.*' She fingered the golden chain around her neck, where the ruby hung. '*I wish you were the daughter of my blood. I would like to see you rule over all of Ceredys.*'

Honora's smile faded. '*I don't know how to manage the estate. I haven't the knowledge to—*'

'*You have the heart.*' Marie touched her shoulder. '*You know what needs to be done.*' An iron glint sparked within her blue eyes. '*And you will do it. Rid this place of the evil that grows within it…*' Her voice drifted off, and Honora helped her ease onto the bed. '*I pray for the day when you will put to rights all that has fallen into disarray.*'

Honora held the two pieces of her knife, bowing her head in memory. When she rose, she slid the ruby back inside the pommel, fitting the dagger back together. She would not allow John to find this.

It was not stolen; it was the reminder she'd needed. And she owed it to Marie, to help the people of Ceredys.

Her sister was sitting on the bed, her head bent down. As soon as Honora entered, Katherine raised her chin. The cool expression on her face was quickly masked, and she looked away without a word of greeting. It was no less than what she'd expected.

Honora had bound the broken pieces of her knife to her waist, beneath her girdle. She sat down, waiting for her sister to speak. But a quarter of an hour passed, and Katherine said nothing. At last, Honora attempted an apology. 'I'm sorry. I never expected—'

'What? That Ewan would want you instead of me?' Katherine's eyes raged with unshed tears. 'You're my sister. I cannot believe you would do this to me.'

'I never asked for his attentions. I don't even know why it happened.'

Katherine swiped at her cheeks, her skin pale. 'I know why.

It's because you've always been bolder than me. Stronger, with more courage.' She made a fist and clenched her hands together. 'I'm not like you, Honora. He wants what I'll never be.'

Katherine paced across the room, releasing her anger. 'I blame myself for bringing you along when we were together. I should have known that he would prefer you, between the two of us.'

Honora didn't know how to respond, for Ewan hadn't truly wanted her. He hadn't suggested that she go with him to Erin, not even after they had almost become lovers. He'd chosen to walk away from both of them.

Her chest constricted, and she struggled not to think about what she would do next. If she did, she might lose her senses.

Gripping her arms tightly, Honora admitted, 'Ewan is leaving Ardennes at dawn.'

'Are you going with him?'

'No. I won't see him again.'

For a long moment, Katherine stared at her. Then she said, 'You're a fool. If he wanted me, I would go.'

'He never asked.'

Accusations hung over the room, and though Honora wanted to make her sister feel better, she had her own troubles to worry about. Namely, where she would go.

She sat down on the floor in front of her trunk. All of her belongings were already inside, along with her chainmail armour. Ewan had returned it to her, after her fight with John.

Honora traced the iron bindings, the rough wood, trying to think of whom she could turn to for help. Then she opened the trunk and began setting aside the belongings she intended to pack.

'What are you doing?' Katherine asked, her expression sharpening.

Honora shook her head. 'Father wants John to accompany me to Ceredys. But I can't go back with him. Not after he threatened me.' She set aside a linen shift, staring down at the creamy fabric. 'Perhaps I'll go to Normandy. We have kin there.'

Katherine approached her and commanded, 'You won't go to Normandy. Go with Ewan.'

'I can't. Not after what I did to you—'

'This isn't about me any more. He told me he thinks of me like his sister.' Bitterness rose up within Katherine's voice. 'Do you know how I felt? The man I fell in love with doesn't want me at all.' She sat down and drew her knees up to her chest, her sapphire gown falling in waves onto the coverlet. Angry tears spilled on to her cheeks. 'If I can't have him, at least I can be sure that he's happy without me.'

Katherine dried her tears, her face pale and cold. 'Go with him, Honora. And don't return here again. I've no wish to see you.'

Dawn broke across the sky, and Honora rose from her pallet on the floor. She hadn't slept at all last night, but had stared at the door. Her skin was cold from not having a coverlet, and her body felt worn down and fragile.

Katherine had left late that night, spending several hours alone before she'd returned to their chamber. Honora hadn't asked where her sister had gone, but accepted that she'd wanted time to herself.

Quietly she rose, and picked up the small bundle of clothes she'd chosen to bring with her. The armour remained inside her trunk, for she intended to leave it behind.

The morning light brushed the horizon with hints of rose and gold. She donned a cloak over her gown to guard against the chill. The choice she'd made was one that troubled her still, the burden weighing down upon her shoulders.

For she'd decided to ask Ewan for help.

It frightened her, to reach out to him. She'd thought about it all night, questioning the wisdom. But he was the one man she trusted. He wouldn't turn her away, not when she needed him.

She looked back at her sleeping sister. She'd never intended to hurt Katherine, but apologies could not change anything. Nonetheless, she murmured, 'I am sorry.' The coverlet stirred, and she wondered if Katherine had heard her.

Honora cast one more look towards the sleeping figure. With lowered shoulders, she opened the door to leave. Just outside, she recognised two of John's men-at-arms.

'Good morn, Lady Honora.' A soldier stepped forward to block her path.

Icy fear rippled through her. 'What do you want?'

'We've come to escort you to Lord Ceredys's chamber,' the taller soldier said. 'You will be returning home, upon his orders.'

Before she could retreat, they seized her arms.

'Katherine!' she yelped before they closed the door and dragged her off. Honora cursed, fighting to free herself, but one man grasped her wounded wrist. Any motion at all caused a searing pain.

Damn John for this. He had no right to take her captive within her own home.

'Let go of me!' she demanded, but they ignored her, forcing her into another chamber. Behind her, she heard the sounds of two men fighting. The soldiers shoved her forward until she hit the stone floor. Her belongings were tossed at her feet.

'Honora.'

She raised her head and saw John seated upon a chair. His face was a mottled blend of black and purple bruises. A dark red split marred his lips, and the expression in his eyes was of a man bent upon vengeance. 'I hope you slept well last night, in preparation for our journey this day.'

Honora made no reply, while her eyes searched for a way out. There were four men in the chamber, along with herself and John. Too many. Her spirits sank, for she would rather die than return to Ceredys with him.

'Why would you think that you can take me captive within my father's *donjon*?' she demanded. 'I never agreed to go with you.'

'You are not a captive,' he corrected. 'We are merely escorting you home as a courtesy. Your father preferred that we accompany you, so as to keep you from harm.' His words held a trace of irony as he gestured for one of his men to help her to her feet.

'Ceredys is not my home.' Her heartbeat quickened as she struggled to think of a way out of this. 'And you cannot force me to go back.'

'Oh, you'll go willingly,' John said. 'For if you don't, I'll order my men to attack Ewan MacEgan. He's on foot, isn't he? It would be easy enough to send an arrow through his back.' He gentled his tone. 'But if you come with me without protest, I'll let him go.'

She'd sooner trust a spider. But now was not the time to argue. Ewan would be leaving very soon. Likely, he would travel west, towards the coastline. He'd be out in the open, exposed to any attack.

No, she couldn't endanger Ewan by protesting. Best to feign surrender, waiting for the right moment to escape.

'I don't have a choice, do I?'

John smiled. 'I'm glad to see you understand. I'll give the orders for our departure and see that the rest of your belongings are brought.'

He glanced down at her waist, his gaze narrowed. 'Your knife is broken. How curious.'

Before she could move away, he ripped the blade free from its binding. The pommel separated, and the ruby clattered on to the floor. Triumph dawned in John's eyes. 'So. You thought to hide it from me.'

'I only discovered it yestereve.'

'Liar. And now you're going to tell me where the rest of the treasure is.'

'I don't know—'

His fist moved towards her face, but Honora threw herself to the ground, dodging the blow. John tossed the dagger grip at her feet, keeping the blade and ruby for himself. A hardened look crossed his face. 'Rest assured, I will find the rest of the Ceredys jewels. You will tell me everything I want to know. Or you'll suffer for it.'

To his men, he ordered, 'Guard her while I see to the horses. Let no one except me into this chamber.'

When they had left, a single soldier remained while another stood just outside the door. Honora forced herself to behave like her sister, quiet and demure. It would be easier to catch the guard by surprise when the time came to make her move.

Whether hours or minutes had passed, she couldn't be sure. The chamber remained darkened, since the guard had closed the shutters. Jesu, she wished the battlements were closer. The window was wide enough to crawl through, and it was possible to reach the stone walkway if she took a strong leap. But a misstep would cause her death. It was too great a risk.

Her guard seemed less interested in her as time passed. She had not spoken once to him, nor behaved as though she were a threat. Luring him into complacency, that was critical to her escape.

The broken grip of her knife lay upon the ground at her feet. Although it was made of metal, it was ineffective as a weapon. She didn't know why, but she tucked the grip into the girdle about her waist. It was familiar, it was hers, and perhaps a new blade could be added one day.

She stared at the contents of the chamber once more. There was only the chair, the bed and the gowns she'd taken with her. And though she'd prefer to use the chair as a weapon, the guard was seated upon it. Not a good choice.

But there was another possibility. She considered the options, weighing them over in her mind.

When she heard a faint noise approaching, a creaking sound, she tensed. Time to do something instead of waiting for John to return.

'I am cold,' she murmured to the guard. 'Might I put on another gown?'

He hesitated, but could find no reason to deny the request. With a shrug, he tossed her the bundle of clothes. Honora unwrapped it, sorting through the garments until she chose a linen underdress.

He was still watching her.

'Turn your back, please,' she begged. 'You've no need to watch me dress.'

She was startled when he obeyed. Fumbling with the clothes, she made it sound as though she were getting dressed while she drew closer to him. Gripping the fabric tightly with both hands, she sprang forwards and wrapped the garment around the guard's throat. Twisting it tight, she suffocated him, praying that he would soon lose consciousness. She didn't want him dead, only weakened.

When he slumped to the floor, she threw open the shutters. To her shock, a thick rope hung down. Glancing outside, she saw Sir Ademar moving downwards.

'What are you doing?' she whispered.

He swung himself inside the chamber. 'Your sister told me what…happened. She thought you might need help.'

Katherine? Honora gripped her shoulders, stunned that her sister had sent the knight to her.

'Why didn't you alert my father?'

He shrugged. 'This way was, ah—that is to say, I found it would be…m-more interesting. Get you out without anyone kn-knowing about it.'

A hopeful smile perked upon her lips. 'More interesting?'

He nodded. 'Less trouble. And, no-no one gets hurt.' He flushed at his stammer, but she didn't mind it at all.

He was right. If she could escape before John noticed it,

she might gain as much as a few hours of riding. But then, a frightening prospect occurred to her. Was Ademar expecting her to jump from here?

'How do you suggest I get down?'

He struggled with his words, speaking slowly. 'I'll help you…to the battlements. We need to move now.'

Honora winced at the thought of swinging the rope to the stone walkway. It wasn't directly below the window, and there was a very real possibility that she wouldn't make the leap.

'I'd rather fight the guards outside the door.' She was about to suggest that they do exactly that, when the door started to open.

Sir Ademar threw himself against it, and ordered, 'Go!'

With her stomach fighting to stay calm, Honora reached out for the rope. *It's not so very far*, she told herself. Perhaps if she repeated it enough, she might begin to believe that.

'Swing towards the battlements,' Sir Ademar urged. 'You'll find what you need to g-get out of the castle.' He strained as a harsh pounding on the door rattled the frame. 'Ewan will b-be miles from here by now.'

Honora crawled through the window, balancing on the sill as she reached for the rope. Glancing back at him, she sent him a thankful smile. 'You're a true hero, Sir Ademar.'

And with her heart pounding, she lowered herself down.

Twilight dimmed the horizon, and Ewan stopped by the river to drink. He'd followed the sun's path west, his feet sore from all the walking.

The taste of failure was bitter upon his tongue. It would take a fortnight to reach the coast without a horse. He'd considered defying Lord Ardennes's orders and stealing his mount back. But in the end, he'd decided to keep peace with the man, even if it meant abiding by fines he didn't agree with.

The path he trod was as worn down as his spirits. He'd

expected to come here and find a bride, fulfilling a destiny he'd dreamed of. Land. And a lovely woman at his side. It was meant to be the beginning of a new life for him, one in which he had his own kingdom instead of his brothers' castoffs.

Instead, he was walking away empty-handed. Aye, his temper had gotten him tossed out of Ardennes without even a horse. But he didn't regret defending Honora. He'd do it again, given the chance.

She had grown into a woman of strength. Though she had endured her share of hardship, not once had she indulged in self-pity.

Ewan admired her bravery. And whether he wanted to admit it or not, already he missed her. Honora had been his equal in all ways, both with her sword…and in her passionate spirit.

The night they'd shared together in the garden haunted him still. The scent of her hair, the sweetness of her mouth…the silk of her skin.

He should have brought her with him, despite all the problems it would cause. At least then he'd know she was protected.

The sky grew dark, the sun sinking below the horizon. Ewan built a fire and set up a pallet for the night. He had coerced the castle cook into packing provisions for the journey. While he was unloading the sack, he heard a single horse approaching.

Ewan reached for his sword, staring out into the distance. Chainmail glinted in the dying sunlight, and he hid himself within the tall grasses, waiting for the enemy soldier to approach.

Had Lord Ardennes sent a man? Or John of Ceredys? He wasn't certain, but he wished he had a bow and arrows.

He crept to the far edge of the riverbank, his sword hilt in his hand. As he watched the rider approach, something was wrong. The soldier was not seated upright, but instead lay slumped across the saddle. He wore the Ardennes colours, but carried no shield.

Was the man wounded? Or was this a ploy to lure him closer?

Cautiously, Ewan emerged from his hiding place when the rider drew to a stop. The soldier attempted to dismount, but slid off the horse, falling to the ground.

Críost. It was Honora.

Ewan sheathed his sword and ran to her, helping her to sit up. Her body folded against his, and he didn't know how she'd managed to stay atop the saddle for the many hours she'd been riding.

He glanced around, but saw no one else with her. 'Are you all right?'

He lifted the iron helm and chainmail coif off her head, and she ventured a tired smile.

'I am now.'

Chapter Fourteen

Ewan helped her drag off the remaining armour, peeling away the chainmail until she had on nothing but a crumpled bliaud and shift. The fabric clung to her body, dampened with perspiration.

'I'm so tired,' she murmured, letting him hold her. 'I was afraid I wouldn't find you.'

Ewan let her rest against his chest, stroking her hair away from her face. 'I'm glad you came.'

He couldn't believe she was truly here. Though he wanted to know why she had followed him, he was afraid to ask. As if she'd slip through his fingers and disappear.

He tilted her face towards his and kissed her lightly in a kiss of welcome. Though he craved her touch, he didn't press her for more. 'I have food, if you're hungry.'

Her smile deepened. 'Thank goodness for that. I was hoping you would.'

He opened up the provisions and chose a delicate pastry filled with chopped figs and almonds, smeared with honey. Breaking off a piece, he fed it to her.

'Oh, this is so good.' Honora moaned with pleasure. She looked like a woman who'd been made love to, and Ewan gritted his teeth to stop himself from the lusty thoughts racing through his mind.

'Wine?' he offered, handing her the flask. Honora drank, then sat down to finish devouring her food. Ewan let her eat her fill, satisfying his own hunger with cheese and fresh bread.

Honora licked at her fingertips after she'd finished. The sun had sunk beneath the horizon, while the orange flames of the fire cast a glowing light amid the darkness.

Her hair stood out against her shoulders, wild and rumpled. She smoothed her wrinkled gown and drew up her knees. Her feet were barefoot after she'd abandoned the boots.

'I suppose you want to know why I followed you.' She looked embarrassed and added, 'You were the only one I could turn to for help.'

'What happened?'

She moved towards the fire, warming her hands. The flames illuminated her face and the dark bruises encircling her left wrist. 'John took me captive and locked me in his chamber. He was planning to force me back to Ceredys.'

She rubbed at her wrist, her voice quiet. 'If it weren't for Sir Ademar's help, I might not have escaped.'

'Sir Ademar?' Ewan tried to keep his tone neutral, but the knight's name caused a ripple of jealousy. 'He was the one who rescued you?'

Honora nodded. 'My sister sent him.'

'What of your father? Did he allow this to happen within his own walls?' Ewan had seen the way Nicholas of Ardennes disregarded his daughter, and it provoked his own sense of justice.

'He wanted me to leave.' At the confession, Honora drew up her knees. Though she tried to mask it, he saw the fear rising up.

'Why?' He couldn't keep the outrage from his voice. A father should protect his daughter, not subject her to the dangers of men like John.

She glanced back at the horizon, her face troubled. 'Because I betrayed Katherine with you.'

Though she didn't say it, he was responsible for her exile. Ewan sat down, resting his hand upon one knee. 'I won't apologise for wanting you. Or for refusing to wed your sister. It would have been wrong.'

Her clear green eyes stared into his, filled with regret and guilt. 'What we did was wrong. I should have stayed away from you.'

'It wouldn't have made a difference.' He reached out and touched her face. 'Would it?'

Guilt stained her cheeks, and she looked away from him. 'I have to decide what to do now. I thought I might go to Normandy, if you'll escort me. I have kin there, and—'

'Come to Éireann with me,' he interrupted. 'You'll be safe.'

Honora hesitated, risking a glance back at him. Her green eyes were filled with worry. 'I could go…for a time. But I can't abandon Ceredys and the folk to John's mercy. I made a vow.'

He wanted to argue that it wasn't her responsibility, that she should stay far away from Ceredys. But it would do no good. Honora kept her promises, regardless of the risk to herself.

'Recruit help from among my tribesmen,' he suggested. 'They are trustworthy, and you may be able to coax my brother Patrick, the King of Laochre, into helping you.'

Honora expelled a sigh. 'I suppose I'll try. I've nowhere else to go.' She turned away, and he moved beside her, drawing her back against his chest.

'You're not alone, Honora.' With her hair at his lips, her body leaning upon his, every sense went on alert. The soft strands smelled lightly of flowers, and his hands encircled her waist.

In silent answer, she held fast to his arms, squeezing lightly. For the first time, she wasn't fighting herself or pushing him away. Instead, she returned the embrace, resting her head beneath his chin. It startled him, that it would feel this good to hold a woman.

'What about you?' she asked. 'Will you find another heiress to wed?' Though her tone remained even, he felt her posture shift, as though she were afraid of his answer.

It was a question he hadn't been able to face. After everything that had happened, it now seemed dishonourable to wed a woman for her lands, though it was the reason for most marriages.

'I don't know,' was all he said. 'I'll make that decision after I return home.' Too much had changed. The plans he had made now seemed unrealistic, a fool's dreams. Still, he was unwilling to surrender them yet.

'Any woman would be fortunate to wed you,' Honora said softly. She turned to face him, and he saw the flush of embarrassment on her cheeks. As though she'd said too much.

'I don't want to think about what lies in the future,' he admitted. 'I'd rather just be with you now.'

'As friends,' she murmured, her hand resting on his shoulder.

'No, Honora.' He rose onto his knees, his hands sliding into her hair. 'Not friends.' He ravaged her mouth, kissing her in such a way that she would know exactly what he wanted. She shivered in his arms, but didn't pull away. 'I can think of no better way to spend this night than to make you cry out with pleasure.'

She looked stunned, her mouth parting. Her green eyes filled with uncertainty and a trace of fear. 'Ewan…I feel like we're starting over again, as strangers.'

'We're not strangers, Honora.' He touched her shoulder, sliding his hand down her arm. 'We're going to be lovers.'

His body went rigid, and he drew her hips close, palming her bottom. 'I want to watch you fall apart. Again…and again.'

She rested her forehead against his chest, and he heard her shuddering sigh. 'I'm not…good at it.'

'Good at what?' He forced her to look at him, and her cheeks were fiery red with humiliation.

'Being with a man. I was a disappointment to my husband.'

Behind the hurt words, he saw her fear. She'd been misused, and the scars of her marriage had not healed.

Though he could easily let her alone, allowing her to sleep apart from him, he didn't want her believing the lies spoken by Ranulf.

'If you were disappointed in your marriage bed, it was the fault of your husband. Not you.'

He held her again, stroking her spine with reassurance. It didn't appear to have any effect, for she could not relax in his arms.

'I hated it,' she admitted.

She was like a terrified bird, poised to fly from his arms. Though it was a physical torment, Ewan loosened his embrace, pulling back. If he pushed her too much now, she would fear him. 'Trust me when I say, I would never do anything to hurt you. If you don't want me to touch you, I'll leave you alone.'

He led her over to the pallet he'd set up earlier, fighting to keep out the pain of his arousal. Gods above, this was going to be a miserable night. 'Sleep now, and gather your strength for the morrow.'

She studied him for a moment, as if making a decision. At last, she removed her bliaud, wearing only her shift. She lay down upon the pallet, while he kept his gaze on the fire, trying not to look at her tightly moulded form.

'Aren't you going to sleep beside me?' Honora asked. 'I know you must be tired from your journey.'

He was, but he didn't trust himself to be so close and not touch her. 'I'll keep watch over you.'

Above them, the night sky glimmered with stars. The moon shed a gleaming light over the clearing, spilling over her skin like silver. Honora turned to her side, her dark hair resting upon one shoulder.

'Ewan,' she whispered. He glanced back at her, then wished he hadn't. The linen shift did little to hide her body, revealing the plump curve of her breasts, the swell of her hips. 'I'm afraid.'

'Don't be. John and his men won't find us. By the morning, we'll be gone.'

Honora shook her head slowly. 'I wasn't speaking of John.' She sat up again, her hands resting in her lap. 'I'm afraid I wouldn't please you if we became…more than friends.'

The vulnerability on her face, the way she had bared her confession before him, made him choose his words carefully. 'There's nothing you could do that wouldn't please me.'

'That night in the garden,' she said. 'I'd never felt anything like that before.'

He didn't move, his control straining taut. If she laid a single finger upon him, he knew he would snap.

Honora leaned forwards, resting her weight on her hands. 'I trust you. But I don't know what to do. Will you show me?'

Honora didn't know what had come over her, to be so bold. But right now, she'd lost everything. Her home, her family…there was nothing left, save Ewan.

When she was in his arms, he made her forget everything. His kiss, the way he touched her…it made her feel restless. Tonight, she wanted the comfort of his embrace. Even if it meant reliving the past.

'You don't know what you're asking me,' he said. His deep voice sounded uneasy, as though she'd crossed a boundary.

'You taught me to use a sword. Surely you can teach me this.' She wanted to experience the secret thrill he had conjured once before, to know what it meant to be desired.

Ewan expelled a curse and stood, walking towards her. His eyes grew heated, and when he removed his tunic, his bare chest appeared like smooth marble. 'You're still afraid, aren't you?'

She nodded.

'Don't be. Any time you say the word, I'll stop.'

Upon her back, she felt his hands caressing her. His mouth dipped down to brush against her nape, and a thousand shivers replaced it. He moved her hair away, kissing her ear, then her cheek.

'I don't want you to stop.' She needed to lose herself in his touch, forgetting everything that had happened. Behind her, she heard a soft noise as he removed the rest of his clothing.

Ewan lay down behind her, drawing her backside against him. She gasped with shock at the feel of his hard length against her bottom. His palms slid beneath her shift, raising up the hem and baring her flesh. She shuddered, closing her eyes as he slid his thick erection between her thighs.

Her body responded with wetness, and he used his shaft to rub and tease her.

'You've always tormented me, Honora. Both when you were a girl…and now, as a woman.'

Goose flesh prickled across her skin. He pulled the linen shift tightly against her breasts, and her nipples speared with arousal. He ran a single knuckle over the fabric, caressing the tips. 'I want to taste you.'

She tried to remove the shift, but he trapped her, his body weight pinning her against the pallet. 'Leave it on for now.'

With a wicked smile, he lowered his mouth to the fabric and licked her nipple through the linen. Honora arched her hips against him, her skin burning hot. He nipped at her breasts with his teeth, while he used the tip of his manhood to torment her swollen flesh. 'Do you feel it?'

Her breath hitched. 'Yes.' The same wildness skimmed through her body, and as she grew closer and closer, he slowed the pace.

'Reach for it, Honora. Let me take you there.'

She cried out, both needing the release and fearing what would happen afterwards. Ewan kissed her, plundering her mouth as he caressed her cleft.

There. His hand rubbed her until she soared, shaking violently as the glorious sensations ripped through her.

Without thinking, she brought her hand to his shaft, wrapping her fingers around the length. As another wave of pleasure shuddered through her, she squeezed him, pulling against him. He held on to her hand, and she moved faster. Over the smooth head, down the length of him, until he let out a groan, spilling his wet seed upon her stomach. He moved against her, stroking her with his arousal a few more times, until he rested his weight upon hers.

'You surprised me,' he said huskily.

He looked embarrassed by what he'd done, and Honora pulled his mouth down to hers for a soft kiss. 'Was it wrong? I wanted to please you.'

'There is no doubt you pleased me,' he said. 'Perhaps too much.' He extricated himself from their embrace, before he went to retrieve her fallen veil. A few moments later, he returned with the linen, which he'd dipped in the river. He cleaned her body, and Honora shivered at the cool water. A few times, he ran the cloth over her breasts, arousing her unintentionally.

Or perhaps, with full intent.

She allowed him to dry her off, wrapping both of them inside his cloak. Ewan held her with her head against his chest. She relaxed against him, soothed by the warmth of his body next to hers.

As sleep drew closer, Honora tried not to think about the future that lay ahead. For she knew, as Ewan did, that there could never be a marriage between them. There was no future for a landless Irishman and a banished widow.

All they had were these stolen moments. And one day soon, those, too, would be gone.

When Honora awoke, she smelled fish cooking. Ewan was seated beside the fire, a fresh trout spitted over the flames. He was fully dressed, and his gaze warmed when he saw her bare skin peeping from beneath the cloak.

She tried not to be self-conscious, though she remembered everything they'd done last night. Perhaps, tonight, he would finish what they'd begun. Her skin prickled to imagine it, though she was uneasy about the joining.

She rubbed her arms in the morning chill. Without Ewan's body heat to warm her, she'd become cold. She'd never been one to leap out of bed in the mornings. More often, she'd snatch the coverlet and roll over, trying to steal another hour of sleep.

'Is that the only fish you managed to catch? It's rather small, isn't it?' she teased. Reaching for her shift and bliaud, she dressed, trying not to feel embarrassed about wearing only her shift.

'There is nothing small about my fish.' Ewan's voice was almost a growl, as if she'd threatened his manhood with the description. 'It's big enough for both of us.'

Catching her about the waist, he added, 'I'll share, if you kiss me.'

She tilted her chin up to meet his mouth, and his tongue slid inside, tangling with hers. Oh, Jesu. He knew just how to unravel her will-power, stripping away her defences.

Unfamiliar sensations poured through her, a fierce need she'd never known with any man, save him. Her body craved his bare skin against her own, his talented hands touching every inch of her.

But they still had a long journey ahead. She pulled back, her hands shaking. 'The food, Ewan,' she reminded him.

His green eyes were dark with desire, but he released her. He removed the fish from the spit and brought it over to a large rock to divide it. With his dagger in one hand, he cut off a piece for her. Honora took her piece and struggled to pull it apart.

'What happened to your dagger?' he asked, eyeing the broken pieces.

'My father broke it,' Honora admitted. She went on to tell him that Marie St Leger had hidden a ruby within the weapon, and that John had stolen it back.

'He thinks it's part of a larger treasure,' she said. 'But I've only seen the ruby.'

'That's why he attacked you that night.'

'Yes. I didn't know Marie had given it to me. Were it not for my father breaking the weapon, I'd never have found it.' Honora rubbed her eyes, sighing heavily. 'John has the ruby now. But I don't know if he'll leave me in peace.'

'If he thinks there is more, I doubt it.' Ewan studied the grip. The pommel had broken off, and he touched the hollowed space with a single finger. 'Do you think a larger treasure exists?'

'John thought so.'

He lifted the dagger grip to peer inside. Inside the hollow where the blade tang was meant to rest, he slid his smallest finger. A moment later, he withdrew a tightly folded piece of vellum, only larger than his thumbnail. 'Honora, have you seen this?'

She hadn't. 'What is it?'

Ewan opened it and she saw strange black markings etched along the bottom, in a foreign design. Above them was a spiral emblem and the figure of a bird.

'What is it?' Honora asked.

'I've seen similar carvings on the chest in the chapel. But I've never seen a bird like that.' Ewan peered closer at the unusual drawing. 'It isn't one bird, Honora. It's six.'

The strange spirals and birds meant nothing to her. Nor did the black markings.

'Should we look for it?' Honora wondered aloud. 'If we ever learn what the markings mean.'

'Perhaps.' Ewan drew closer to her, spanning her waist with his hands. With his mouth, he nuzzled her neck. 'But right now, I think you should finish eating.'

He reached down and fed her from his fingertips. The

flaky trout was delicious, but his warm tongue only caused more desire to spark within her.

They had nearly finished when Ewan froze suddenly, his gaze focused in the distance. Honora shielded her eyes and immediately spied the threat.

A silvery ribbon flashed in the morning sun, the glint of chainmail armour. Whether it was John's men or her father's, it didn't matter. Both were dangerous.

'How many?' she asked, her hand reaching towards the grip of her dagger, out of habit. She'd forgotten it was broken.

'A dozen, perhaps.'

'Do you want to fight them?' she asked. Likely, they could defend themselves well enough, if Ewan had a weapon she could use.

'There are only two of us, Honora. I've no intention of getting us both killed.' Gathering up the pallet and his belongings, he threw the sack of supplies over her horse. 'Get on.'

She kicked dirt at the fire to smother it, then let Ewan lift her up. He swung behind her, urging the horse west. With the sun and their enemy at their backs, he went as fast as he dared. The mare struggled with the extra weight, but managed to break into a slow gallop.

'At least we have a horse,' he murmured in her ear. 'But it will take hours to reach the coastline. With luck, we'll find the caves and can hide from them.'

She sensed a tight fear underscoring his plans. 'What if they catch up to us?'

'We'll make a decision if it comes. In the meantime, we ride.'

She held on tightly to the reins, her heart racing in rhythm to the horse's hooves. The morning shifted into afternoon, and the soldiers were still visible, drawing closer. The mare was growing tired, and Ewan stopped to let the animal drink. He dismounted and helped Honora down.

'The horse needs to rest,' Honora interjected. 'If we push her too hard, she won't be any use.'

'They're gaining on us, Honora.'

'I know it.' Her spirits dragged even lower, but when he lifted her back on the animal, she protested. 'It's too soon. The mare needs more time to recover.'

'We don't have time. But we won't force her to take both of us.' Gripping the reins in one hand, he brought the horse into a light trot as he ran beside them.

Honora wanted to argue with him, but Ewan's face was set with an unbreakable stubbornness. He'd tire, soon enough, and she would take her turn running beside the horse. It seemed foolish, but they did appear to be maintaining their distance from the enemy soldiers.

When minutes turned into nearly half an hour, she couldn't stand it any more. Ewan's face was red, sweat dampening his tunic, but he showed no signs of slowing down. His endurance astounded her. But if he didn't rest soon, he'd collapse.

She jerked the mare to a stop, and Ewan stumbled forwards. 'It's your turn to ride. I'll run.'

'No. We have to keep moving.'

'And you're going to kill yourself if you keep on like this. Ride the damned horse and rest.' She couldn't believe he was forcing himself to such lengths. Dismounting, she took the reins from him.

Instead of mounting, he ran beside her. What was he doing? 'Ewan, don't do this.'

'I'm not weak, Honora. I'll manage.'

Is that what he thought? That she believed him less of a man if he rested?

'I never said you were weak. But you're no good to me if they catch us and you cannot fight.' She stopped running and pulled the mare to a stop once more. Resting her palms on each side of his face, she tried to make him understand. 'I can't run for as long as you. But I can't fight them alone, if that's what happens.'

His answer was to lift her back on the horse. Rigid with exhaustion and determination, he kept on running. The motion of the horse chafed against her thighs, and when at last they reached the coastline, she said a prayer of thanks that they were closer than she'd thought.

Sweet heaven, Ewan's entire body looked as though it had been tortured. His tunic was damp, his shoulders heaving.

'We're leaving the horse behind,' Honora ordered. 'She would only lead the men to us. The soldiers will claim and care for her.' With a glance at the grey waters of the sea, she added, 'And I pray you're right about those caves.'

'I am. I saw them on our journey here.'

She gripped his hand and pulled off the pack of supplies, releasing the horse towards the soldiers. She hated the thought of leaving her mare, but there was no alternative. Their saving grace was that the light had faded, and their pursuers would have to stop for the night.

'How are we going to reach Erin?' she asked as they made their way down the hillside to the rocky coast.

He shook his head. 'Bevan said he would send one of my brothers back with the ship. Or else I was going to ask a fisherman for help.'

Once they reached the beach, Ewan led her into the shallow water. He took their supplies from her, and she was grateful to be relieved of the burden. The weight of her chainmail armour was more than she could manage.

'Why are we walking in the sea?' she asked.

'No tracks. The tide will remove all traces of us.'

The cold water stung her feet, and she bit her lip to keep moving. How far they traversed, she couldn't know. The sky was dark purple, the sun rimming the horizon in a blade of gold.

At last, he stopped. 'Look there.'

Praise be, she saw the cave. She was so tired, she was beyond caring if it was a suitable shelter. If it were large enough, they might be able to build a fire. Her skin was so cold, her teeth chattered.

They stepped across the rocks, still keeping their feet from the sand. Once they reached the entrance, Ewan pressed his back against the stone wall, listening. The pungent sea air filled the interior, and she wrinkled her nose.

'Can we build a fire?' she whispered.

He set down the pack of supplies. 'I think so. The cave is deep enough that we can keep the light hidden. And it's too dark for them to see the smoke. Stay here while I gather some driftwood.'

'Be careful.' She stopped him and brought his mouth to hers in a light kiss. He deepened it, filling his hands with her hair.

'I won't let anything happen to you, Honora.'

'I know it.' But even as he left her, the cold darkness seemed to fall over her like a forbidding cloak. She prayed to God that somehow they would find an escape.

Ewan dropped a load of wood inside the cave, reaching into the pack of supplies for flint. It took a while to get the fire started, but eventually the small space grew warmer. Faint cracks in the ceiling of the high cave kept the smoke from getting too thick.

Honora sat as close to the fire as she dared, her feet bare, her wet shoes discarded. She looked soft, vulnerable. Nothing like the fighter he knew she was.

Though his feet burned from the distance he'd run, he'd not let her see the exhaustion. He wanted to take care of her, to ensure her safety. Never would he let anyone harm her, especially not John.

He saw her guarding her wrist, flexing it gently. 'How is your wrist?'

'It's still bruised. But it isn't broken or sprained, thanks be.' She moved it to show him, and added, 'I can fight if I have to.'

There would be no need for her to risk it, not if they remained hidden. And with darkness to shield them, John's men would not venture towards the rocks.

'You won't have to fight,' he promised.

Honora opened the supplies and pulled out the flask of wine and a half-stale loaf of bread. He sat beside her, waiting for her to eat. But she didn't. Instead, she set the food beside her on a stone and opened her arms to him. 'Come here.'

He didn't understand what she wanted. But given a choice between food and Honora, there was no question which he preferred more. When he tried to hold her, she shifted so that her back was to the wall of the cave. She made him lean back in her arms, his back resting against her soft breasts while her thighs were spread on either side of him.

'You're weary,' she said. 'And it's my turn to take care of you.' She broke off a piece of the bread and fed it to him. Ewan barely tasted the meagre food, though he was famished. They hadn't eaten since that morn, and under normal circumstances, he'd dive at the food.

But it was far more distracting to see her shapely legs emerging from the hem of her gown. He accepted another bite of bread, raising the edge of the bliaud a little higher with his palm.

Now that they were alone once more, his awareness of her deepened. He rested his hand upon her bare knee, letting her know of his interest.

After they'd finished sharing the bread, Honora unlaced his tunic and lifted it away. He didn't know what her intentions were, but so long as she was removing clothing, he didn't particularly care.

Her hands sank into his shoulders, kneading his tired muscles. The sensation of her fingers touching him was exquisite, and he closed his eyes, hardly daring to breathe.

'Honora,' he said softly, 'you're quite good at this.' He

didn't know how in the world she could ever believe her touch wouldn't please him.

She caressed his nape, her fingers sliding through his hair, easing the ache at the base of his neck. Though her touch wasn't meant to arouse him, it was stoking a fire he yearned to quench.

'You're tense,' she whispered. 'Relax and let me care for you.'

Relax? As her palms glided over his skin, he fought a hiss as she caressed his spine. To distract himself, he cupped both of her knees, leaning back against her. His thumbs moved beneath her gown, stroking her thighs.

But when her lips kissed his shoulder blade, he'd had enough. 'Stop,' he gritted out.

'Stop what? I only meant to ease you.'

He turned to face her. Pulling her waist towards him, he set her upon his lap so she could feel the hard length of him straining at his trews. Her mouth opened in shock as he took her hips in his hands.

'There's only one way you can ease me, Honora. And if you don't stop touching me, I'm going to take you right here.'

Chapter Fifteen

His words made her tremble. She hadn't intended to touch him in this way, but once she'd started, it was hard to stop. His warm muscles were so tight, so well formed, she'd used this chance to run her hands over him.

In his eyes, she saw desire, a suffering that only she could alleviate. And tonight, she would endure whatever lay ahead.

Would it be so bad? From the thick ridge resting against her womanhood, she suspected it would be uncomfortable.

She'd endured her husband's attentions, and though it had hurt, she'd learned to ignore Ranulf and wait for him to finish. Never had he inspired any sort of desire, nothing like the way Ewan drew her in.

She was hardly aware of his hands rubbing her back. 'Honora, I spoke in haste,' he murmured. 'You know I would never force you. On my life, I swear it.'

But when she gazed at him, his expression was strained, a man who was on the edge.

'It wouldn't be force,' she found herself whispering. She couldn't put a name upon the feelings she had for him, but even though her life had fallen apart, she was glad to be with him. It wasn't right, it wasn't fair to her sister, but she craved the comfort he could bring. And if she could ease him with her body, it hardly mattered.

The interior of the cave had grown warm, the fire heating up the small space. She stood barefoot before him, her pulse racing with what she was about to do. Ewan's eyes grew shadowed with an overpowering need, and in the golden firelight, his skin took on a darker cast. She wanted to kiss him, to mould her hands to those strong shoulders and let the past fall away.

Ewan looked at her as though he wanted to devour her. He rose up, his hands resting upon her waist. 'Will you let me join with you this night?'

She knew tonight would be different from all the other times he'd touched her. And though she'd hated the act of letting a man inside her, she couldn't deny that Ewan had made her feel like a treasured possession…

'I will,' she whispered. And he closed the distance, covering her mouth with his.

She gave herself up, winding her arms around his neck. His kiss was that of a man trying to be gentle, but underneath it, she sensed a raw need. What would it be like to unleash that power?

Honora opened her mouth, and his tongue slid inside. Wet and sleek, her skin tingled at the taste of him, her breasts tight against her gown. Ewan's hands moved to the laces, and she felt a rush of cool air as he lowered her gown to her waist.

His mouth led a path down to her aching breasts, and when his tongue flicked at the nipple, her breath shattered. He bit at it gently, sucking her, until her body grew wet. Last night, he'd touched her intimately, and his fingers had slid inside easily. Perhaps it wouldn't hurt as much as she thought.

She loosened the ties of his trews, but Ewan didn't lay her down on the sand, as she expected. Instead, he freed both of them of their clothing, laying it down to form a soft bed. From their belongings, he brought out the pallet, setting it atop the clothes to make a silken bed

'Lie down,' he ordered, and she obeyed, feeling the soft fur against her bare skin. He stared at her, as though he couldn't quite believe she was truly about to give herself to him.

'You're the most magnificent woman I've ever known.'

Honora flushed, for she had not the rounded curves of most women. She was too thin, and her arms were rigid and tough from the sword training.

Self-consciously, she tried to cover herself, but he gently trapped her wrists at her sides. 'No. I want to see you.'

His hot gaze travelled all the way down her body, lingering upon her breasts and the juncture at her thighs.

Resting his weight on his arms, he covered her body with his own. At the touch of his erection, she inhaled sharply.

'It's all right,' he soothed, leaning down to kiss her again. She reached down to guide him into her entrance, planning to finish this, to get it over with.

But he held steady. 'You're not ready for me yet, *a ghrá.*'

Not ready? Her body was trembling, and she was moist as she'd never been for Ranulf. Surely it was time.

Ewan kissed a path down her collarbone, moving towards her erect nipple. When she moaned at the sensation, he moved his hand between her thighs, entering her with two fingers.

She arched her back, fighting against the shocking sensation of him caressing her, while his tongue stroked her breast. His thumb found the raised nodule, and Honora gasped at the pleasure when he teased it.

'Wait,' she pleaded, her breath coming in quick gasps. 'I can't bear it. I won't be able to—to stop myself.' She was so close now, so afraid of letting go.

'Don't stop. Let it happen.' His mouth moved lower while he kept up the steady rhythm of his hands. He kissed a path down her ribs, to her stomach. The invasion of his hands forged a fire that rose up, higher and higher. 'It's going to happen more than once, Honora. Prepare yourself.'

Then, abruptly, his mouth moved between her legs, his tongue plunging into the heart of her. Oh, dear God. She bucked at the wild, wanton touch of his tongue. Licking at her, sucking at her flesh, until she bit back a scream, her body riding out the surge of spicy fulfillment.

He raised his head up and smiled wickedly. 'Not yet, Honora.'

Not yet? Her hands dug into the silky pallet as his tongue caressed her folds, nudging her towards yet another release. She was half-crying, desperate for him.

'Ewan, enough of this. I need you.' Her very skin burned for him, her body craving the joining.

Ewan rolled over to his back, raising her body above his until she straddled him. 'I am yours to command, Honora.'

He guided her on to his hard length, and like a dagger meeting its sheath, she slid down upon him. It didn't hurt, but her body still had to adjust to his size.

She wasn't used to this, being in command. From the dazed expression on his face, she gathered that he was fighting his instincts, barely in control of himself. Gently, she raised herself up, then lowered her hips again, taking him deep inside.

The answering growl from his throat gave her confidence. Again she moved, and the sensation of him filling her was starting to become sensual.

He moved his hips in counterpoint to her rhythm, penetrating gently, but in such a way that it was like a caress.

'Faster, *a ghrá*,' he urged. His voice, like rough velvet, commanded her to seek out the pleasure he offered. She experimented with a quicker pace, and a shudder flooded through her as she took him deep inside, her body trembling with each thrust.

Ewan reached up to fondle her breasts. With his thumbs, he rubbed the hardened tips, moving faster as she arched against him.

'More,' he ordered, grasping her hips. He slammed her body against his, and she gasped at the violent bliss that surrounded their joining. 'Ride me.'

She did, her hips slapping against his until the fist of

pleasure caught her in the gut, spilling over until her inner muscles spasmed around his length.

It was then that he lost his control. Shoving her to her back, he lifted her legs around his waist. Grinding his hips, he plunged deep inside, pounding until she jerked back, straining hard until everything melted into a blinding pool of ecstasy.

She closed her eyes, feeling the rock-hard length of him sheathed deep inside. Instead of resisting, she welcomed it. Another unexpected climax overtook her, and she clung to him in desperate surrender.

Ewan groaned, thrusting once more until he lay motionless upon her body. A moment later, his mouth pressed lazy kisses against her throat, his body still joined with hers.

She held him close, utterly exhausted, and yet not wanting him to move at all.

This, this was what she'd been missing with Ranulf. Her husband had never taken the time to caress her, nor teach her anything. It was an awakening she'd never expected.

Honora ran her fingers down his back, over the lean, muscled hips, learning his body.

'Are you all right?' he mumbled against her skin. He hadn't stopped touching her, his hands stroking every part of her he could reach.

She shivered, her body suddenly cold. Ewan rolled to his side, withdrawing from her body. Outside, she heard the rolling of thunder and the sound of rain.

She sat up and reached for her gown. Ewan stopped her. 'Leave it. I want to sleep beside you, my skin against yours.'

She dropped the shift, settling back against him. 'You'll have to keep me warm, then.'

'That will not be a problem, *a ghrá*.' He pulled her against him, pulling his cloak atop their naked bodies.

'What are we going to do about John's men?' she whispered. She could imagine his men, gathered in wait for the dawn. Their chances of escape were minimal. 'What if they find us?'

'I won't let them take you.' His arms tightened around her. 'No matter what happens.'

The next morn, Honora dressed at dawn, moving quietly so as not to awaken Ewan. She'd slept badly, worrying about John and his men. If they left the cave, they would be exposed. And she couldn't let herself be taken back to Ceredys. Not until she'd gathered her own army against John.

Worry settled in her stomach, taking root. She sat down upon a large stone, watching Ewan sleep. It was then that she noticed his feet. Blisters and matted blood covered the soles.

He'd not said a word about his discomfort. It was from all the running yesterday, and she could only imagine the pain of it.

Ewan's eyes flickered open, and he caught her staring. 'What is it?'

'Your feet. You should have told me, and I'd have tended them.'

'They'll be fine. It's nothing.'

She winced when he stood upon the sand, imagining the abrasion of the granules against his flesh. 'At least let me bind them for you.'

'I've my shoes. It's enough.' He reached out and donned his clothing and footwear, and as he covered up his body, she blushed. He'd made love to her twice more that night, and from the heated look upon his face, he was contemplating another round.

'What are we going to do about the soldiers?' she asked, pulling his attention back to the dilemma at hand.

'You're going to stay here. There's a village a few miles from here, and I'll try to convince one of the fishermen to help us get away.'

Stay behind? Oh, not likely.

'We'll go together,' she corrected.

'You're safer here. John doesn't know where you are.'

'And you think you can get away without them seeing you?' She shook her head.

'I'm good at that, Honora. Trust me.'

'At least if we go together, I can guard your back,' she argued. Did he think he was invincible?

Irritation swept across his face, and Ewan fastened his sword belt around his waist. 'I don't need your help, Honora.'

'If you think I'm going to remain behind, MacEgan, you're sorely mistaken. Put away your pride and let me help you.'

He crossed the cave and grasped her by the waist. 'Do you think I'll allow anything to happen to you?' His hand palmed her spine, rubbing in small circles. 'Stay here. Be safe.'

He was treating her as though she had no courage at all. As though she should hide in the shadows while he went off to fight.

'Would you do the same?'

He tilted his head, not understanding her question. 'What do you mean?'

'If you were being hunted, would you stay behind while I went off to fight?'

'It isn't the same. You're a woman.'

She reached out and seized his sword, her anger rising up. 'A woman, am I? I was trained, the same as you.'

'You're not as strong.'

'My technique is just as good as my father's men. I'm more help to you at your side than staying behind.' She couldn't believe the sudden change in him, as though she were incapable of defending herself. She might not have the same strength as a man, but she could certainly hold her own.

Ewan leaned in to kiss her, but Honora wasn't about to be talked out of it, even if he did make her knees weak from the melting touch of his mouth on hers.

'You're a distraction,' he said. 'If I'm to fight, I'll be thinking of you and whether or not you're safe. If you're here, I'll know that no harm has come to you.' He grasped her shoulders. 'Stay in the cave.'

His arrogant decree didn't sit well with her. She wasn't a dog, trained to stay behind while he went off to fight. No. She was tired of being told what to do and how to behave. Ewan was going to get her help, whether he wanted it or not.

She waited until he'd left. Then she gathered up the supplies and followed behind, her movements stealthy so he would not hear her. When he moved along the rocks, she struggled to balance the load and stepped out of the cave. The daylight half-blinded her, and she shielded her eyes, staring out at the sea.

In the distance, she thought she saw a vessel approaching. A mixture of hope and trepidation rose up inside, and she stared hard at the boat. Was it her imagination, or was the boat coming closer? She took a hesitant step forwards, glancing around. Perhaps it was one of Ewan's brothers, as he'd claimed.

When she glimpsed the top of the hillside, her heart plummeted. Wearing full chainmail armour, she spied John of Ceredys upon his stallion.

She cursed, realising that Ewan was right. John wasn't going to give up, not when he believed she knew the location of the treasure. He'd grown obsessed with it, and no doubt he would continue to search until he drew his last breath.

Her fingers bit into the rocky limestone, and she remained in the shadow of the rocks. The army was waiting for them to leave their sanctuary. She glanced at the sea, wondering if she could swim out to the boat. Although she wasn't a good swimmer, the vessel was their best hope of escaping.

Ewan crept along the edge of the caves, moving towards her. He motioned her back, his face hardened and furious. 'You were supposed to stay here.'

She ignored the order and kept her voice low. 'There's a boat not far away. Do you want to try and swim for it?'

'It's my brother's boat,' Ewan said. He took her by the elbow, guiding her back inside. 'The one Bevan sent back for me.'

'That's good, isn't it?'

'Only if we can reach it before Ceredys's men attack.' He

trapped her against the wall, his hands resting upon the limestone. 'You risked too much, leaving the cave. I told you to stay.'

'And I told you, I'm not going to hide like a coward. I fight at your side, MacEgan, not in your shadow.'

He stared at her, his jaw tight with anger. 'Don't defy me, Honora.'

She faced his fury, lifting her chin. 'I make my own decisions, MacEgan.' The sound of men's voices and horses seemed to draw closer, and her pulse quickened. 'They're searching the coastline, aren't they?'

Ewan nodded, lifting his hands away. 'We haven't much time. If we don't leave, they'll trap us here.' He gripped her hand while he led her to the entrance.

'Give me your knife, and we'll fight together,' she argued.

'They have arrows.' He shook his head. 'Without a shield, we're dead. Wait until the boat is closer, and then I want you to swim out. Tell my brother what's happened. He'll know what to do.'

'We could risk the swim together,' she offered.

Ewan didn't seem to hear her words. 'I'm going to let Ceredys take me captive. He'll try to ransom me, or use me to get you. Go with my brother, and he'll bring back our own army.'

His idea might work, but Honora didn't trust John. He wasn't the sort of man to take prisoners. He'd sooner kill Ewan than hold him for ransom.

No, it wasn't worth the risk. They had to do something unexpected, something that would startle John enough that he wouldn't react in time.

Her idea took form, solidifying. Ewan wouldn't like it. But the only way to ensure that he followed her was to seize the moment.

Before he could stop her, she dropped their belongings and ran from the cave.

Chapter Sixteen

Honora raced across the sand, running towards the sea as fast as she could. Her feet hit the icy water and the waves slowed down her pace. Horses galloped towards her, but she dived beneath the surface, drowning out the mingled sounds of men shouting and hooves pounding upon the surf. Her gown weighed her down, dragging her further in.

Her mouth filled up with water, and Honora started to panic. She'd never been a good swimmer, and now her life depended upon it. As she reached up for air, her body stung with the crippling chill. She could barely move, but she forced herself to keep paddling.

If she didn't reach the boat, everything was lost. She thrashed through the water at first, her head bobbing beneath the waves. Then abruptly, her mind calmed. She was strong. She'd trained since she was a girl.

Use your strength. Fight back.

Her arms cut through the waves, and though she considered removing the soaked gown, she would need it for warmth later. The wool clung to her body, while she used her legs to keep herself afloat.

With a quick glance back at the coast, she saw that she had made it far enough that John's horses could not follow.

She was still in range of the arrows, but they made no move to shoot her.

Just as she'd suspected. John wanted her alive, not dead.

But there was no sign of Ewan. Where was he? Fear drove her to swim faster, her arms burning as she swam closer to the boat.

Cold. And so tired. She'd never swum this distance before, and her energy was waning. Her mouth filled up with briny water, but she forced herself to keep going.

Another glance back, and she saw two of John's men swimming towards her.

Damn. She churned her shoulders, fighting her way to the boat. So close now.

After endless minutes passed, a wooden oar reached out and she grasped it, the man pulling her aboard. He was fair-haired and one hand was misshapen. His face was similar to Ewan's.

'A cold day for a swim, I'm thinking,' he said.

She trembled with the chill, her teeth chattering. 'Where is Ewan? Did you see him?'

'He dived into the water not long after you.' The man pulled hard at one of the sails, adjusting it until the boat moved further out in the water, increasing its speed.

'We have to wait for him,' Honora argued. She peered over the edge of the boat, unable to believe the casual tone in the man's voice. Her heart clamored, for she hadn't once seen Ewan. The thought of him drowning made her want to dive in after him.

'Oh, Ewan can swim a great distance underwater. I wouldn't worry about him.' The man calmly picked up a crossbow, eyeing the swimming soldiers. 'I am Connor MacEgan. You must be the Ardennes heiress.'

Honora didn't know quite how to respond. It wasn't as if she could introduce herself as the woman who'd destroyed Ewan's chances of marrying her sister.

'I am the daughter of Nicholas de Montford, Lord of

Ardennes. Widow of the Baron of Ceredys,' she hedged. 'Honora St Leger is my name.'

Connor flashed a crooked smile. 'He spoke of you when he returned to Éireann, after his fostering.'

Did he? It fired her curiosity, wondering what Ewan had said. But Connor ceased the conversation to aim at one of the soldiers swimming towards the boat. He fired his crossbow, and the bolt struck true. The soldier floated a moment upon the sea before the body began to sink.

Connor reloaded the weapon, nodding at the waves. 'There's our Ewan. Look.' She followed his gaze and saw a head bobbing in the water, perhaps fifty yards away.

Honora held her breath while Connor kept firing the crossbow, taking out one man after the next. When only four men remained on the beach, she saw John fall into a retreat. Silently, she sent up a prayer of thanks. 'Did Bevan send you here?' she asked.

Connor nodded. 'Ewan has a knack for trouble.' With a glance towards the beach, he added, 'As you can see.'

A few moments later, Connor lowered his oar into the water. Ewan grabbed on, and his brother helped him into the boat, seawater sloshing inside the vessel.

With a cocky grin, Connor said, 'I see you've made a good impression with the Normans.'

Ewan did not appear amused. 'Set the course, Connor.'

Honora studied the bottom of the boat, well aware of Ewan's furious gaze. Connor tossed her his cloak, and she huddled beneath it, her soaked clothing making her teeth chatter. 'Do you want to share the cloak?' she offered Ewan.

His gaze was hardened with unspoken chastisement. 'No.'

He turned to Connor. 'I never thought I'd say this, but I am glad you came when you did.'

'When you've warmed up a bit, you can tell me about it.' Connor glanced over at Honora. 'Now if a fetching *cailín* asked me to share her cloak, I doubt if I'd be clutching my pride and shivering.'

'Close your ears, my brother. I've words to say to Honora.'

To her embarrassment, Connor moved to the front of the vessel, feigning interest in one of the sails. He would hear every word, she knew.

Honora pulled the edges of the cloak around her. 'Perhaps sharing this with you would not be such a wise idea.'

'You could have been killed,' Ewan ground out. 'Running out into the open like that? One arrow, and you'd have been dead.'

Fury tightened his jaw, his eyes blazing. 'I've never seen something so foolhardy and dangerous in all my life. You were supposed to wait for *me* to make the first move.'

'While you gave yourself up to become a captive?' His accusations ignited her own temper. 'Do you think John would have let you live? He'd have killed you at the first opportunity.' She tossed the cloak at him, ignoring Connor's amused expression. 'I saved us both by what I did. And I won't regret it.'

'How can you think your actions made any sense at all?'

'Because John doesn't want me dead. He wants me alive, because he believes I know about his damned treasure.'

And so he can control me, she thought angrily. Just as Ewan was trying to do now.

'I make my own decisions,' she snapped. 'And that was a good one, I'd say.'

'She's right,' Connor offered. 'She did an excellent job distracting them so you could make your own escape.' He reached up, grasping one of the ropes, and Ewan helped him adjust the sail. Honora retrieved the fallen cloak, wrapping her freezing body inside the warmth. If he wasn't going to wear it, then she would.

Connor tied off the sail and added, 'Shouting at a woman isn't the wisest idea, Ewan. Best to kiss her and tell her you're sorry.'

'Don't you dare.' She wasn't interested in false flattery, nor meaningless apologies.

Ewan moved towards her, and were it possible to get away, she would have. As it was, she was trapped at the bow of the boat. 'You left our belongings in the cave.'

'There was nothing of value.'

'A suit of chainmail armour has great value.'

Honora rubbed her arms, staring out at the dark water of the sea. 'None of it was worth our lives.'

He reached out and took her hand. Lowering his voice so that Connor would not hear, he murmured, 'Why did you do it, Honora? You nearly stopped my heart.'

'I couldn't let you give yourself into captivity.'

He touched his forehead to hers, and forgiveness slid over her.

Connor cleared his throat. 'Are you going to kiss her or not?'

Ewan's answer was to pull her tightly into his arms, his mouth grazing her lips.

The green colours of his homeland welcomed them, conjuring a smile on Ewan's face. Though it had only been a few weeks since he'd seen it last, he'd missed Éireann. And from the expression in Honora's eyes, she saw the beauty, as he did.

His brother's ring fort Laochre was no longer a blend of stone and wood, but rivalled some of the strongest castles in England and Normandy. Patrick had designed it with tall square towers, built out of limestone with twelve-foot-high outer walls, and a deep fosse filled with water, to keep out invaders.

Thankfully, their tribe had strong ties with the Normans, and they had survived the difficult transition when King Henry had claimed Éireann for his own. They had been permitted to keep their lands, largely due to their alliances with the Norman lords Thomas de Renalt and Edwin de Godred.

Although Norman by birth, his brothers' wives had become so deeply a part of the tribe, few would know their heritage. No doubt Honora would get along well with them.

'Is this where you live?' she asked as they crossed through the gates of Laochre Castle.

'It is where my brother, the king, lives,' he corrected. The awe on her face made him slightly uncomfortable, for his own dwelling was far more humble.

Ewan walked slowly to hide the discomfort in his feet. The blistered soles had begun to heal, no thanks to the seawater. But he'd not reveal any of his pain to his family. His wounds would close up, soon enough.

When they reached the inner bailey, he heard a female voice mingled with a child's laughter. 'Liam, come back here, I say!'

His eight-year-old nephew came fleeing across the courtyard while Queen Isabel chased him. She reached for the boy just as he jumped with both feet into a large mud puddle. Dirt and water flew up into her face, splashing the front of her gown.

Abruptly, his laughter stopped.

'Now you've done it, Liam.' Ewan shook his head. Glancing around, he pointed towards the far gate. 'I imagine your mother will put it over there.'

The boy's face turned puzzled. 'Put what over there?'

'Your head after she removes it.'

Isabel was already gripping her young son by the arm. The boy grimaced and pleaded, 'But, *a matháir*, I couldn't help myself.'

'Yes, you could have. And not only will you beg my pardon, you'll also beg the pardon of your uncle Ewan's guest.' She ventured a smile towards Honora, switching into the Norman tongue without effort. 'My apologies for this young scamp. I am Isabel MacEgan.'

Ewan glanced at Honora, suddenly realising that she hadn't understood a word of the exchange. He was accustomed to both languages, for his older brothers had forced him to learn the Norman tongue at an early age.

He put his arm around Honora, smiling at his brother's wife. '*Queen* Isabel,' he corrected, 'this is Honora St Leger of Ceredys, daughter of the Baron of Ardennes.'

Honora started to curtsy, but Isabel waved her hand. 'You

needn't treat me any differently. My husband may be a king, but I am simply his wife.'

Her gaze studied both of them, and Ewan realised that both he and Honora looked travel-worn. Although their clothing had dried upon the journey, Honora's gown had torn in a few places, while her cropped hair was unveiled and standing out against her head.

'You'll want to bathe and refresh yourselves after your journey,' Isabel invited.

Honora grew flustered at the mention of her appearance. Wincing, she reached out and touched the ends of her hair.

Ewan didn't miss the piercing gaze his sister-in-law shot him, along with the silent question of whether or not Honora would be his wife. He shook his head slightly, warning her not to say anything.

While his mother was distracted, Liam used the moment to escape, ducking behind Connor who had just joined them. 'You won't let her behead me, will you?'

Connor ruffled the boy's hair. 'Not today. But you must make amends, or you'll find yourself cleaning the stables.'

Liam wrinkled his nose, and Isabel exchanged a glance of amusement with Connor.

'I am glad you are home, Ewan,' Isabel continued.

'As am I. It's as it should be, all of us together for Midsummer's Eve.' He followed her inside the hall, holding Honora's hand. Connor walked behind them, but with Liam firmly in his grip.

'Will you have a Midsummer's Eve feast?' Honora asked.

'We will,' Ewan said. 'MacEgans enjoy any reason to hold a festival.'

She braved a smile. 'I suppose you enjoy the food and drink.'

He nodded and took her hand, stroking her skin. Though he said nothing, he saw the colour rising in her cheeks. The two nights they'd spent alone together had only whetted his appetite for more.

Isabel led them through the castle, explaining the different rooms to Honora. When at last she reached the solar, she stopped them both. 'Wait here, Honora, and I'll arrange your bath before the welcome feast this eventide.' With a hesitant smile, she glanced at Honora's attire. 'And I can bring you an extra gown, should you need it.'

Honora's expression was grateful. 'Thank you.'

Once Honora was inside, Isabel closed the door and confronted Ewan. 'Are you going to wed her?'

Though Ewan had expected the question, his denial seemed caught up in his throat. 'We're friends. She needed my help after her father forced her to leave.'

Isabel pursed her lips in a tight line. 'You didn't answer my question, Ewan. And what happened to the heiress you were supposed to wed?'

'It's complicated,' was all he could say. 'I refused the match with Lady Katherine.'

'And you brought Honora home instead?' Isabel glanced back at the solar. 'She's fair enough, I'll grant you. I suppose I could make wedding preparations, if you'd care to celebrate the ceremony at Midsummer's Eve.'

He held up his hands to slow her down. 'She's not going to marry me, Isabel.'

'Why wouldn't she want you?' With her hands on her hips, the Queen looked ready to wage battle.

'Peace, Isabel. She has no plans to wed any man. She was widowed a year ago, and her husband was not kind to her.'

The Queen's anger softened. 'I'm sorry. I didn't know.'

'I want her to be safe here.' Ewan put a hand on her shoulder. 'And she means a great deal to me.'

Isabel touched his cheek. 'She may remain here at Laochre as our guest. But *you* must stay in your own dwelling.'

Ewan shot her a lazy grin. 'Are you protecting my chastity, Isabel?'

Isabel shook her head and let out a sigh. 'Behave yourself,

Ewan. In the meantime, I'll send word to Genevieve and Bevan to come and join us tonight. They will want to know you're home safely.'

Ewan nodded, and opened the door to the solar once more.

At the interruption, Honora turned to Ewan. 'Did you need something?'

He didn't answer, but pulled her to him for a kiss. He hadn't touched her for what felt like days, and he needed to feel her mouth upon his. 'Yes. I needed this,' he whispered against her mouth.

When he pulled back, her face was scarlet. She glanced over at Isabel, as if to apologise, but Ewan saw only a look of amusement upon the queen's face.

'Out, Ewan,' Isabel ordered. 'Honora does not need you to wash her back.'

'I should be happy to be of service,' he offered, lifting his hands up. Isabel shoved him out of the room, laughing as she did.

Honora huddled inside the steaming tub, wishing she could stay inside the warmth forever. A maidservant helped to wash her hair while another servant tended to her old clothing. Queen Isabel busied herself, choosing a new gown for Honora to wear.

Honora grimaced to think of just how disastrous her gown had looked. The colour had leached out from the seawater, and the hem was ripped in several places. Neither Connor nor Ewan had said a word about it. Not that she could have done anything, but she hated the thought of meeting strangers while she was dressed like a serf.

She'd never felt so awkward in all her life. Here, the tribe spoke the Irish language. She hadn't understood a word of their speech, and already she could see how different their customs were. It brought back her old feelings of helplessness at Ceredys, though she tried to push them away.

The Queen picked up a vivid saffron-coloured gown, and

shook her head. 'No, this colour would make you look too sallow. Rose, perhaps.' She held up another gown, then shook her head. 'The colour isn't dark enough for you.'

Honora said nothing, feeling more and more uncomfortable. The Queen was a stunningly beautiful woman, with fair hair and deep brown eyes. As she picked up each gown, Honora felt more and more uneasy.

She owned a number of gowns, but she'd never really cared much about her appearance. Ranulf had wed her without even meeting her first, and he'd paid little attention to what she wore.

'I am sorry,' she said to the Queen. 'I don't mean to take clothes that belong to you. I could purchase a gown, perhaps...'

With what? She hadn't even brought a sword with her. She felt banished from her family, unable to ask them for help.

'You are my guest,' Isabel reminded her. 'And I can sympathise with how you feel, for I went through it myself.' A wince crossed the Queen's face, but Honora couldn't picture her in such a situation.

'I imagine you have a good reason for not having any belongings,' Isabel continued.

The questioning tone made Honora feel compelled to explain about John and the army. 'I don't know if I'll be able to return,' she finished. 'But I can't leave the people of Ceredys at John's mercy. They need help.'

She knew they would suffer from his wrath in her absence. Shame curled over her, the memory of her earlier failure like a festering wound that would not heal.

The Queen opened a trunk, gathering up an armful of gowns. 'Did you ask Ewan? He may have a strategy in mind.'

'He thinks I should recruit from among his tribe.' Honora stared down at the water. 'But I don't have enough coins to pay them. For that matter, I don't even speak their language.'

'Is Ewan planning to fight on your behalf?' Isabel lifted up a gown, pretending to be interested in the colour, but Honora didn't miss the concern in the Queen's voice.

'It isn't his battle,' Honora said softly. She didn't want to bring Ewan into the fight, not when he could be killed.

She'd been so afraid when she hadn't seen him swimming towards Connor's boat. So many things could have gone wrong. She might have lost him.

Her hands fisted beneath the surface of the bath water, her heart wrenching at the thought. She needed to know that he was safe among his tribe. That nothing would happen to him.

And, she needed to face John on her own terms. He had defeated her once, but he'd not do it again.

Honora sank back against the wooden tub, holding her knees tightly. The maidservant helped Honora rinse her hair and wrapped her in a linen drying cloth. Isabel led her beside the fire and, as the maidservant combed Honora's hair, she directed the servants to make preparations for the evening feast.

'We'll need extra trestle tables brought in. And tonight we'll have Ewan's favourite, roasted lamb.' Isabel continued giving more orders for ale and describing what she wanted for the festivities. Honora's head tumbled with all the details. All of this, for the two of them?

'It isn't necessary to go to this trouble,' Honora began. She didn't want to imagine being the centre of everyone's curiosity. Her apprehensions tripled at the thought.

Isabel ignored her and dismissed the women. 'Ewan is like my own brother. And he deserves no less than our best welcome.' The words were spoken with a slight air of chastisement, and Honora hid her discomfort.

The Queen held up a deep blue gown, the colour of cornflowers. 'Now this will set off your hair.' Tilting her head, she asked, 'Why is it so short? Were you ill?'

'No. That isn't the reason why I cut it.' Honora didn't say anything further, for she didn't want to answer questions. 'May I borrow a veil?'

Isabel looked at her sharply, her gaze narrowed. She stared

at Honora, as though she were trying to understand her. But thanks be, she did not ask a second time. Instead, she pulled out a linen veil from inside a trunk of clothing.

Honora breathed a sigh of relief. The veil would hide her shorn hair, avoiding further explanations.

Isabel helped her to don a strange garment, a white fitted underdress called a *léine* and the blue overdress with voluminous draping sleeves. The silk fabric was very fine, and Honora vowed not to soil it in any way.

A soft knock sounded on the door a moment later, a female voice speaking the Irish language. Honora didn't know what was said, but the Queen opened the door.

A dark-haired woman, clad simply in a cream *léine* and a grey overdress, walked inside. Her warm smile was genuine and welcoming.

'This is Connor's wife, Aileen,' Isabel said. 'She is the most skilled healer I've ever met. She wanted to meet you, but she cannot speak your language. I am happy to translate for you.'

Your language, she'd said. Not *our* language. It seemed that Isabel had shed her ties to their homeland.

'I am most grateful to your husband, Connor. He saved our lives,' Honora said to the woman, and the Queen translated. Then Honora added, 'Will you ask her to examine Ewan's feet? He injured them a few days ago, and I know he'll not ask for help, though he needs it.'

After Isabel made the request, Aileen nodded and reached out to squeeze her hand, speaking rapidly to Isabel. The Queen added, 'Aileen says she is glad to help. And she welcomes you as Ewan's bride.'

The acknowledgement was a slice to her heart, for Honora saw the protective glint in Isabel's gaze. 'I am not his bride,' she admitted. 'But I will always be his friend.' She met Isabel's disapproving gaze with her own firm vow. Ewan had never once spoken of marriage, nor would he. She had always known it.

And…the truth was, she didn't know if she could be any man's wife. Marriage had stripped away her freedom, chaining her to her husband's will. She didn't deceive herself into thinking Ewan would be any different.

All men wanted a woman who relied upon her husband to defend her—not one capable of defending herself. Like her father and her husband, Ewan would never welcome her fighting skills, never accept her for who she was.

It hurt to think of it, for with every passing moment, she was growing closer to him. Too close. The nights she'd spent in his arms had gone beyond her imaginings. Even now, her skin warmed to think of how he'd touched her. And tonight, she would go to him once again.

Later that evening, amid the large crowd of Irish men and women, she found Ewan immediately. Though he was speaking to a kinsman, his attention turned to her, his eyes heated with the reminder of what they would share in each other's arms. She couldn't move, held captive by his gaze.

He broke off his conversation, heading straight towards her. A tremor built up in her knees, the undeniable desire spreading straight to her core.

When Ewan reached her side, he took her hand without speaking a single word. Honora could hardly keep up with his long strides, but his tight grip made arguing impossible.

'Where are we going?' she asked. 'Your family—'

'—can wait,' he finished. 'The feasting won't begin for an hour. And I've a need to spend time with you.'

He pulled her up a spiral staircase, covering her mouth with his. He feasted upon her lips, her tongue, as though he couldn't get enough.

Honora couldn't catch her breath, her heart racing within her chest. She wound her arms around his neck, surrendering to the hunger of his kiss.

'You're mine, Honora,' he said against her throat. She

gripped his hair, letting him seize her mouth in another heated exchange. Her heart was crumbling, at war with her mind. These stolen moments were all they had together. And though she knew they wouldn't last, she clung to him.

When his hand started to move against her skirts, she realised that he wasn't thinking clearly. She could *not* let him take her upon a stone staircase, in front of anyone who happened by.

'Ewan, wait—'

'Shh…' he murmured in her ear, nibbling at the lobe. He pulled at her hips, drawing her flush against his body.

And Honora realised that words were not going to break through to him. Only actions would make him see reason.

Wrenching her mouth away, she unsheathed his dagger and stepped from his embrace. 'MacEgan, keep your trews on, and gain control of yourself. You can have me later.'

'Well said,' came a voice from behind her. Mortified, Honora turned and saw a richly dressed man descending the stairs. From the gold circlet he wore upon his head, there could be no doubt he was King Patrick of Laochre.

'My brother…' the King smiled '…I think you've finally met your match.'

Chapter Seventeen

Ewan held out his hand, and Honora returned the blade to him, grip first. He introduced her to his brother, and Honora looked as though she wanted to disappear into the wall.

'Welcome home.' Patrick clapped him on the back, then turned his attention to Honora. His eyes glinted with amusement. 'You remind me of Isabel. A time or two, she's drawn a knife on me as well.'

'It's a bad habit of mine,' Honora confessed, her cheeks flushing. Then she turned back to him. 'I'm sorry, Ewan. I shouldn't have done that.'

He gripped her hand, squeezing it tightly. Beneath his breath, he warned, 'Don't do it again.'

Honora had simply taken his breath away when he'd seen her. Dressed like one of his kinswomen, the rich cornflower-blue overdress and creamy *léine* made Honora's skin the colour of moonlight. The gown hung in soft folds, accentuating her slender waist.

Before she could respond, his brother intervened. 'Ewan, take Honora and introduce her to the rest of the MacEgans while I find Isabel. We will talk of your trouble at the Welsh coast later.'

Ewan took Honora's hand and led her into the Great Chamber. All of his kinsmen and family were gathered around, sitting at the long trestle tables while Queen Isabel waited at the dais for her husband the King. There were places for each of his brothers and their wives, but he noticed that his brother Trahern's place was empty.

Gazing around at the dozens of tables heaped with food, the harpists and bards, Honora paled. 'I never expected this much.'

'Kings are expected to give large entertainments.' Ewan led her to the dais and the chairs waiting for them. Aileen and Connor's twin boys raced in front of them, nearly causing Honora to stumble. Ewan picked the pair up by their tunics, handing them off to their father.

Connor grimaced and carried a boy under each arm. 'No sweets for either of you.'

When they reached the dais, Ewan brought Honora to the centre of the table, where they would sit near his brother Patrick. All eyes turned towards her with curiosity, and he heard the low murmur of gossip.

Although Patrick introduced her as an honoured visitor, Ewan knew everyone believed Honora was going to be his bride. For once, he was thankful she didn't speak the Irish language, for she wouldn't hear the jests of his kinsmen.

Through their eyes, he saw her loveliness. Brave and strong, she was a woman worth fighting for. A woman any man would want to wed.

It troubled him to realise that he didn't want to let her go, despite her vow to Ceredys.

When at last they were seated, Honora leaned in, whispering in his ear, 'I feel like running away. I've never seen so many people staring at me.' The warmth of her breath against his skin caused an involuntary shiver.

'Then run away with me. Later tonight, as you promised.' Ewan rested his palm upon her hand beneath the table.

Honora took a long sip of wine, but didn't smile at his teasing. Instead, she appeared lost in all the conversation and the people watching her.

'Ewan, stop casting eyes upon Honora,' Connor interrupted, speaking the Norman tongue for her benefit. 'I want to hear the story of how you managed to be trapped by Norman soldiers and rescued by a woman.'

Ewan glared at his brother, sending Connor a silent warning to cease his questions. He wanted Honora to enjoy the feasting, not endure an interrogation. 'Misfortune seems to find me,' was all he said.

But Honora turned towards Connor, apologising. 'It was my fault. When I travelled with Ewan, we were pursued by a dozen men.'

Patrick had leaned in to hear her explanation, and Honora turned to both of them. 'Were either of you familiar with my husband, Ranulf of Ceredys? Or his son, John?'

Ewan expected Patrick to deny it, but instead his brother inclined his head. 'Unfortunately, I did make the Baron's acquaintance, years ago. But not his son.' From the look on the King's face, it was clear he'd had no liking for Ranulf.

'John causes far too much suffering,' Honora said. 'They do not deserve to live as they do. I vowed to return to Ceredys and help them.'

'I suppose John is like his father,' Patrick said quietly.

'Yes.' Honora picked at her food, then confessed, 'I tried to hire mercenaries. But they stole the money and did nothing to help.'

Mercenaries? Ewan's hand tightened upon Honora's. He hadn't known she'd resorted to such desperate tactics. She was lucky they'd merely stolen her coins and not tried to harm her in other ways.

Patrick's expression grew dour. 'Overthrowing Ceredys wouldn't help your people. The King would not support your efforts, nor would he allow you to take possession of the land. Does the Baron have an heir?'

She shook her head. 'I don't think so.'

'Even if Ceredys were dead, his portion of the estate and his title would pass onto another heir. Perhaps to a cousin.'

Honora palmed her eating knife. 'I cannot abandon the people. I feel responsible for them.'

Patrick studied her for a long moment, his gaze passing to Ewan. Then he said, 'God be with you on your venture.'

His brother's response wasn't at all what Ewan had expected. It would be a simple matter to spare twenty men, but the King had ignored the unspoken request for help, turning the topic back to the Midsummer's Eve preparations.

It was clear his brother didn't want to involve the MacEgan tribe in a war against the Baron of Ceredys, not for Honora's sake. And while he understood Patrick's desire to keep their people separated from the conflict, Ewan wasn't about to let Honora go to Ceredys alone.

Now it seemed finding an army was going to be a problem. His kinsmen would not cross the sea and risk their lives out of friendship. Honora would need silver or another means of payment.

As each hour passed, Ewan sensed Honora was growing more overwhelmed. Her smile was forced, and she didn't understand any of the conversations without his translation.

'Walk with me,' he said softly, taking her hand once more. Honora stood, and Ewan made their excuses. His brothers shot him teasing remarks as he left, but he ignored them.

He led Honora to a more private corner, at the top of the battlements. Here, they could look out over the landscape, towards the glittering sea and the vast kingdom that belonged to his brother.

'You aren't happy here,' he said to her. 'I can see it in your eyes.'

She sat down upon the stone staircase and rested her hands on her knees. 'I'll be fine. I'm just feeling uncertain about the future.'

He sat beside her. 'I'm not sorry you're here.' It bothered

him to see her so troubled, and he wondered how he could set her at ease.

Honora leaned her head against his shoulder and stared out at the castle. Torches flamed against the stone walls while dozens of soldiers kept watch. 'I suppose I can feel safe from John within these castle walls.'

'Patrick believes in a strong defence.'

She frowned a moment later and pointed to a segment of the inner bailey wall where a medium-sized hole remained. 'What happened there? Shouldn't you repair that breach?'

His mouth tightened. 'It's nothing. Just a hole.' And one he'd wanted Patrick to mend for the past nine years.

'Why is it there?'

'Because my damned older brother thinks it's funny.'

She turned to face him, her face curious. He didn't want to explain it to her, but she asked anyway. 'What happened?'

When he didn't answer, a smile perked at her lips. 'It bothers you. Should I ask King Patrick about it?'

His brother would enjoy telling her, Ewan was certain. The entire tribe knew about it, and now the soldiers touched the hole for luck before going into battle. How that tradition had begun, he'd never know.

Expelling a sigh, he confessed, 'Patrick was converting the old walls into stone. I was thirteen, I think. One of the stones fell out. Not enough mortar to hold it together, I suppose, but the rest of the structure stayed intact. Connor dared me to crawl through the hole.'

Honora's lips twitched. By God, she'd better not laugh about this.

'Did you make it through?' Though she posed the question with complete seriousness, he sensed she was trying to hold back mirth.

'I didn't. My head and shoulders made it through, but I couldn't get past my ribs.'

The humiliation was one he'd never lived down. He

couldn't forget how his brothers had laughed at him, while he'd struggled to free himself.

'Were you stuck within the wall?'

He glared at her. Of course he'd been stuck. 'One of the top stones slipped down on top of me. I nearly dislocated my shoulder trying to get out.'

'What did your brothers do?' Honora covered her mouth with a hand, colour rising in her cheeks.

'What any older brothers would do…they left me there for the rest of the day. Laughed at me every time they passed. Connor set a crown of daisies on my head that I couldn't get off because I couldn't move my arms. Bastard.'

'Who set you free?'

'One of the kitchen maids took pity on me. But Patrick left the hole there in memory.'

She did start laughing then and put her arms around him. 'Oh, Ewan. I wish I could have seen that.'

'I'm glad you didn't.' He cut off her laughter the best way he knew how. With a kiss.

Honora kissed him back, letting herself fall into the embrace. Ewan slipped his hands inside the sleeves of her overdress, shaping her body, caressing the curve of her breasts.

She gasped against his mouth as Ewan continued his devastating onslaught. The softest flick of his thumb against her nipple sent an unexpected rush of wetness between her thighs. She caught herself before she moaned, but when his hands touched her bare ankle, sliding up her leg beneath her skirts, she couldn't stop herself. The rough texture of his palm against her thighs made her shudder. Higher still, he stroked her legs, lingering against her flesh.

'I want to be with you again.'

She was glad her burning cheeks were hidden by the shadows of the night sky. Though she wanted him desperately, she was even more afraid of sleeping in his arms. 'I don't know if that would be wise.'

'Not here,' he corrected, his lips gentle against her cheek. 'I'll take you to my hut. No one will bother us.'

She struggled to calm the breath rising and falling. Her head and her heart were at war, her sense of reason battering against her body's desires. 'Your tribesmen thought I was going to be your bride, didn't they?'

Ewan's hands framed her face as he leaned in. 'Don't worry about them. All that matters is what's between us.'

'You're waging a battle I can't win,' she whispered. She touched her forehead to his. 'Each time I lie in your arms, you're breaking down my heart. And we both know I'll be leaving Erin.'

Somehow, he had laid siege to her feelings, slowly tearing down the walls until she could hardly imagine a life without him. Even now, she wanted to embrace him, to breathe in his scent and know that he was hers.

'You don't have to make that choice,' he said. 'You can stay with me here.'

'I can't, Ewan,' she said, holding him close. 'One day, you're going to wed an heiress. And I don't want to be here when that happens.'

He held her close, not denying it. 'Don't think about the future, Honora. Just be with me now.'

She let him hold her, afraid that these moments with him would never last.

Later that night, Ewan took her back to the chamber Isabel had set aside. It seemed best to let her sleep alone after the long journey. Though he longed to comfort Honora, to sleep with her body beside his, her warning had resonated with him.

She was right. The more time they spent together, the worse the risk of hurting her. She still believed he was going to wed an heiress, though he'd given up that idea.

He didn't want to face a future without her, but there

seemed to be no alternative. Honora would never let go of her vow to Ceredys. She would put her life in danger, and there was nothing he could do to stop her.

Not unless he went with her.

The thought of her lifting a sword against John, or worse, watching her be struck down, was unthinkable.

The morning sun pierced through the doorway, and Ewan walked outside. He took care of the animals first, then took a hard look at his property.

His circular hut was constructed of limestone and thatch, with a packed earthen floor. Half-a-dozen cattle gorged themselves on the dried corn he'd stored over the winter, protected by a low stone wall.

It wasn't enough. Even if he sold off each of the cows, he'd still need more coins to buy land and to build a larger home.

A small section of the stone wall had begun to crumble, so Ewan busied himself correcting the fallen stones. His muscles tightened as he hefted a stone, placing it atop the pile. He worked over the course of an hour, sweating as he finished the wall. The work made it easier to think, to make his plans.

The Midsummer's Eve festivities were approaching. During the *aenach*, visitors would come from the neighbouring tribes to intermarry and to compete in the contests of strength and skill. Often there were prizes for the winners, sometimes a silver cup or a horse. It might be, he could win the contests and use the coins to help Honora.

He glanced back at his meagre hut. Honora deserved better than this. She deserved a fine estate, with an army at her command to cast out John of Ceredys.

And he wished he could be the one to give it to her.

'There he is.' Liam MacEgan pointed to Ewan, who was repairing a stone wall. Honora sent a silent prayer of thanksgiving that the boy spoke her language, else she'd never have found Ewan's dwelling.

Honora thanked Liam, and he waited, a slight smile on his face. 'Was there something you wanted?'

He shifted his weight from foot to foot. 'My uncle sometimes gives me a sweet or a honey cake when I'm helpful.'

Another shrewd smile.

'If I had one to give you, I certainly would,' Honora apologised. 'But perhaps Ewan has something.'

At the sound of their voices, Ewan looked up. Liam scampered into his arms, chattering in Irish at a speed she couldn't comprehend.

Even as Ewan found a treat for his nephew, she didn't miss his look of discomfort, as though he were ashamed of his home.

There was no reason for it. The small stone hut had fresh thatching, and the walls were sturdy. It reminded her of the roundhouses she'd seen, not far from her homeland. The welcoming aroma of peat smoke surrounded the space, and the lowing of cattle broke the stillness. Behind the hut was a small garden, with rows of onions and peas already planted.

Honora didn't wait for an invitation, but ducked inside while Ewan was talking to Liam. The interior was cool and dark, the earthen floor immaculate. A small sleeping pallet lay in one corner, while a fire glowed in the centre. A shelf contained cooking pots and dishes made of fired clay.

There were no decorations of any kind, and Honora doubted if he'd had time or the inclination. It needed a little more care to make it into a home. She sat down on the bench beside the table, and it wasn't long before Ewan entered.

'This is where you live?' she asked.

He gave a brusque nod. 'For now. One day I hope to leave it behind.'

She crossed the small space, standing before him. 'Why? There's nothing wrong with your home.' Truth to tell, she preferred it to the vast castle, for no one would criticise her here, nor note her sorrowful lack of skills.

'Save your pity. I know what this place is. But it won't be this way always.'

Did he believe she was lying to him? It wasn't pity, not at all. 'Why would you say that?'

'I want to provide more for my family and the woman I'll wed one day.' He stared at the beams of the house, not looking at her while he spoke.

Jealousy slashed through her common sense at the mention of a wife. She found herself blurting out, 'Have you picked her out already?'

His eyes flared with sudden desire. 'I have one in mind.'

Before she could speak another word, he trapped her against the bench and table, gripping her head while he kissed her. It felt like years since he'd touched her, and desire rippled through her instantly. His hands moved fast, tearing through each layer of clothing while she fought to free him from his tunic and trews.

A savage need poured over her like water, racing through her veins in the need to join with this man. She kissed his chest, running her hands over his shoulders and arms. 'I want you inside me.'

'You're going to have to wait, then. For I've not finished touching you.'

After her clothes lay upon the ground, Ewan laid her back on the table, her spine pressed against the wood. He fastened his mouth upon her nipple, using his teeth and tongue to drive her into a deeper need. He wrapped her legs around his waist, his hard shaft pressed against her wet centre. 'I'm not letting you return to Ceredys, Honora. I won't risk your safety with John.'

He squeezed her bottom, forcing his length to ride against her cleft. Easing the tip of himself inside, she tried to sheathe him, but he wouldn't allow it.

'It's my choice to make,' she breathed, hissing when his mouth moved down to her navel. He lowered himself until he was kneeling on the ground, her legs wide open before him.

'Not any more,' he growled against her sensitive flesh. With his tongue, he tasted her intimately. He stroked a rhythm upon her flesh, the building pressure rising high inside her.

'I made a vow to the people,' she gritted out, gasping when he stood, lifting her hips to his.

'And I'm making a vow to you. You're going to stay here. I'll go in your place and free them, if it means that much to you.'

'It's my battle. Not yours.'

'Argue you all you want, *a ghrá*. But I'll let no man harm you.'

He plunged his erection inside her, and she shattered, the white-hot pleasure making her climax. Ewan lifted her ankles to rest upon his shoulders while he invaded and withdrew. She felt every inch of him penetrating, and each stroke brought her closer to another fulfillment.

She didn't like his supercilious declaration. 'I won't be pushed aside again, Ewan. I'll face my own enemies.'

He withdrew his thick length, gently turning her over until her elbows rested on the table, her knees spread wide on the bench. 'Not John.'

A moment later, he filled her from behind, driving himself so deeply, Honora found it impossible to think clearly. Her body was shaking violently as he brought her to the edge of madness and sent her flying across. She half-screamed when he impaled her, over and over. He grew even harder as he pumped inside, roaring as he reached his own climax.

Honora slumped over the table, unable to move. Ewan rested his face upon her back, still within her. 'When I return,' he breathed, kissing her skin, 'I'll hire my sword out until I've made enough silver to give you your own estate.'

Did he think he had to buy her affections? Was he expecting her to wait for a year or longer, until he felt he had enough wealth?

'I don't need an estate. It means nothing to me.' Especially if Ewan wasn't there. Couldn't he see that he would chain himself to a life of wandering? He would become a mercenary, a man whom she would hardly ever see.

'It means everything to me.'

His words left her cold. This wasn't about wanting to provide a good place for her to live. It was about besting others, lifting himself up to the wealth of his brothers. He hadn't heard a word she'd said.

Why? Why was he behaving like this, as though she needed more to be happy? But then, he'd said it himself, hadn't he? *He* was the one who wanted an estate, not her.

After a time, he withdrew and cleaned himself, donning his clothes again. Honora struggled with the *léine* and overdress, and Ewan helped her with the laces.

'You should return to Laochre,' he said, kissing her cheek. 'I am staying here tonight, to take care of some things. I'll see you on the morrow.'

Just like that, he dismissed her. Not a word about whether he wanted to marry her, whether he wanted her to live with him—nothing. Only a promise that he intended to go to Ceredys and leave her behind. To do what? Spin wool? Sweep the floors?

Honora strode away from his dwelling without a farewell. Right now she wanted to work off her irritation. She crossed his land, minding her step through the cow pasture. Hot tears swelled up in her eyes, for Ewan's ambitions were blinding him to the truth.

She didn't want a kingdom. The fear of failure haunted her, knowing that she'd let the people of Ceredys down. She didn't want to be responsible for dozens of families, and whether they had enough food to last through the winter.

But Ewan did.

A heaviness rose up in her throat. She'd never known how important this was to him. She couldn't give him the kingdom he wanted; her dower lands were controlled by John. But neither did she want Ewan to waste years of his life in search of gold he might never have.

No matter what he'd promised, she refused to stay behind in Erin while he went to fight her battles.

This was about more than vengeance or redemption. It was about proving to herself that she could fight her greatest enemy and win. That she could swallow her fears and become a true warrior.

She shielded her eyes from the morning sun, staring out at Laochre. The stronghold was filled with countless soldiers, Irishmen who walked with the quiet confidence of fighters.

And not a single one of them knew her secret. She'd hidden herself for so long, denying her abilities. Was it any wonder that Ewan could not see her as an equal, when she hid behind the shadows of her father's disapproval?

She stood, taking a deep breath. It was time to change that.

Chapter Eighteen

As Honora passed the homes of the MacEgan tribe members, she was surprised to see children gathering herbs, tying fresh sage, St. John's Wort and lavender into bundles. But what startled her most was the abundance of firewood.

'It's for the fires,' Connor remarked as he approached from behind her. 'The ashes and embers will guard against bad luck. And all will jump across the coals for protection.'

'A dangerous custom.' She eyed the large pile of wood, thinking that it was impossible for anyone to leap over such a fire without catching their clothing ablaze.

'It is. And the children love it most of all.' A noticeable wince crossed his face. 'My boys in particular.'

'Do you burn all of the herbs?'

'Not all. Some are twisted into bundles for luck. I usually give my wife, Aileen, a bundle of lavender. The problem is, she keeps grinding it up to make medicines.'

Even so, he walked over to one of the baskets of lavender and gave her a small handful. 'Twist this into a bundle and make a wish. Then toss it into the fires tonight.'

Honora accepted the fragrant herbs and began twisting the strands into a knot. There was so much to wish for, she hardly knew where to begin.

They walked alongside one another, and Connor suddenly tensed at the sight of a young maiden standing with a group of girls. Her long dark hair was twined with ribbons and flowers.

'Is something wrong?' Honora asked.

Connor looked murderous. 'She's too young for this.'

'Who?'

'My daughter, Rhiannon.' He crossed his arms across his chest, and it was then that Honora noticed the young men watching the girls. Connor looked as though he wanted to cut their throats and leave them out to bleed.

'Too young for what?'

A savage look glittered in his eyes. 'Too young to be thinking of kissing a lad. Or, worse, taking a lover. She's only thirteen, for the love of Danu.' His left hand went to his sword hilt, and it was then that Honora noticed the scars.

Connor saw the direction of her gaze. 'Don't worry. If any of them dares to lay a hand on my daughter, I can use my sword well enough.'

Honora spied similar scarring upon his right palm. That one looked even more injured, the fingers twisted into an unnatural shape. 'What happened to you?'

He sobered. 'I was punished for a crime I did not commit. But thanks be, Aileen saved my hands. And my life.' He held them up for her inspection. 'If it weren't for her, I might have lost them.'

'Do they hurt?' She couldn't imagine such a life, being unable to fully use her hands.

'No. They're not as pretty as my face, but they can do what's needed.' Connor winked, and his teasing nature set her at ease once more. 'Now if you'll excuse me, there are some lads I need to kill.'

'Your daughter will be humiliated.'

'She might,' Connor admitted. 'But she'll keep her virtue.'

As he stalked towards the young men, Honora hid her smile. All around her, she smelled the yeasty scent of fresh bread. The blacksmith's hammer rang out amid the sounds of girls giggling and the lowing of cattle being gathered together. Though it was only the day before Midsummer's Eve, she could already feel the rising excitement.

Children practised against one another in foot races, while she heard the sound of steel upon steel in a nearby training field.

Just ahead, she saw several targets set up, while four women practised archery. While two of them were fairly skilled, the other two kept aiming too low, their arrows embedding in the ground.

With their hair braided back, wearing only the tight-sleeved *léine* underdresses, the women had more freedom of movement. But when Honora watched them make the same mistakes over and over again, she couldn't stop herself from approaching a red-haired woman, slightly younger than herself.

'Forgive me,' she said, knowing they would not understand her. The red-haired woman stopped, her expression confused. Honora pointed to the bow and asked, 'May I try?'

The woman exchanged a glance at her friends, but nodded. Honora picked up the weapon, feeling the wood, testing the bow string. It was a good bow, and she fitted an arrow, aiming it towards the target. She ripped at the bowstring, sending the arrow directly into the centre of the target.

The woman beamed at her, and started chattering at her in Irish. Honora gestured for the woman to take the bow back again, and she adjusted the woman's aim, slightly higher than where she had intended to shoot.

'You have to allow for the arrow to fall when you shoot,' she explained, feeling ridiculous for speaking to them in a language they didn't understand. But then Connor returned and translated her words. The woman tried again and this time, her arrow struck the straw target. Her smile beamed, and Connor said, 'I think you've made a friend with Noreen. She wants you to show the others. They are competing against the

Ó Phelan tribe in archery later on. If you could help them to win, they would be in your debt.'

Honora ventured a smile towards the women, nodding. The woman named Noreen took Honora's hand and introduced her to the others. Before long, Honora was showing each woman how to shoot properly. She took pride in watching them succeed. For this was something she knew well enough, even if she was not an adequate mistress of the household.

An hour later, the women bid her farewell, and Honora crossed over to watch the swordfighting. One of the older men wore the armour of a Norman knight. He ran the men through sparring exercises that she'd seen hundreds of times at her father's castle.

Entranced, she watched them, wishing she could join them. Like a violent dance, they slashed their swords, dodging blows and parrying thrusts. Her hand rested on the broken grip she'd tucked beneath the overdress, longing rising up within her.

When they stopped to rest, King Patrick approached her. Honora tried to curtsy, but he waved a dismissive hand. 'Was there something you needed? Or did you merely wish to watch?'

Actually, she'd wanted to participate. But first, she needed a sword of her own.

'I wanted to watch the warriors.' Truthfully, she hoped to choose the men who could join her in the fight for Ceredys. Though she had nothing to offer them here, she could promise them silver and jewels if they followed her to England.

The King led her to the training field. 'The men compete to be named the strongest. I suspect that will be Ewan.'

'He's changed a great deal since his fostering.' Honora walked alongside the King towards the *donjon*. 'In many ways.'

She stared up at the tall castle with its stone walls, wincing a little when they passed beneath the murder hole. As a girl, she'd never liked the sense of being watched. Sure enough, she caught a glimpse of young Liam before he thought better of throwing the mud cake he held in his grimy hands.

'Are you going to wed my brother?' King Patrick asked. There was a note of disapproval in his voice.

Honora stopped walking, startled at his confrontation. 'He hasn't asked.' And though it broke her heart to think of it, she wasn't certain she could say yes if he did. She didn't want to wed a man who was constantly in search of riches, falsely believing it was what she wanted. 'And I must first protect my own people. Ewan knows this.'

Patrick pointed to the practice field. 'Sir Anselm, the Norman knight you saw training my men, can help you to address the men. I cannot promise any of them will join in your fight, but you can ask. When you are ready to leave, we will provide you with safe passage.'

Honora finally looked up at the stony grey eyes of the King, grateful for his assistance. Though it was no guarantee she'd find any men to help, it was the first time she'd seen any hint of assistance. 'Thank you.'

She tried to curtsy, but he stopped her, shaking his head. 'I've seen the way Ewan watches you. And all of us want only his happiness.' Like an over-protective brother, he made his feelings clear.

'I would never do anything to hurt him.'

The King studied her, as though reaching inside to determine her worth. 'Then we understand each other.'

The morning of Midsummer's Eve cast a mystical veil over the MacEgan tribe. Flowers hung everywhere, and not a single hearth burned. All had been extinguished in preparation for the fires that night.

When Ewan reached Laochre, the air was buzzing with excitement. He saw his brother Bevan arriving with his wife, Genevieve. She leaned heavily upon her husband, her stomach rounded with pregnancy.

'You're looking well, Genevieve,' Ewan remarked, giving her a kiss of welcome.

'I feel like you should be herding me along with the other cows,' she teased. Ewan embraced her warmly, and her gaze turned shrewd. He didn't know what Bevan had told her, but Genevieve was studying him as though she didn't like what she'd heard. 'I didn't realise you chose Honora over her sister. My father told me many stories about her. Where is she?'

'I haven't seen her since yesterday,' he admitted.

Genevieve cast a look towards her husband, and Ewan quickly changed the subject. 'Will Trahern be here?'

His older brother was curiously absent. Renowned for his storytelling, Trahern rarely missed a festival.

Bevan shook his head. 'Not this time.'

'Why? What happened?' Ewan couldn't imagine anything that would keep Trahern away.

'Something to do with a woman.'

The pointed look Bevan sent him was undeniable. Ewan did not shirk from the discerning gaze. But instead of reacting to his brother's unspoken question, he commented, 'Trahern will be missed. I hope he changes his mind.'

Bevan gave a nod. 'So do I.' He kissed his wife on the cheek and added, 'Go and rest, Genevieve. You're looking pale. I'll join you later.'

Ewan excused himself and walked towards the crowd gathering. He bypassed the children's games and the horse racing, until he reached the games of skill. He watched the men wrestling, mentally noting which of the fighters had the greatest abilities.

The sound of metal striking metal rang out in the field, and after a time he went to join the sword contests. A large crowd had gathered around, and he could hardly see the fighters. All around him, men cast wagers upon the match.

Ewan reached for a silver coin of his own. He didn't often wager on a match, but this one had caught the eye of his kinsmen.

Ruarc MacEgan, his cousin, was cheering along with the others. Ewan moved in, straining to see the fighters.

'Is it Connor?' he asked Ruarc.

Either his brother or Patrick must be one of the swordsmen, for such a large group to encircle the area. Men and women alike were calling out for their own champion.

'It's one of the Ó Phelan bastards.' Ruarc grinned. 'And a woman is skinning his arse.'

Ewan's good humour evaporated. No. She wouldn't dare.

But then again, Honora St Leger was as unpredictable as the rain. No other woman was as skilled as she, nor as bold. Without another word to his cousin, he forced his way through the crowd.

Honora stood, facing off against one of the Ó Phelan tribesmen. She wasn't wearing a *léine* or overdress, but instead wore a pair of man's trews, held up by a rope. The trews were tight against her form, and he doubted if he was the only man who'd noticed the curve of her hips. Around her torso, she wore a tunic and *ionar* jacket. Her hair was tied in a short braid against the back of her neck.

Arrogant and cocky, Ó Phelan let out a roar and charged towards Honora. His sword slashed down, and Ewan reached for his own sword, ready to move into the fight.

But Honora parried the blow, nimbly leaping out of the way. Ó Phelan circled her, rage glittering upon his face. 'Are the lot of you such cowards that you send a woman to fight?'

'Even our women are stronger than the best of the Ó Phelans!' Ruarc shouted back, to the approval of the crowd.

But Ewan didn't share their laughter. All he could see was his woman, facing a dangerous enemy with nothing but a blade. She'd insulted the man's pride, and Ó Phelan would not grant her mercy. He might not kill her, but he would not hesitate to break a bone or draw blood.

Damn her. Why had she done this? There was no need for it. He tried to move into the circle, but a strong arm held him back. It was Patrick, his brother.

'No. Let her finish this.' There was a glint of approval in Patrick's eyes. 'You never told me she could fight.'

'I trained her.'

'Well done of you.' Patrick nodded thoughtfully. 'It isn't a bad idea. There are several of our own women who might do as well. It would double our forces.'

'You're not serious.'

His brother shrugged. 'Against a trained Norman army, one does what one must. And few would expect a woman to be so skilled.'

Honora braced herself with the shield, then stepped neatly away, sending her opponent sprawling.

The Ó Phelan let out a foul curse, but found himself facing the point of Honora's sword at his throat.

'I win,' she said quietly. Although few understood her Norman language, the victory was clear.

The combined noise of the crowd was nearly deafening. Ewan was struck by the coins changing hands and the large bag of silver that Honora received. Against the odds, she'd defeated her enemy.

Ewan moved forward, but he was nearly trampled by the men and women trying to reach her.

Honora tried to keep her smile, but as the people swarmed around her, she grew less confident.

Ewan pulled Honora free, and didn't hesitate to let his tribesmen see his displeasure. They backed away, eventually leaving them in peace.

'Now what in the name of Belenus was that about?' he demanded of her. 'You just humiliated one of the Ó Phelans.

Our peace with that tribe was fragile enough before you destroyed it.'

She held out the bag of silver, her eyes cool. 'Here. For the land you want so badly.'

The weight of the coins was heavy triple what he'd received from the sale of his cattle. Ewan shoved the coins back. 'I don't want them. I want to know what possessed you to fight where anyone could see you.'

Her eyes flashed, and before he realised it, she'd drawn her blade upon him. With a sword pressed against his throat, she snarled, 'Because I won't hide any more. This is who I am. It's who I've always been. And I am tired of pretending to be someone I'm not.'

Her flushed cheeks and the rigid anger made her face deeply alluring. In spite of the sword pressed against his skin, he wanted to drag her against him and kiss her. He wanted to mark her for his own, to make her understand that she was his.

'And who are you, Honora?'

'I am a warrior.'

Honora left Ewan standing there, the bag of coins at his feet. A sense of liberation filled her up inside. She should have done this long ago.

Ewan didn't like it, not at all. She'd seen the way he'd watched her fight, his hand resting on his own sword hilt as though he were ready to rescue her. He lacked faith that she would win.

Her spirits fell, and she knew that Ewan, unlike his tribesmen, was not pleased by what she'd done. She removed herself from the festivities, walking back towards Laochre Castle.

He would not want to stay with her now; she was certain of it. And while the thought should have been reassuring, it cast a darkness over her heart.

She walked up the winding stone staircase to the solar,

where she found Genevieve MacEgan seated next to a tow-headed young boy, who was pushing a wooden cart across the floor. She was spinning, the thread easing through her fingers with practised ease.

'I brought your sword back,' Honora said, setting the weapon beside Genevieve.

The dark-haired woman smiled. Of Norman heritage, like herself, she had offered Honora the blade after speaking to her husband, Bevan.

'My father told me of your skills,' Genevieve admitted. 'He was quite proud of you.'

Honora let out the breath she hadn't known she was holding. 'The Earl of Longford was a kind man. I suppose I wasn't meant to enjoy my exile.' A chagrined smile met her lips. 'I didn't realise he knew about my secret.'

'He never minded. And he would be glad to see you marry Ewan, if that is your desire.'

Honora avoided answering the unspoken question. She sat down beside the young child and pushed the cart across the floor. The boy beamed and raced off to chase it.

'That is Connor's son Finn,' Genevieve said. 'He is being fostered with Bevan and myself, along with his twin brother, Dylan.' She put her spinning aside, resting her hands upon her swelling stomach. 'I hope this new baby is another son. I love boys.'

'I wish you well with the birth.' Honora ventured a smile, though the idea of bearing her own child sent a panic through her.

Genevieve's serenity calmed her. 'It will go well enough. I have faith.'

Finn sent his wooden cart racing across the floor until it bumped against Honora's knee. He pursued it and plopped down in her lap as he picked up the cart. The familiarity of the child startled her, and she couldn't resist offering him a hug.

'Do you want children of your own?' Genevieve asked.

Honora shook her head. She couldn't imagine anything more terrifying. 'I would not be a good mother. I was never taught how to care for a child.'

A laugh escaped Genevieve. 'No amount of training is ever enough to be a mother. But your instincts guide you. That, and your babe won't stop crying until you discover what it is they want.'

Turning the subject to another, she added, 'I understand you fought well today.'

'I defeated the Ó Phelan tribesman,' Honora admitted. 'But Ewan was not pleased with me.'

'He probably wishes he had been given the opportunity first.' Genevieve smiled. 'If I know Ewan, he's likely jealous.'

'It's more than that,' Honora confessed. 'He'd be happy if I never touched a weapon again. He'd prefer it if I stayed home and tended the hearth.'

Genevieve tilted her head to the side. 'Don't be too sure of that. You aren't the first woman he trained.'

Honora's gaze narrowed. The sword she'd borrowed was thinner and lighter, easier to wield. 'This was yours?'

'I used to practise swordplay with Ewan when I first came to Laochre,' Genevieve admitted. 'My father wasn't pleased at first, but after I married Bevan, he relented. Then, of course, he told my mother that it was entirely his idea.' She continued spinning, her fingers moving across the wool. 'I haven't used a sword in many years, though. And I was never as skilled as you, from what Ewan tells me.'

She reached out for the sword hilt and offered it back to Honora. 'Take this. It was a gift from Ewan, long ago. I should like you to have it. He won't mind.'

The lightweight sword was perfect, its blade well-balanced and the hilt polished. But Honora declined the gift, saying, 'I really shouldn't.'

'Keep it,' Genevieve insisted. 'And if you don't mind my

interfering, I think you should return to Ewan.' With a wicked smile, she continued, 'Greet him naked in his home, and let him beg your forgiveness.'

Chapter Nineteen

That night, the tribesmen and women lit the fires upon the hillsides. The priest, Father Brían, offered a blessing of his own for the forthcoming summer. Every man, woman and child circled the fires three times in a clockwise direction, stopping to drop handfuls of pebbles upon the flames.

Then young men took turns, leaping across the flames. A newly wedded couple joined hands and jumped across the fire, laughing and sharing in a passionate kiss afterwards.

Ewan stood back, unwilling to watch them. It made him think of Honora and the power she held over him. He'd tried to stay away from her, but it was like trying to give up food and drink. He'd missed holding her, stroking her smooth skin and tasting the hint of apples when he kissed her.

When he'd seen the Ó Phelan's sword swinging towards her earlier, he'd wanted to drag her away from the match. She could have been killed in a heartbeat, and he'd have been too late to stop it.

Then she'd cast the bag of silver at his feet, and his anger had deepened. Her win had bothered him, not only because of the unnecessary danger, but because she'd cast up his desire for wealth in his face. He couldn't accept them.

He'd asked Patrick to hold the silver for safekeeping, and

Honora could use it to buy her army. He sobered at the thought. It was a fool's errand, wanting to overthrow John of Ceredys. But it meant everything to her. Honora would never belong to him until she had laid the past to rest.

And he would do what was necessary to relieve that burden.

From behind him, he scented Honora's light floral fragrance. 'You're angry with me,' came her voice.

'I was.' He hadn't wanted her to risk her own safety against an enemy tribe.

Honora stepped into view and he saw that she had discarded the men's trews. An emerald overdress and white *léine* accentuated the lines of her figure, while around her shoulders she wore a long crimson *brat*. The shawl offered warmth against the evening chill, the flash of colour bright against her skin. At her waist, she wore a sword he had once given to Genevieve. As if embarrassed by it, her hand covered the hilt.

'Genevieve offered this to me. She said it was a gift from you, years ago. Would you rather I returned it to her?'

'No.' The sword reminded him of his awkward youth, when he'd sparred against Genevieve. He'd had the weapon made as a wedding gift, and the weapon was lighter, intended for a woman's palm. 'Keep it. Your dagger isn't of use to you any more.'

'Thank you.' She stood beside him, as though she didn't know what else to say. Her cropped hair was longer now, brushing her shoulders. He wanted to touch it, to draw her close in a warm kiss. But there was a cool distance surrounding Honora, an invisible warning.

'Will you walk with me?' He reached out to take her hand. 'I want to show you something.' He pointed towards the hillside where one of the fires had burned down to glowing embers.

She looked doubtful, but nodded. 'All right.'

He led her up the hillside, trudging through the long grasses. The night air was warm, but it did little to assuage the uneasiness he felt inside. He sensed that there was more Honora hadn't said.

As the incline grew steeper, they used both hands and feet to climb higher. One side of the hill levelled out, and from the vantage point they could see across the land, to the sea upon the horizon. Above them, one of the fires blazed. Encircled by earth and stones, the fire had burned upon this sacred hillside for as long as he could remember.

He sat down upon on outcropping of stone, leaning back against the hill. Honora did the same, and for a time there was nothing, save the popping of the fire and the distant sound of rolling waves. Below, near the festivities, came the sounds of laughter, conversation and music.

Honora reached down and plucked a handful of grass, twisting it into a bundle. 'Is it true what Connor said? That if I toss this into the fire, I can make a wish?'

'It is.'

She grew pensive, as if imagining her heart's desire. When she tossed the grass on to the embers, it smouldered, the edges flaring briefly before it died into smoke.

'What did you wish for?' he asked.

A wistful smile touched her lips. 'Victory.' She lay down beside him upon the hill, a short distance away from the fire. Her fingers twined with his, and together they stared up at the stars glowing against the night sky.

'It's beautiful,' she said, the curve of a smile at her lips. 'It reminds me of the night we spent outside when we were younger.'

'The Earl had me whipped for sneaking out.' He propped his head up on his elbow, watching her. 'And you thought it was a wonderful adventure.'

'It was. I have no regrets. I'd never slept out of doors, and it felt like I was one of the soldiers, going off to battle.' She turned to look at him, her body reclining against the grass. With only the firelight and the moon shining upon her, she looked like the goddess Danu, waiting to greet her lover.

'You fought well this afternoon,' he said at last, leaning upon one elbow to face her. 'But I don't understand why you felt the need to compete against the men.'

'Because there were no women to fight me?' Though she spoke the words with a light teasing note, he didn't smile.

'Why?' he repeated.

She kept her gaze upon the stars. 'You've always been able to fight. At any time, any place. You never had to hide your skills.'

Her hand lowered to touch the sword hilt at her waist. 'I've hidden behind a suit of chainmail armour so that no one would know I was a woman. And I am weary of it.'

She continued. 'My father would have whipped me, had he known. And Ranulf—' She stopped speaking, her chest rising as if to shut out the words. 'He forbade me to touch any blade, ever again. Not after that first night.'

'What happened?'

'He was rough with me during the bedding,' she admitted. 'I didn't think. I just grabbed my dagger.' Her knuckles tightened. 'I cut my own husband.'

'Good.' It was all he could manage to strike back the jealous rage. The bastard had hurt her, taken her innocence. If Ranulf weren't already dead, he'd have had no difficulty killing the Baron.

'They kept me a prisoner in my own home,' Honora continued. 'Only Marie helped me.' She sat up, drawing her knees to her chest. 'I'd never felt so helpless. I was afraid of Ranulf and John.'

'Anyone would be afraid, after what you endured.'

'I didn't like the woman I became when I was there.'

He sat up and moved behind her, pulling her back to his chest. With his arms around her, he tried to grant her comfort.

And though she held him in a light embrace, his senses warned that she was slipping away, like water through his fingers.

'You couldn't accept me fighting openly, could you?'

Ewan thought about lying to her, of saying what she wanted to hear. But it wasn't about her abilities—it was about wanting to protect her. It went against every instinct he had, to let her fight.

Slowly, he shook his head. 'It isn't that I don't believe you can fight. You've proven that before. But I'd never allow another man to hurt you. I couldn't stand back and watch.'

Though he understood her desire to cast off the façade of helplessness, neither could he go through his own life waiting for the moment when someone would strike her down. For warriors tempted fate at every turn.

She pulled out the broken pieces of her dagger and set them in his hands. 'If I can't fight, this is all I am. I have no value, no use at all.'

He took the pieces and returned them to the girdle at her waist. Then he set her hand upon the sword hilt at her side. 'You can fight, Honora. But not alone.'

He lowered his mouth to her neck in a soft kiss. He felt the wetness of her silent tears.

'I'm going to Ceredys in a few days,' she said. 'Your brother Patrick offered to let me talk to some of his soldiers.'

'No.' His arms tightened around her. 'Putting yourself in John's path is foolishness. It's a battle you can't win.'

She coloured at the reminder. 'I'd rather fight him and lose, than remain here like a coward.'

'Don't you understand?' Ewan wanted to shake some sense into her. 'He desires you. He will force himself upon you if you go near him again.'

Her face turned furious. 'And what do you think he's been doing to the women of Ceredys? He made me watch while he took them, one after the other. Because I refused him.'

Her rage ignited, and she pulled free of his embrace, rising to her feet. 'With every day I'm here, they continue to suffer. I can't stand back and let it continue.'

There would be no dissuading her. He could see the futility of it. But he'd not let her go alone. He would follow her and ensure that she was safe, regardless of her arguments.

Honora let out a shuddering sigh. 'It was my fault he violated them. Mine, because I would not endure his advances. I threatened his life if he touched me.'

'It isn't your fault at all,' he argued. 'You aren't accountable for what he did.'

'I still blame myself.'

There was nothing he could say to ease her guilt, but he pulled her back into his arms, caressing her cheek with his knuckles. Without thinking, he touched his mouth to hers in a light kiss.

A mistake.

Her mouth met his with hunger and fire, and he held her tightly, showing her with his body and his kiss how much he desired her. The fierce possessiveness, the need to keep her safe, drowned out all reason.

Honora broke free and took a step back, as if she needed the physical distance. Her breathing was rushed, her arms wrapped tightly around her. 'I can't lie with you tonight, Ewan. I am sorry.'

She was widening the distance, separating herself in preparation for the forthcoming fight. With a chilling clarity, he realised what this was about. She didn't expect to come back alive. She was expecting to die in this battle, giving up her life for her people.

'You're not going to face John alone, Honora.' He took her hand, walking back with her towards the castle.

'Of course not,' she argued. 'I'm hiring men of your tribe. With the silver I won from the fight with Ó Phelan.'

'I'll be among them,' he said quietly. He didn't care how

angry she was. This was about her life, her safety. And he'd not remain at home.

'I don't need you stepping in as though I can't protect myself.' She pulled her hand away, anger punctuating her words.

'Oh, I've no doubt that you are quite capable.' He reached out and touched her chin with his finger. 'But I would give up my own life, before I'd let John harm you.'

Honora didn't speak a word, her eyes filled with defensive fury. She mistakenly believed that he lacked faith in her skills.

'We aren't finished yet, Honora,' he murmured. 'Not at all.'

Chapter Twenty

T he silver was not enough. Honora had suspected as much, but she'd managed to hire two men. She had selected a younger fighter, a man named Bres, whom she'd seen in the competitions earlier. He would be hungry to prove himself. After Bres, she'd chosen Conand, a man who was half-Norse and had a great deal of experience fighting against the Normans. King Patrick had also granted her the knight, Sir Anselm, who would accompany them to England.

An army of three. Dear saints, she needed a miracle.

'Farewell,' Genevieve said, kissing her cheek. 'If you happen to see my father, give him my love.'

Though she was unsure of how things would transpire at Ceredys, Honora managed a smile. 'When all of this is over, perhaps I will visit him.'

Queen Isabel walked over to join them. She held out a wrapped bundle to Honora. 'I had your gown repaired. But you are welcome to keep the *léine* and overdress I gave you.'

Honora thanked her, and the Queen held her hands a moment longer. With a serious expression, she noted, 'You don't have enough men for this battle.'

'No,' Honora admitted. 'But the men of Ceredys will help

us.' *Especially those seeking vengeance on behalf of their wives and daughters,* she thought darkly.

'You have my prayers,' Isabel offered. 'And I bid you a safe journey.'

'Will you grant me your prayers as well, Isabel?' a male voice asked from behind them.

Honora turned and was struck to see Ewan wearing a full suit of chainmail armour. His dark blond hair hung down below a metal helm, and a sword was sheathed at his waist.

Oh, Jesu. Ewan had really meant it when he'd said he was coming with her. She didn't want this, didn't want him commanding the attack. She'd warned him before that this was her battle to face.

Dressed like a Norman fighter, he was every inch the warrior. Honora's mouth went dry, just to look at him. Powerful and dominant, Ewan held the confidence of a man who knew he would win.

'You will always have my prayers, Ewan.' The Queen stood on tiptoes and kissed him on the cheek. He bid farewell to his brothers and their wives before striding towards the coastline.

Before she could voice a protest, Ewan spoke rapidly in Irish to his kinsmen, giving orders. They nodded in agreement, walking along the shore where the boat was waiting. The vessel was larger than the one they had arrived on, and it enabled them to take horses. Each man had his own mount, and Honora had surrendered the last of her silver for her own mare.

Bres was helping the horses on board the boat, leading them through the water and onto an elevated ramp. Ewan had reached the water's edge and was following the path of the horses.

Honora hurried faster until she caught up. 'Where do you think you're going?'

His eyes gleamed. 'You already know the answer to that, Honora. As I've said, you'll be getting another fighter.' He removed his helm and stepped into the boat, reaching for her waist to help her inside.

'And one more,' came a different voice, speaking her language. Honora glanced over her shoulder and saw a man with a terrifying appearance. His head was shaved, his face devoid of any hair. Cold grey eyes stared into hers.

Ewan stood, his face transfixed with shock. 'Trahern. My God, when did you arrive? What's happened to you?'

The man was so large, Honora had to lean her head back to see his face. Built like a giant, his excessive height would intimidate anyone.

'I arrived last night. Patrick told me you needed fighters.' His steel eyes bored into her own, and Honora forced herself to stare back. She would not let him intimidate her.

When she got a closer look at the man, her wariness deepened. This was a man who didn't care if he lived or died. Perhaps he was seeking death, from the look of it.

'This is my older brother Trahern,' Ewan introduced, clasping his brother's hand in greeting.

Honora gave a nod. 'I have no more silver,' she managed. 'I'm afraid I cannot pay another fighter.'

'Like Ewan, my services require no coin.' He barked out an order in Irish to the men who were moving the ramp away from the vessel. 'I fight of my own will.'

The giant sat down, fixing his gaze upon the sea. Not towards his family, nor his kinsmen.

Ewan lifted his hand in farewell as they set their course for England. But not once did Trahern look back. Only when Erin was far in the distance, did he shift his attention to the occupants of the boat.

'Did you find her?' Ewan asked. 'The woman you sought?'

Anguish flashed over the man's face, and Trahern shook his head. 'She's dead.'

Honora wondered if the woman was someone he'd loved. But Trahern offered no further explanations. It was clear, he had no desire to talk about it.

When she met Ewan's gaze, she understood his unspoken

message. He was here to protect her, whether she wanted his help or not.

It hadn't resonated with her earlier, the realisation that Ewan was not going to let her go. Aye, she'd been angry, feeling that he didn't trust her abilities.

But that wasn't why he was here.

It struck her that she'd have done the same. If he were about to face an enemy in a battle he might not win, she would be at his side. Her throat closed up, her gaze drifting downwards.

She would be as lost as Trahern if anything happened to Ewan MacEgan. For she was falling in love with him.

They ate a light meal that night, of bread, roasted mutton and crisp spring peas. Trahern didn't speak, though Ewan attempted to coax his brother into conversation.

Before the evening light faded, Honora decided to seek Ewan's help with the parchment. She reached into a fold of her overdress and withdrew the broken dagger grip. Removing the scrap of vellum, she handed it to Ewan. 'I've decided to look for the treasure. Marie would have wanted me to find it, else she wouldn't have hidden the parchment.'

'It might not exist.'

She knew it, but if it did, Marie had tried to protect it from John.

Ewan unfolded the vellum. 'I think the markings across the bottom are runes. I'll ask Conand. His mother was Norse, and he might be able to translate it.'

He spoke to the Irishman, handing him the parchment. Conand stared at the pattern of runes, his mouth moving silently. When at last he looked up, his expression was a mixture of interest and fear. 'It's a curse. Upon those who seek to gain the fortune of the gods.'

Ewan adjusted one of the sails, tying it down, but Honora could tell he was listening. 'Go on,' she said.

'The birds represent gold,' Conand explained. 'And the man who seeks to find it must overcome the power of Ægir.'

'Who is Ægir?' Honora asked.

'The Norse sea god.'

His revelation made perfect sense. Marie St Leger had been fond of the sea, taking many walks along the shoreline. Honora had often accompanied her, and they'd walked barefoot in the sand.

If any treasure was to be found, it could be hidden somewhere along the coast.

'We'll make camp on the shoreline,' Honora said. 'Search along the beach. If you find anything, I'll offer you a share in the gold.'

The men's eyes brightened with anticipation. Bres, in particular, had the eagerness of youth. Barely nineteen, he reminded Honora of Ewan. She smiled, thinking of it.

Ewan took off the *ionar* he'd worn, folding the jacket to form a soft pillow. 'Get some sleep, Honora. I'll mind the boat.'

'We'll take turns,' Trahern corrected.

Honora knew nothing about sailing and was content to let them guide the vessel. She closed her eyes, resting her head upon Ewan's garment.

It was a mistake. She could feel the warmth of his body, smell his scent. It was like sleeping beside him, and an uncomfortable awareness crept into her mind. Her eyes flitted open, and she saw him watching her.

His body was silhouetted by the dying sun, his posture tense. He carried the weight of the chainmail armour as though it were nothing. Muscles seemed to strain against the tiny links, the armour moulding around his large form.

She wanted to touch him again.

Troublesome thoughts mulled around in her head, and she shifted her position so as to watch him without his knowledge. The night air was growing colder, and she huddled against the side of the boat, as if the wood could warm her.

* * *

When the sky finally turned dark, only the stars and moon-light remained to guide them. Ewan took his turn guiding the vessel, and when Bres replaced him at the helm, she sensed movement coming closer to her.

'Honora,' Ewan whispered. There was a warmth in his voice, as well as a questioning tone.

'I'm cold,' she admitted.

'Will you allow me to warm you?'

She nodded, but then realised he could not see her response. 'Please.'

Before he did so, he eased her towards the back of the boat, away from both horses and men. Isolated from everyone, she could almost pretend they were alone.

She huddled close, and at first, the cold chainmail links were a shock against her skin. Ewan settled her upon his lap, wrapping his cloak around her like a warm blanket. Beneath her cheek, she could hear his heart beating faster.

No one broke the silence of the night. Only the creaking of the boat and the light sound of wind whipping the sails interrupted the stillness. Honora tried to close her eyes, but all she could think was how right it was, being in Ewan's arms.

She didn't want to leave him. She needed the warmth of his embrace, to be intimate with him. The very thought of any other woman being a part of his life made her want to reach for a sword.

'Ewan?' she whispered, her voice barely audible.

His reply was to hold her closer, his mouth leaning down to her ear. 'What is it?'

The hardness of his body pressed up against hers made her ache for him. She didn't know what to say, nor how to tell him that she wanted him desperately. She turned around in his lap to face him, her legs straddling his waist. Her hands moved up to his cheeks, feeling the coolness of his skin.

Already her body was warming. Except for Bres, the rest of the men were asleep. They were virtually alone, and in the darkness, she could see no one.

Beneath the cloak, they had complete privacy. Honora slid her hands beneath the heavy armour, reaching under his tunic to touch his bare skin. Ewan let out a soft hiss, and she pressed her mouth against his.

He didn't ask questions, but devoured her lips. Instantly, she grew liquid, her body melting into his. The metal links of his armour seemed to brand against her skin, while his palms cupped her bottom. She tightened her legs around his waist, and his hard length was evident beneath his trews.

Jesu, she never should have started this. Although the men were asleep and it was so dark she couldn't see her fingers in front of her face, she was afraid of being discovered.

Just a kiss. That was all it was.

Her mouth moved against him as though she couldn't get enough. She fought to keep silent, but when his hands inched beneath her skirts, she nearly let out a cry.

'Can you remain quiet?' he whispered against her ear. His mouth closed over the lobe, sending shivers through her. 'How strong are you?'

She rose up to his own ear, tasting the curve of him. 'Strong enough for you.'

Beneath the cloak, his hand moved against her wetness, arousing her deeply. His fingers slid inside, flexing into her body. Entering, then withdrawing. Slow and smooth.

With each stroke, Honora bit her lips to keep from making a sound. She shifted against him, her body straining for the fulfilment he could bring. It was the most intensely carnal sensation she'd ever experienced, to be surrounded by others while the man she loved was touching her.

Forbidden. Wicked.

He fumbled his hand beneath her and a moment later, his fingers were replaced with something else. Without warning, her weight slid against the thickness of his manhood, and he filled her. Making love like this, with others around them, was something she'd never done—never expected to do. And because it was Ewan, she climaxed immediately.

Her womanhood convulsed around him, his unexpected motion sending her over the edge. Ewan cut off her sound with his mouth, kissing her fiercely. He held her tightly as her wetness spasmed against his length. And then, when she was pliant against him, her body spent, he let the quiet rocking of the boat move them together.

Her knees rested against the bottom of the boat while Ewan sat back. She couldn't see the expression on his face, but she lifted herself a fraction and sank back down. He was buried so deep inside, she could feel his sac resting against her womanhood.

His mouth came down on hers again, relentless and driven as he fused their bodies together to the rhythm of the waves. Her fingernails bit into the chainmail armour, and she tasted blood. She was past caring where they were or who was around them. All that mattered was joining with him, telling him without words just how much she loved him.

The barest movement of the waves sent her weight thrusting down upon him. It was taking Ewan apart while he tried not to make a sound. Her unexpected kiss and his own lust had sent all reason spinning into madness.

He didn't know what had caused Honora to kiss him, but he wasn't about to turn her away. He sensed that she needed him, and though he could not guess why she'd changed her mind, he couldn't stop himself from claiming her.

The problem was, she had become the conqueror this time.

It had seemed like an interesting way to shock her, to see what she would do if he became her lover again. But he'd fallen under her spell now, and it was too late to turn back. Though he wanted to press her down into the boat, thrusting deep inside until she cried out her release, he couldn't. And knowing that they could be caught at any moment added a delicious new aspect.

She was close to another climax now. Pressing her lips against his, her tongue slid inside his mouth. He captured it, tangling with her in a different type of battle.

His length was so hard, he gritted his teeth. He adjusted the long cloak again, though likely no one could see them. Gripping the fabric closed with one hand, he used the other to guide her up, and then down again upon his erection.

'Let yourself go,' she whispered against his ears. Her silky wetness bounced against him, squeezing him tight. He drove in as deeply as he dared, making her ride him, just as the boat skimmed the waves again.

And then his body erupted, spilling into her depths and giving him one of the most intense releases he'd ever had. Her arms gripped his neck so tightly, she dipped down again. He was rewarded with her body shaking, and he kissed her again to cut off any sounds she might have made.

She rested against him, her thighs around his waist, her skirts tangled up. Laying her head against his chest, he held her so close their hearts might have become one. Against her ear, he murmured, 'There will never be any other woman for me but you.'

Her lips kissed his temple. 'None other, but you,' she promised.

For now, it was enough.

When the boat landed within Morecambe Bay, along the northwest shore of England, Honora guided them to a safe place to land. 'There are areas of quicksand,' she'd warned.

Ewan had deferred to her knowledge and when she had found a safe place for them to disembark, they set their anchor and brought in the horses.

Honora wanted Bres and Conand to begin traversing the beach for anything that could lead to the treasure. In the meantime, Ewan planned to study the area with Trahern and discern what John was up to.

'I want to go with you,' Honora had said. 'I know Ceredys better than either of you.'

'They'll recognise you too easily,' Ewan argued. 'We're not going to confront him—we're going to scout out his location. I'll come back, and we'll form a plan together.'

His promise pacified her, and Honora stayed behind with Bres and Conand while they rode east.

Several dozen sheep grazed in the meadow, while a narrow stream ran towards the castle. A small grove of trees stood a slight distance from the village, and Ewan motioned for his brother to follow him. They dismounted, hidden within the copse of oak and rowan. 'Tether the horses, and we'll split up,' Ewan ordered. 'I don't want anyone knowing we're here.' He sent a hard look to his older brother. 'Don't be caught.'

'Watch your own skin, my brother. And I'll watch mine.'

Gone was the teasing nature of Trahern. There was a time when Ewan had relied upon Trahern to break a darker mood with his lighthearted stories. But now, the change in his brother was palpable. Trahern had confessed that he'd lost Ciara, the woman he'd planned to marry. It had cut his brother down as badly as when Bevan had lost his first wife.

Ewan wasn't about to let the same happen to him. Honora was his, and he would guard her at all costs. Though he didn't know what had prompted their night together on the boat, it gave him the greatest hope of all. She had promised that there would be no other man but him. And God help them both, he would see to it that no man ever harmed her.

A premonition seized him, his skin prickling. He'd left her back on the beach, with only two men as her protection. It wasn't enough. If John approached…

But then, Ceredys would have to ride past them to reach the shoreline. Ewan pushed the apprehensions away, forcing himself to concentrate upon the fortress. The motte-and-bailey structure showed signs of disrepair, with breaches in the outer walls and vines covering the spaces. A square fortress, it was still built mostly of wood with a few stone walls.

The village was composed of thatched roundhouses, and more than one showed signs of being burned. Charred straw hung from the rooftops, while other sections were hardly repaired at all. Perhaps the Baron's form of punishment, to those who could not pay their rents.

The fields were sparse with grain, showing signs of a weak harvest, come the end of the summer. Neglect and death seemed to permeate the lands. As they moved in closer, an unnatural silence seemed to hang over the land.

Ewan kept his hand upon his weapon as they crouched low. Two serfs saw them, but made no greeting. There was hopelessness in their posture, as if they no longer cared. Ewan motioned for Trahern to move to the right side of the outer wall while he investigated the breach at the left point.

He spied several guards patrolling the gates, so he kept low as he traversed the outer perimeter. It was possible to move inside the wall by squeezing through the stones, but as he eyed the crevice, he had a vision of getting stuck, just as before.

Too late to worry about that now.

Ewan moved slowly, working his way through the breach. The vines kept him hidden, while the fallen stones offered a clear view of the outer bailey. He hoped to God that the entire wall would not collapse on him as he slipped inside.

Peering within, Ewan spied holes everywhere. The castle grounds had been torn apart, as though John had ordered his men to dig up the entire bailey. He heard voices arguing, and John's voice mingled with another man's. Glancing towards his brother on the far side of the entrance, Ewan motioned his intent to move in.

Not far from his vantage point was a wooden cart, waiting to be unloaded. It was a possible hiding place, one that would offer protection from the guards.

Ewan waited for the right moment, then kept his position low as he dived beneath the cart. Though he couldn't see John clearly, he could hear the argument.

'Find her. It won't be hard to locate the MacEgan lands in Erin. I want her brought back to Ceredys.'

'My lord, we are doing all that we can.'

'You should have loosed your arrows upon them both,' John cursed. 'She knows where the St Leger treasure lies. And I'll see her flesh stripped away, piece by piece, before I'll let Honora take what belongs to me.'

Ewan had heard enough. He didn't like leaving Honora alone on the beach, especially now. But before he could make his way back to the outer wall, a rider entered the gates at full speed. After he dismounted, Ewan overheard the rider talking to John.

'My lord, she is here. A boat just arrived.'

'Bring her to me,' John ordered.

'As you wish, my lord.' The rider cleared his throat. 'But you should know she and her escorts are digging amidst the sand.'

'Are they?' John's voice turned softer. 'Good. Prepare my horse so that I may welcome the Lady of Ceredys home again. And bring the prisoner.'

A prisoner? Ewan didn't know what John meant by that, but he was running out of time to reach Honora's side. He held his position steady until he was able to abandon the cart. Racing back towards the wall, he pushed his way through the vines until Trahern followed. Once he saw that his brother was clear of any danger, Ewan quickened his pace back to the horses.

It seemed he would have his chance to kill John of Ceredys sooner than he'd thought.

There was nothing. Not a trace of the treasure, and Honora had scoured most of the pathway she had walked with Marie. She didn't even know what she was looking for.

'It's useless,' she remarked, but neither of the men understood her language. With no way to communicate with them, she was forced to wait for Ewan and Trahern's return.

Her mind felt disconnected, her fears rising. Though she had encouraged Ewan and Trahern to recruit other men from the village, she didn't know if the people of Ceredys would trust them. Visions of failure haunted her, and she feared for their safety.

She envisaged Ewan's face, his ragged blond hair and fierce green eyes. He had come here for her, though it meant risking his own life.

Last night, the truth had suddenly crystallised. Ewan wasn't at all like other men. Instead of taking over the assault plans on Ceredys, he had allowed her to take command, deferring to her orders. He could easily have imprisoned her back in Erin while he went off to fight. Instead, he'd remained at her side, steadfast and treating her as an equal. He meant everything to her, and once they made it through this ordeal, she was never going to leave his side.

A pensive smile tugged at her lips. And, if she somehow managed to find the St Leger treasure, she would give every last coin to him, to make his dreams into reality.

Sitting down upon a large rock, Honora studied the shoreline. A large expanse of sand lined the edge of Morecambe Bay. She had walked through the grasses nearly every day. Marie had warned her not to go beyond the path, saying, 'The tides are never predictable, and you must be careful not to stray.'

Honora had seen the bodies of men, washed up from a sudden flood. And so she had always heeded Marie's advice.

Rising to her feet, she began to walk down the hillside path, a worn stretch of dying grasses that she'd travelled often. Though Marie St Leger could not walk quickly, she'd often spoken of her love for the sea.

Honora thought again of the parchment and the curse of the sea god. She shielded her eyes, staring out at the water. Could the treasure be hidden beneath the waves? Such a location would be nearly impossible to find, for the tide was constantly shifting and changing. Nothing was constant.

Unless…

She stared back at the pathway, and then at the water. The tide was starting to reveal sand embankments, stretches of buried land. It was possible…

The tip of a stone outcropping emerged from the water. Honora's heart pounded as she saw the stone shaped like a bird. There.

She waved to Bres and Conand, pointing at the stone. There wasn't much time, only a few hours before the tidal patterns would shift again.

But if any man wanted to bury a treasure and make it difficult to find, this was the perfect spot, for it was the only stable ground. A haven in the midst of ever-changing waves.

When Conand approached, she motioned towards a small leather pouch he wore. 'I need that, if you don't mind.' He understood her gesturing and unlaced the pouch, handing it to her. When Honora pointed towards the stone outcropping, a smile spread over Conand's face.

'We need rope.' She gestured to the length of string that had bound the pouch to his belt, and pointed towards the boat in the distance. Conand spoke to Bres in Irish, and a moment later the younger man returned with a length.

Honora held on to the rope, testing her footing as she eased on to the grey sand of the Bay. The tide had eased back, revealing more of the beach. She gripped the rope, skirting a patch of quicksand that was revealed.

Slowly, steadily, she inched her way towards the rock. She didn't dare move any faster, for she could not trust the ground beneath her. Marie had filled her head with too many stories of folk who had been swept away by the tide. Or, worse, those who had stumbled into quicksand, buried alive.

When she reached the rock, she let go of the rope and ran her fingertips over the edges. Made of smooth limestone, it was buried deep below the sand. She knelt at its edge, feeling around for any crevices or fissures. There was a palm-sized opening near the side of the stone, and she reached deep within. Her hand closed over something small and round. Excited, she grasped it, but before she could examine it closely, she heard horses approaching.

Her mouth tightened when she spied John of Ceredys, not Ewan. Damn him. There was no time to search further.

She took the rope and used it to guide herself back to shore. Though she tried to move faster, still she kept her gaze firmly upon the sands. In the distance, the waves were getting rougher, the tips capped with white.

The sky grew darker, the afternoon shifting into evening. Honora reached Conand just as John and a small escort of men arrived. There was no sign of Ewan or Trahern, and a knot formed in her stomach.

Let them not be dead. Let them be safe, she prayed.

Amid their horses, John forced a prisoner to walk, bound and hooded. The figure wore shapeless clothing, and Honora could not tell if it was a man or a woman. The captive was smaller than she'd expected, perhaps an adolescent or a tall child. She reached for her sword, preparing herself for the worst.

The Baron brought his horse up to the edge of the path, his smile dark. 'I bid you welcome, my Lady of Ceredys.'

'What have you done?' she demanded, pointing towards the prisoner.

'I've brought you a gift. Find the Ceredys treasure, and I will let the prisoner go.'

'Who is he?' She tried to move towards the prisoner, but John stopped her with the tip of his own sword.

'Patience, my lady.' He dismounted, keeping his weapon directed towards her throat. 'I see you've been busy this day. What did you find?'

'Nothing.'

'But Marie told you to look here, didn't she? You know where the treasure lies.'

Honora didn't answer. 'Who is your prisoner?'

A harsh laugh erupted from John's throat. 'Someone who tried to rescue you. A fool.'

With a gesture towards his man-at-arms, the hood was ripped away.

And Honora stared into the eyes of her sister.

Chapter Twenty-One

‘**I**’m going after Honora. Stay here, and recruit more men to help us.’ Ewan readied his horse, preparing to mount. It had taken longer than he’d hoped to reach the safety of the trees and their horses. He had to move quickly, to reach the coast before John did.

‘You’re not going alone,’ Trahern argued.

Years of being told he was too young, too weak to fight, suddenly snapped his temper. Ewan grasped his taller brother and rammed him against one of the trees. ‘These people are the reason Honora returned. Free the captives, and get the women out. I’ve no doubt you can find their husbands and brothers to help us.’

While John was distracted, this was their chance to solicit help from the villagers. And they desperately needed more fighters.

‘I need you here,’ Ewan said quietly. ‘Bring as many men as you can.’

He saw the hesitation in Trahern’s eyes, the unwillingness to let him go. And so he struck the final blow. ‘Free them, the way you would have freed Ciara.’

Trahern’s dark grey eyes were cold and silent. But, at last, he gave a nod of assent, turning his back.

Ewan urged the horse into a hard gallop. As he rode, his mind seized up with fear. A dark hollowness invaded his heart at the thought of Honora coming to harm. He couldn't let it happen.

Though she wasn't alone, he didn't want her to face John without him. He couldn't strike out the memory of seeing her on the ground of the training field, John's sword at her throat. Or, worse, envisioning Honora as John's prisoner.

Wind tore at his face, while a light rain began to fall. When he reached the pathway, Ewan slowed the gelding slightly, to prevent the horse from stumbling. He hardly noticed Bres and Conand lying wounded on the beach, or Lady Katherine held prisoner by John's soldiers. All he could see was Honora, her sword in her hand, while John threatened her with his own weapon drawn.

Ewan urged the horse faster, not even aware of the sounds tearing from his throat as he charged towards the mounted Norman. With his sword raised, he slashed it downwards. His strike landed harmlessly upon Ceredys's shield when he turned.

The Norman wore full chainmail armour, his helm hiding the clipped fair hair. A faint red scar lined his cheek, the mark Honora had given. And it would not be the last scar he received.

Raising his own weapon, the Baron swung hard, and steel struck steel. Ewan drew his horse up beside Ceredys's and threw himself at the man, forcing him off his mount. The Norman twisted, and Ewan struck the sand first. The air knocked from his lungs, but he had no time to dwell upon it, for Ceredys shoved him towards the rearing horse's hooves.

Críost. Ewan tried to lurch sideways as he saw the animal stumble. John kept him pinned, but as the stallion started to fall, Ewan used all of his strength to avoid the crushing weight.

His right shoulder popped from its socket, the pain ripping through him. Ewan cursed, but his arm hung limp at his side.

He reached for his fallen sword with his left hand, but another weapon slid between them.

'He is mine, Ewan.' Honora's cool voice intruded, and she never took her eyes from John. 'This fight belongs to me.' Her face was flushed, her green eyes focused upon her quarry. There was no fear, only determination.

John got to his feet, a sneer upon his face. 'You haven't the strength to lift that sword for longer than a minute, Lady Honora.'

'Haven't I?' she mused. 'We'll find out.'

Ewan rose to his feet slowly, his left hand gripping the sword. Though every instinct told him to interfere, to move Honora to the side, he didn't. Until he could force his shoulder back into its socket, his sword arm was useless. She had a better chance at defeating John than he did.

But if she faltered in the slightest, he fully intended to intervene.

'Do it, then.' He met her gaze, offering her a confidence he didn't completely feel.

Her reaction was disbelief, before a faint smile spread over her face. This meant something to her, he realised. Not whether or not she won, but the chance to try.

'Are you going to hide behind a woman's skirts, MacEgan?' John taunted. He stood, gripping the sword in a tight grasp.

'I'd rather watch her defeat you,' Ewan found himself saying. Wincing at his shoulder, he stepped back, trying to ease the joint back into place.

Moving into her line of sight, Ewan urged, 'End this quickly, Honora.'

Honora adjusted her stance, waiting for John to make the first move. The Baron's patronising expression showed amusement. 'Your sister brought me great comfort in your absence.' He tapped his sword against hers, making mockery of his opening strike.

'You are a fool,' she said softly. 'My father will have your head removed if you've harmed a single hair upon her head.'

He exerted pressure against her blade, trying to disarm her. 'I thought the Lady Katherine might be useful in coaxing you home to Ceredys. It seems there was no need.'

Honora stepped backwards onto the sand. John swung hard, and she blocked his blow. He tried to force her blade away, but she held steady, her muscles tight. 'Let my sister go,' she commanded.

'Oh, she'll not be harmed, so long as she obeys.' He glanced towards Katherine, his expression hard. 'And so long as you show me the location of the treasure.'

'You don't know that it exists.'

'The ruby is proof of that, though you tried to steal it from me.' He lunged forwards, pressing his blade close to hers. 'But that isn't the only reason I want you at Ceredys.'

His eyes grew hooded with unspoken desire. It made her skin crawl, the way he seemed to touch her with his gaze. 'You could also do with a lesson on how to obey a man.'

'I am not in the habit of obedience,' Honora gritted out.

'Nor in womanly pursuits, it seems.' His sword struck hers once again, aggressively seeking a weakness. Honora met each blow with her own parry.

Though this fight went on longer than the last, she took satisfaction that she was not tiring beneath the onslaught. Over and over, her blade struck his, while Ewan watched.

He had stepped aside, letting her be the warrior she was. And, by God, giving her this chance to fight made her love him even more.

When John tried again to use his strength to disarm her, Honora leaned hard against his sword, forcing his weight sideways before she tripped him to the sand. His stunned expression made her seize the advantage. He tried to roll away, but she pinned him, her blade resting against his throat.

For a hard moment, she stared at him. This was the moment she had trained for, the chance to free her people. One slice was all it would take to end his life.

She stared into his eyes, this man she wanted to kill. And still she didn't move.

'Honora,' Ewan said softly. In his voice she sensed his silent support. And that he would finish what she could not.

John smiled. And seconds later, a handful of sand struck her eyes, burning and blinding her. He backhanded her face, and she saw stars. Out of instinct, Honora guarded her eyes, her hand reaching out to defend an unseen blow. Then suddenly, Ewan's sword struck John's, and the two men grappled together. She cried out, trying to clear the grit from her eyes.

With his shoulder dislocated, Ewan could only fight left-handed. Honora raced into the shallow water, scooping it into her eyes to wash the sand free. When her vision eased, she ran back to assist him.

She was too late. John had him trapped, a knife pointed at Ewan's bared throat.

'You can save his life, Honora,' he whispered. 'Find the treasure I've been seeking. Bring it to me.'

'There is no treasure.'

John stared at her, his eyes mad, disbelieving her words. 'Bring it to me, or I kill him now.'

Ewan's shoulder burned with a vicious pain. Where the hell was Trahern? Was he off telling stories instead of recruiting fighters? The blade was tight against his throat, and he sensed that John was going to kill him anyway, regardless of what he'd promised Honora.

Ewan glanced over at Bres. The young man's face was crimson, his breathing laboured. An arrow stuck out from his ribcage; not a mortal wound, but he was of no use to them. Conand lay unmoving, the sand stained red beneath him. Ewan prayed the man wasn't dead, but he could not be sure.

Damn it, if he could just pop his shoulder back into place,

he could bring Ceredys down. As it was, he had no movement in his right arm.

Ewan could see Honora's mind working rapidly, as she moved closer to John. He didn't like the look in her eyes; she was up to something.

'What if I find nothing?' she whispered to John. Her hand reached out to touch the Baron's shoulder, moving downwards. An involuntary growl emitted from Ewan's throat. What the hell was Honora doing? If he were able to move, he'd wrench her away from the bastard.

'Promise me you won't harm him.'

John's breathing quickened. 'I might allow you to bargain for his life. With your body.'

Ewan could feel her reaching to John, and though he could not fathom her purpose, his jealousy reared out of control. 'Don't, Honora.'

Honora sent him a warning look, but her hands released John. What in the name of God was she trying to do?

With no answer to the question, she stepped backwards towards the sandbar. In the distance, a storm was rolling in, the dark waves tipped white.

Her foot slipped, and she stepped into a patch of quicksand. Throwing her body sideways, the shallow wave soaked her, but she managed to elude the death trap.

Ewan started to breathe again when she regained solid footing. Honora didn't need to be taking such chances, not on a treasure she wouldn't find. He couldn't understand what her intentions were, but the danger was unacceptable.

'You don't have much time,' Ceredys warned. 'The tide is coming in.'

Honora made no reply, walking towards a strange stone outcropping. Recognising the bird shape, Ewan wondered what she'd found. She knelt in front of it, digging further. Her hands disappeared as she reached inside an opening.

'Did you lie with Honora?' John asked softly.

Ewan drove his elbow into the Baron's gut, and in return a burning sensation sliced his throat. Warm blood dripped down the chainmail he wore.

'I can see that you did.' John lifted the blade again. 'I should kill you for it. She belongs to me.'

Before he could break free of the Baron's grasp, Honora cried out in triumph. The tide was moving closer, the waves now reaching her ankles. Within moments, her knees were covered by the water.

Too fast. He'd never seen a tide move in that quickly.

'Honora, get out of there!' Ewan warned.

But she kept pouring handfuls of something hidden into a sack at her waist. He didn't trust it. It was too simple. Was she trying to trick John by filling the sack with sand and rocks? Or had she truly found something?

'Bring it to me,' John commanded.

Honora trudged through the sand, trying to reach the shore-line before the tide came in. More than once, she stumbled, while the water had risen up to her waist.

She stood a few paces from Ewan, her body soaked, her teeth chattering. 'I have the treasure. Now let him go.'

'I don't believe you.' John tightened his grasp, the point of his dagger sharp against Ewan's throat. 'Show it to me.'

As surely as he knew he was about to die, Ewan believed Honora had nothing but sand inside the sack. Though he didn't fear his own death, Ewan couldn't allow the Baron to take Honora prisoner again. And he didn't know how to save her.

Honora's hesitation only infuriated the Baron. 'I said show it to me!'

With a broken expression, Honora whispered, 'I am sorry, Ewan.' She reached into the bag and withdrew a handful of silver coins. They slid from her fingers, and in that moment, the blade eased from his throat.

Ewan gripped the Baron's arm, twisting the knife away. He

heard a bone crack, and John grasped his wrist, howling in pain.

Ewan lunged for the bag of silver. 'No, wait!' Honora protested. But he ignored her, using his left hand to hurl the silver into the sea. Then he pulled Honora to him, grasping his sword in his left hand.

John stared hard at him. And seconds later, he rushed after the silver coins.

Chapter Twenty-Two

Ewan let out a hiss when Honora embraced him tightly. 'Help me with this shoulder, Honora.'

She winced, as though she'd rather tear her own arm off, rather than cause him pain.

'Do it quickly,' he ordered. Bracing himself, he focused his attention on John while she bent his elbow inward and then back again. When the shoulder would not move, he groaned with the wave of agony that radiated through him.

'I'm sorry,' she fretted, moving his elbow once again.

'Just finish it.' He bit his lip until he tasted blood. Honora bent his elbow back sideways until he nearly passed out from the pain. At last, he heard an audible pop, and his shoulder slid back into its socket.

The Baron was clawing at the water, searching for the bag he'd thrown. The waves had risen higher, covering up the sandbar.

Ewan held Honora in his arms, watching as John searched for the treasure. 'You didn't have to throw it into the sea,' she whispered.

'Your life is worth more to me than any treasure.' He pressed a kiss against her brow. 'Let it go, Honora.'

'But, you don't understand—'

She was cut off by the murmuring of voices upon the hillside. Trahern approached on horseback with a gathering of men and women behind him. The men looked murderous, with weapons of every sort in their hands. Knives, sickles, even hammers were grasped in their fists while the women hung behind.

As a group, they advanced down the pathway, and behind them was Honora's father, Lord Ardennes. The Baron was filthy, his hair matted. In his hands he carried a sword, and he brought up the last of the people with his own army.

The two guards holding Katherine clenched their weapons, eyeing John for his orders.

'Kill her,' John snarled over the din of the waves. Honora jerked, her gaze terrified. Ewan raced towards her sister, even as he feared he wouldn't make it in time. Honora followed behind him, her own sword in hand.

The guard held Katherine with both arms across her shoulders. The other soldier lifted his own dagger. With her hands bound in front of her, Katherine could do nothing.

Then a figure appeared above the hillside. Sir Ademar dismounted from his horse, roaring, 'Katherine, the sword!'

Katherine struggled against the soldier, bashing her head against his nose. Grasping his sword with her bound hands, she unsheathed the heavy weapon.

Ewan could hardly believe what he was seeing. Gentle Katherine swung the soldier's sword against two attackers. She shouldn't have been strong enough to lift the weapon, but she moved with the same lethal swiftness as Honora. Even with her hands still bound.

When he and Honora arrived at her side, Ewan finished the fight, killing both soldiers. Honora could only stare at her sister. 'I never knew. All this time, and you never once spoke of it.'

Katherine managed a weak smile. 'You weren't the only one who learned to wield a sword. I knew that one day you'd do something foolish. Someone had to protect you.'

'That night…in the chapel,' Honora breathed. 'It was you. You defended me against John's man.'

'I did.' Katherine lowered the weapon, but did not relinquish the hilt. 'I saw you leave our room, and I knew someone had been searching your belongings.'

Sir Ademar reached Katherine at last, his face rigid with fury and fear. 'Katherine,' he breathed. He embraced her tightly, touching her hair, her face, to ensure she was all right.

'You're alive,' she whispered. 'I can't believe it.'

Ewan exchanged a glance with Honora as the pair kissed, murmuring softly to each other. Honora squeezed his hand. 'I am glad for them.'

'It's not over yet.' Ewan gestured towards the sea, where John stood, immersed up to his chest in water. In his hands, he held a dripping sack. And his face held dark fury.

'Did you think I wouldn't find it, bitch?' He strode towards the edge of the beach, but the people of Ceredys blocked his path.

Incredulous, John raised his sword. 'I am your overlord. Let me pass.'

Before he could move, one of the larger men smashed a wooden hammer into John's face. 'You violated my wife, damn you to hell!'

Enraged, John slashed his weapon down, blood pouring from his nose. Trahern stepped forwards and blocked the sword with his shield. The fight was short-lived, for Trahern disarmed him within moments.

The people of Ceredys closed in. Grimly, another man lifted John up, tossing him backwards into the tide. The weight of his armour pulled him down, and Ceredys scrambled to regain his footing.

A wave crashed into him from behind, knocking him down. Though his head bobbed up, another wave sent John slamming against the large rock. When the water receded, blood stained the surface of the stone.

Ceredys did not rise again.

* * *

Honora stood before Ewan, about to become his bride. Upon her head, she wore a crown of hawthorn flowers. The light scent mingled with the beeswax candles, and she was both nervous and overjoyed to be at his side.

They were surrounded by family—all of the MacEgan brothers and their wives, children and foster-children chattering eagerly. Even her father stood witness, his face sombre as they stood before the priest. Nicholas had reluctantly offered his apology for his earlier stubbornness, and Honora had thanked him for bringing his own army against John's forces back at Ceredys only a month ago. Despite his gruff demeanour, he admitted that he'd never wanted harm to come to either her or her sister.

Katherine had already married Sir Ademar, and both of them had accompanied Nicholas to the wedding, her sister nearly floating with happiness.

Ewan held her hand as they murmured their vows. And when the priest bade him give her a kiss of peace, Honora's knees wobbled at the heated embrace her new husband gave her. At the end of the Mass, Genevieve's newborn daughter gave a lusty cry.

'We should go and make one of those,' Ewan whispered beneath his breath.

The blood seemed to drain from her head at the thought of motherhood, but Honora managed a laugh. Ewan swept her up into his arms, ignoring the crowds as he took her back to their own private chamber within Laochre Castle, where a soft bed awaited them.

Their belongings littered the floor, for Ewan had been so eager to wed her, they would return to his own dwelling on the morrow.

He undressed her slowly, each layer of clothing falling away. The warmth of the fire kept the stone chamber warm, and new spring rushes lined the wooden floors. Honora opened her arms to him, a smile upon her face. A secret swelled inside her, and the need to tell him was nearly bursting.

'I am going to give you a castle like this,' Ewan swore. 'One day. No matter how many years it takes.'

She gave him a sidelong glance. 'I don't need a castle, Ewan.'

'I would lay the world at your feet, if I could.' His expression was so serious, so intent, that she held him tightly, resting her cheek against his heart. 'But none of it means anything without you. If you're with me, I could live inside a stable and be happy.'

Ewan stroked her hair, his breath against her ear. 'Although…I wouldn't have minded if we had found the treasure before John lost it.'

'He lost nothing,' Honora said. 'When you cast the treasure into the water, it was nothing but a bag full of stones and sand I picked up off the beach.'

He drew back, frowning. 'But there were silver coins. I saw them.'

Honora sent him a cheeky grin. 'I picked John's pocket when he was holding you prisoner. The only coins lost were his own. I knew he wouldn't believe me unless he saw it for himself.'

'I wed a woman of great intelligence,' he remarked, kissing her again.

'Yes, you did. And I believe you are wearing too many clothes,' Honora said, stripping away his tunic and trews, until they stood naked together. She ran her hands over the firm muscles, replacing each touch with a kiss. Lower still, she moved, over his stomach and down to his hardened manhood. With her hand she stroked it, eliciting a groan of response.

The power of showing him how much she loved him was intoxicating. So much, that she nearly lost sight of her purpose.

Tell him now, her conscience urged. The excitement rose up inside her.

'I have something for you,' she said seductively, taking his hand.

'Do you, now?' Ewan followed her over to the bed, where Honora brought out the small chest Marie St Leger had once given her.

'It's my wedding gift to you,' she said, holding it out to him. 'But you'll have to earn it.'

He opened the chest and saw hundreds of multi-coloured precious stones. Emeralds, rubies and sapphires gleamed amid a small pile of gold.

'Where did you get this?'

Honora beamed. 'Remember when I was searching for the treasure along the bay, near the bird-shaped stone? I happened to look back at the shore.' Her expression turned chagrined. 'It wasn't so difficult to find. The shrubbery upon the hillside is shaped like a spiral. And in the centre of the spiral, I dug up the chest.'

She reached in and picked up a handful of gems. 'Marie wanted me to have it, Ewan. It was her gift, and with it, I'm going to give you the kingdom you always wanted. Patrick has the rest of it. It's enough for a lifetime.'

He started to shake his head, but she put a finger to his lips. 'I know you're too proud to accept it, but trust me. You'll be earning every last stone and every coin.'

Lying back against the bed, she placed the gemstones upon her body. With a wicked smile, she added, 'Come and get them, Ewan.'

Ewan picked her up, letting the stones fall to the coverlet. 'Later, perhaps. After I've made love to you.'

His hot mouth roamed over her throat, pressing endless kisses upon it. 'You are my greatest treasure, Honora. Not a handful of stones.'

He lifted her up, and she wrapped her legs around his

waist, shocked when he sank deep within her. His mouth covered her puckered nipple, sucking hard until she trembled in his arms. 'Take them, Ewan. And me.'

Over and over, he penetrated her, urging her closer to a release. 'The treasure is yours, to do with as you will,' he said. 'Just as I am yours.'

Honora clung to him, her body going liquid. Flesh to flesh, becoming one body, she arched her spine. He grabbed her bottom, lifting her against him, pounding until she shattered in his arms.

Laying her back upon the soft coverlet, he withdrew from her body and scattered the gem stones over her bare skin. 'You're beautiful, Honora.'

'I love you, Ewan.' She lifted her mouth up to his in a soft kiss.

'And I love you,' he whispered against her mouth. 'Now, and always, my warrior.'

Epilogue

John's cousin Edward had taken possession of Ceredys, as the next heir in line. A soft-spoken man with a fair sense of justice, he had been appalled to learn of John's doings. Within a matter of weeks, he had restored peace among the people, helping them to rebuild their lives and their homes.

Though Honora would continue to own one-third of the estate, she was happy to let the new lord of Ceredys govern the property and collect the rents on her behalf. Once Honora was confident that the people were in good hands, she returned to Erin.

True to his word, Ewan began building their castle. Their estate lay beyond the Norse settlement, further inland from the rest of the MacEgan tribe. Though she missed the sea, Honora loved the vast acres of land for riding. Several hundred sheep grazed in the north pasture, while cattle dotted the hillsides.

Although he had initially agreed to use the jewels and gold to buy the land, as his profits increased, Ewan had repaid Honora beyond measure. Unlike most men, he did not gift her with useless earrings or torques. Instead, he'd given her an arsenal of swords, daggers and spears, each honed to razor sharpness. Embedded within each pommel, he'd placed a gemstone to replace those he'd used.

But his greatest gift to her was an army, made up entirely of women. Though they numbered fewer than a dozen, the women trained hard and were an asset to their growing number of tribesmen. Honora watched as the women lifted stones, helping the men build the inner bailey wall. Though the castle was hardly more than a skeleton, her days were filled with directing the folk and overseeing the construction.

Because she worked alongside them, learning their language, the people welcomed her. She didn't feel at all intimidated, because Ewan consulted her and made her feel that her opinion was valued.

Aileen and Connor had spent time with them over the past few weeks while Connor had helped Ewan build some of the interior walls. Though her grasp of the Irish language was still weak, Honora could now understand most of the woman's words.

'You'll be able to live within the *donjon* by next winter,' Aileen predicted.

Honora stifled a yawn, nodding. 'It won't come soon enough for me.' She'd been so tired lately, she didn't understand what was wrong with her. Yestereve, she'd fallen asleep with her face in the trencher, to the amusement of the others.

'And I should think it will be in time before your babe arrives,' the healer added.

Aileen's prediction was like a bucket of frigid water upon Honora's mood. She shook her head. 'I am not having a baby, Aileen.'

With a kind smile, Aileen patted her shoulder. 'Few of us are ever prepared for it. But it will be fine.'

'It's not true.' Honora shook her head. 'There are too many things to be done.'

'You haven't had your courses in a few months, now, have you?'

'Well, no, but so much has happened, I haven't had time.

I've missed them before, when I've been under a great deal of pressure.'

'True, but you have the other signs as well. Most women are tired in the first part of the pregnancy.'

Honora pressed her hands to her flat stomach, and the world seemed to pitch and toss. 'No. It's too soon for me to have a baby. I have to train the women,' she insisted.

Aileen gave a bemused smile. 'You can still train them, so long as you do it while you're sitting down.'

Honora covered her mouth with her hands, shaking her head. Ewan and Connor joined them, and as soon as he saw her face, Ewan grew concerned. 'What is the matter, *a ghrá*?'

'She's going to have a baby, but she doesn't feel ready,' Aileen explained, patting her hand.

At her sister-in-law's matter-of-fact tone, and Ewan's incredulous delight, Honora started to weep. 'I'll make a terrible mother.'

'No, you'll be fine,' Ewan reassured her, wiping a tear away.

'There will be many tears in the next few months,' Connor warned. 'Childbearing women do cry quite often.'

Aileen swatted him. 'And so would you, if you had to carry a child within your womb, your belly growing as large as a pumpkin.' She grimaced. 'And mine were twins, to make it worse.'

The very thought of two babes made Honora's knees buckle. Ewan caught her and pulled her onto his lap. He leaned in and kissed her, framing her face with his hands.

'I'm afraid of this, more than any sword I've ever faced,' she admitted.

Ewan held her close, tucking her head beneath his chin. 'I have no doubt that you will love our child as much as I love you.'

As he rested his hands upon her womb, Honora kissed him

wholeheartedly, thankful beyond words that this man belonged to her.

And always would.

* * * * *

*Celebrate 60 years of pure reading pleasure
with Harlequin®!*

To commemorate the event, Silhouette Special Edition
invites you to Ashley O'Ballivan's bed-and-breakfast in
the small town of Stone Creek. The beautiful innkeeper
will have her hands full caring for her old flame Jack
McCall. He's on the run and recovering from a mysteri-
ous illness, but that won't stop him from trying to win
Ashley back.

*Enjoy an exclusive glimpse of Linda Lael Miller's
AT HOME IN STONE CREEK
Available in November 2009
from Silhouette Special Edition®*

The helicopter swung abruptly sideways in a dizzying arch, setting Jack McCall's fever-ravaged brain spinning.

His friend's voice sounded tinny, coming through the earphones. "You belong in a hospital," he said. "Not some backwater bed-and-breakfast."

All Jack really knew about the virus raging through his system was that it wasn't contagious, and there was no known treatment for it besides a lot of rest and quiet. "I don't like hospitals," he responded, hoping he sounded like his normal self. "They're full of sick people."

Vince Griffin chuckled but it was a dry sound, rough at the edges. "What's in Stone Creek, Arizona?" he asked. "Besides a whole lot of nothin'?"

Ashley O'Ballivan was in Stone Creek, and she was a whole lot of somethin', but Jack had neither the strength nor the inclination to explain. After the way he'd ducked out six months before, he didn't expect a welcome, knew he didn't deserve one. But Ashley, being Ashley, would take him in whatever her misgivings.

He had to get to Ashley; he'd be all right.

He closed his eyes, letting the fever swallow him.

There was no telling how much time had passed when he became aware of the chopper blades slowing overhead. Dimly, he saw the private ambulance waiting on the airfield outside of Stone Creek; it seemed that twilight had descended.

Jack sighed with relief. His clothes felt clammy against his flesh. His teeth began to chatter as two figures unloaded a gurney from the back of the ambulance and waited for the blades to stop.

"Great," Vince remarked, unsnapping his seat belt. "Those two look like volunteers, not real EMTs."

The chopper bounced sickeningly on its runners, and Vince, with a shake of his head, pushed open his door and jumped to the ground, head down.

Jack waited, wondering if he'd be able to stand on his own. After fumbling unsuccessfully with the buckle on his seat belt, he decided not.

When it was safe the EMTs approached, following Vince, who opened Jack's door.

His old friend Tanner Quinn stepped around Vince, his grin not quite reaching his eyes.

"You look like hell warmed over," he told Jack cheerfully.

"Since when are you an EMT?" Jack retorted.

Tanner reached in, wedged a shoulder under Jack's right arm and hauled him out of the chopper. His knees immediately buckled, and Vince stepped up, supporting him on the other side.

"In a place like Stone Creek," Tanner replied, "everybody helps out."

They reached the wheeled gurney, and Jack found himself on his back.

Tanner and the second man strapped him down, a process that brought back a few bad memories.

"Is there even a hospital in this place?" Vince asked irritably from somewhere in the night.

"There's a pretty good clinic over in Indian Rock," Tanner answered easily, "and it isn't far to Flagstaff." He paused to help his buddy hoist Jack and the gurney into the back of the ambulance. "You're in good hands, Jack. My wife is the best veterinarian in the state."

Jack laughed raggedly at that.

Vince muttered a curse.

Tanner climbed into the back beside him, perched on some kind of fold-down seat. The other man shut the doors.

"You in any pain?" Tanner said as his partner climbed into the driver's seat and started the engine.

"No." Jack looked up at his oldest and closest friend and wished he'd listened to Vince. Ever since he'd come down with the virus—a week after snatching a five-year-old girl back from her non-custodial parent, a small-time Colombian drug dealer—he hadn't been able to think about anyone or anything but Ashley. When he *could* think, anyway.

Now, in one of the first clearheaded moments he'd experienced since checking himself out of Bethesda the day before, he realized he might be making a major mistake. Not by facing Ashley—he owed her that much and a lot more. No, he could be putting her in danger, putting Tanner and his daughter and his pregnant wife in danger, too.

"I shouldn't have come here," he said, keeping his voice low.

Tanner shook his head, his jaw clamped down hard as though he was irritated by Jack's statement.

"This is where you belong," Tanner insisted. "If you'd had sense enough to know that six months ago, old buddy, when you bailed on Ashley without so much as a fare-thee-well, you wouldn't be in this mess."

Ashley. The name had run through his mind a million times in those six months, but hearing somebody say it out loud was like having a fist close around his insides and squeeze hard.

Jack couldn't speak.

Tanner didn't press for further conversation.

The ambulance bumped over country roads, finally hitting smooth blacktop.

"Here we are," Tanner said. "Ashley's place."

* * * * *

Will Jack be able to patch things up with Ashley,
or will his past put the woman he loves in harm's way?
Find out in
AT HOME IN STONE CREEK
by Linda Lael Miller
Available November 2009
from Silhouette Special Edition®

This November,
Silhouette Special Edition®
brings you

NEW YORK TIMES
BESTSELLING AUTHOR

LINDA LAEL
MILLER

At Home in
Stone Creek

Available in November
wherever books are sold.

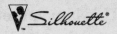

SPECIAL EDITION

FROM *NEW YORK TIMES* BESTSELLING AUTHOR

Ashley O'Ballivan had her heart broken by a man years ago—and now he's mysteriously back. Jack McCall *isn't* the person she thinks he is. For her sake, he must keep his distance, but his feelings for her are powerful. To protect her—from his enemies and himself—he has to leave...vowing to fight his way home to her and Stone Creek forever.

Available in November wherever books are sold.

Visit Silhouette Books at www.eHarlequin.com

SSE65487

REQUEST YOUR FREE BOOKS!

HH Harlequin® Historical
Historical Romantic Adventure!

™

2 FREE NOVELS PLUS 2 **FREE GIFTS!**

YES! Please send me 2 FREE Harlequin® Historical novels and my 2 FREE gifts (gifts are worth about $10). After receiving them, if I don't wish to receive any more books, I can return the shipping statement marked "cancel". If I don't cancel, I will receive 6 brand-new novels every month and be billed just $4.94 per book in the U.S. or $5.49 per book in Canada. That's a savings of 20% off the cover price! It's quite a bargain! Shipping and handling is just 50¢ per book.* I understand that accepting the 2 free books and gifts places me under no obligation to buy anything. I can always return a shipment and cancel at any time. Even if I never buy another book, the two free books and gifts are mine to keep forever.

246 HDN EYS3   349 HDN EYTF

Name	(PLEASE PRINT)	
Address		Apt. #
City	State/Prov.	Zip/Postal Code

Signature (if under 18, a parent or guardian must sign)

Mail to the **Harlequin Reader Service**:
IN U.S.A.: P.O. Box 1867, Buffalo, NY 14240-1867
IN CANADA: P.O. Box 609, Fort Erie, Ontario L2A 5X3

Not valid to current subscribers of Harlequin Historical books.

Want to try two free books from another line?
Call 1-800-873-8635 or visit www.morefreebooks.com.

* Terms and prices subject to change without notice. Prices do not include applicable taxes. Sales tax applicable in N.Y. Canadian residents will be charged applicable provincial taxes and GST. Offer not valid in Quebec. This offer is limited to one order per household. All orders subject to approval. Credit or debit balances in a customer's account(s) may be offset by any other outstanding balance owed by or to the customer. Please allow 4 to 6 weeks for delivery. Offer available while quantities last.

Your Privacy: Harlequin Books is committed to protecting your privacy. Our Privacy Policy is available online at www.eHarlequin.com or upon request from the Reader Service. From time to time we make our lists of customers available to reputable third parties who may have a product or service of interest to you. If you would prefer we not share your name and address, please check here. ☐

HH09R

Silhouette *Desire*

FROM *NEW YORK TIMES* BESTSELLING AUTHOR

DIANA PALMER

THE MAVERICK

A BRAND-NEW LONG, TALL TEXAN STORY

COMING NEXT MONTH FROM

HARLEQUIN®
HISTORICAL

Available October 27, 2009

- **A REGENCY CHRISTMAS**
  by **Lyn Stone, Carla Kelly, Gail Ranstrom**
  (Regency)
  'Tis the season for romance! Share the promise of Yuletide with a
  helping of festivity, family, warmth and passion....

- **ALASKAN RENEGADE**
  by **Kate Bridges**
  (Western)
  Victoria Windhaven is shocked to discover that her bodyguard on
  her dangerous journey through the Alaskan wilderness is none other
  than Brant MacQuaid—a man she'd never wanted to see again! But
  rugged bounty hunter Brant soon becomes the one man Victoria finds
  impossible to resist, and in the confines of their stagecoach their
  passion quickly escalates....

- **THE RAKE'S WICKED PROPOSAL**
  by **Carole Mortimer**
  (Regency)
  Lucian St. Claire, one of the wickedest rakes around, needs an
  heir—so it's time to choose a wife! High-spirited Grace Hetherington
  is definitely not the spouse he wants, yet there's something irresistible
  about her.... And when they're caught in a rather compromising
  situation, he has no choice but to make her his convenient bride!

- **THE WINTER QUEEN**
  by **Amanda McCabe**
  (Elizabethan)
  Lady-in-waiting to Queen Elizabeth, Lady Rosamund Ramsay lives
  at the heart of glittering court life, though she never quite feels
  fulfilled.... Charming Dutch merchant Anton Gustavson is a great
  favorite among the English ladies—but only Rosamund has captured
  his interest! Anton knows just how to woo Rosamund, and it will be a
  Christmas season she will never forget....